Sex, Lies & Secret Lives

Also by Thea Devine

His Little Black Book
Bad as She Wants to Be

Gallery Books
A Division of Simon & Schuster, Inc.
1230 Avenue of the Americas
New York, NY 10020

First Gallery Books trade paperback edition April 2010

GALLERY and colophon are registered trademarks of Simon & Schuster, Inc.

For information about special discounts for bulk purchases, please contact Simon & Schuster Special Sales at 1-866-506-1949 or business@simonandschuster.com.

The Simon & Schuster Speakers Bureau can bring authors to your live event. For more information or to book an event contact the Simon & Schuster Speakers Bureau at 1-866-248-3049 or visit our website at www.simonspeakers.com.

Designed by Jacquelynne Hudson

Manufactured in the United States of America

10   9   8   7   6   5   4   3   2   1

Library of Congress Cataloging-in-Publication Data is available

ISBN 978-1-4165-6265-8
ISBN 978-1-4165-6280-1 (ebook)

Sex, Lies & Secret Lives

Thea Devine

G

GALLERY BOOKS

NEW YORK   LONDON   TORONTO   SYDNEY

To Doris—we will love you forever

To Vogle

And John, as always

Sex, Lies & Secret Lives

Jillian Dare's website:

Impeccable, impressive, indulgent, intriguing, incomparable
Discreet and discriminating
Subtle, skilled, sophisticated, selective, seductive

Black tie only

If you dare . . .

Chapter One

Jillian Durant didn't wake up one morning and decide to become an elite traveling companion. If she had to re-create how it happened, she'd have pointed to her first job in the ad agency, her first boss on whom she'd had a massive crush, and that first furtive, forbidden kiss and grope behind his closed office door just before Christmas that first year.

And then the idea that he'd subtly planted with his creative director, that he needed an executive assistant in his entourage of art director, account executive, and producer when he went to pitch to clients outside Manhattan.

Which led to that first trip, that first flirtation, that first *why don't you*—join me for a drink, have dinner with me tonight, have sex with me *now*. And the conscience-suppressing rationalization: *we're so far from home, who would know? Why shouldn't I?*

Why shouldn't I was the philosophy she'd lived by ever since her impoverished childhood, with nothing except her twin sister, Justine, between her and their alcoholic father, the meager welfare and disability checks that barely supported them, their pregnant mother, and Jillian's determination to never be poor again. *Ever.*

And now, as Jillian slowly awakened in an exclusive London hotel in Cadogan Square and saw her lover's Centurion Card propped up on the nightstand for her, she didn't have a single regret.

She ran one hand through her tumbling midnight black curls, then positioned herself so that her hip curved provocatively under the luxurious 800-thread-count Egyptian cotton sheet and her left nipple peeked out enticingly over the silk duvet.

The trick was to make it all seem natural—the bed head, the sinuous movements, the erect, naked nipple—rather than deliberately choreographed to arouse him, though it was. And it worked: his penis shot to attention under his elegant five-hundred-dollar Burberry trousers, and his hands clenched.

"I have a meeting this morning," he told her.

"Let's you and me have a meeting first," she countered huskily.

"We can meet later, and you can model all the flimsy lingerie you'll buy today that I'll tear off your body tonight."

"I don't need lingerie, do I? When I have this?" She stroked her nipple tip, licked her lower lip, and gave him a kittenish look from under her lashes.

"Damn," he muttered, climbing into bed with her. "You do this all the time."

"It's not me—it's you," she whispered, pulling his head down to her nipple. "I can't buy what you make me feel when you"— gasping as his tongue swiped her nipple and his lips surrounded the hard tip and sucked—"do that."

"I could do that all day," he grunted, pushing her onto her back, tearing away the sheets and the cover, and pulling out his penis as he swiftly spread her legs. "But I only have time for this." He shoved between her legs, and she lifted her hips to pull him in deep, hard and fast. He spurted in an instant, totally beguiled by her manipulative morning seduction.

It didn't take much with men like him. They didn't have time for foreplay and could barely spare ten minutes for sex. She had learned early that she would have to do the work and take whatever she could get.

"And now," she whispered as he pumped himself into her, "you'll have my scent all over your penis during this very important meeting, and you'll only be thinking how soon you can fuck me again."

He wouldn't; Clive Ellicott was an expert at compartmentalizing. He had to be, to keep all his lives separate—the business, the competition, the marriage, the mistress, the traveling companion.

"How about now?" Without pausing a beat, he rolled her over onto her stomach, lifted her onto her knees, and drove into her from behind.

She knew to hold still, to let him go at her with the primitive zeal of a caveman while he fondled her. Now he felt totally in control, in a position where she couldn't seduce him with her feminine wiles and it was just his penis dominating her sex, the way he fully believed it should be.

He crammed himself tight against her bottom for a long, grinding ejaculation and then collapsed on top of her, his expensive trousers down around his knees.

"God," he muttered. "I want to root in you all day."

"We should plan such a day." But there never was time for that. He was too tightly scheduled, and running late now because she had enticed him with her brazen seduction.

That was her job, after all. That, and to make him look good when they went out in public.

"Tomorrow." It wouldn't happen. Tomorrow they'd be jetting to France for another meeting, first class, with every amenity, even on the short forty-five-minute hop to Orly.

But tomorrow she could suggest some quick mile-high mischief, encouraging his sense of being above all others at twenty thousand feet. He'd like that idea. And the privacy. And all the hot, kinky sex she could tease out of him.

She'd suggest it obliquely, let it be his idea. Get him revved up thinking about all the deliciously naughty things they could do.

He hadn't moved yet. "God, you're so tight and hot."

"For you," she whispered. "Do me again."

"No time." But he didn't move.

She undulated her hips and felt his penis elongate. "I felt that," she teased.

"Tomorrow." He started withdrawing, but then thrust back into her with a rough possessiveness that was almost obsessive. "God, I can't get enough."

His hands were all over her buttocks, his vigor heightened by the fact that he was dressed and she was naked and open, wholly his for the taking whenever and wherever he wanted to fuck her. There was a third quick, hard fuck, and he came again. "God, no more. I won't be able to think."

"You'll be such a hard-ass today," she contradicted playfully as he reluctantly pulled out of her. "Because you know my soft ass will be waiting for you later. Don't take too long—I'm missing your penis already."

She watched him from the bed, her legs tangled in the sheets but spread to reveal her naked cleft, her nipples hard and prominent, a tableau she'd perfected for her clients and one that worked every time.

A moment later his face burrowed between her legs, his mouth seeking her muff, his tongue probing her irresistible clit. She came in an instant, her orgasm explosive from repressed arousal. It was another good trick, and he hardened up like cement.

"God, I can't," he groaned.

"Hurry back, then," she whispered, stroking her nipple.

"Shit. Fuck." He wrenched away and hurriedly pulled up his pants, then stood looking at her. "I don't want to leave."

"We'll have all night."

"No, we have a dinner."

"True. And the flight tomorrow," she added with a tinge of regret. "A whole hour wasted just sitting on a commercial flight, when we could be—" She shook her head. "But of course, there's always Paris."

"Be ready at five," he ordered abruptly. "And cover your tits and ass *now*. I need to make some money today so I can afford your voracious cunt."

He didn't see her little smile as he stalked out the door. She'd played this and similar scenes dozens of times in dozens of luxury hotels all over the world.

Now he would think about that wasted hour tomorrow. He didn't like to waste time, especially when he could be fucking her.

He'd come up with a way they could be deliciously alone. He'd think of a private jet.

Why shouldn't I?

For some reason, her lover made her think about her first boss, a married guy she was crazy about, with whom she had sex whenever they were on a business trip, or after hours on his office floor, or at lunch, when he'd pin her against his office wall.

It was always on the edge and mind-blowingly exciting.

But she'd been naive to think that no one in the office was aware of what they were doing. People watched. People gossiped. Especially the assistant art directors. Particularly Zach Leshan.

"You two are cozy. Your conversation sounds like forties movie dialogue."

"He's a great guy," she'd said, keeping her tone neutral while her stomach knotted. Zach wasn't a friend, exactly. He was a source of great gossip—if he liked you and felt like telling. She didn't like what he was telling her now.

"He's a great boss. How many trips has he taken you on now?"

"I *am* his executive assistant."

"And the question everyone wants answered is, what are you assisting him with?"

"Company business," she'd said sharply. "Read the new-clients list. Check the new accounts he's brought into the shop in the past year."

"And how many orgasms has he brought in?" Zach had asked slyly. "And why isn't he paying you for your time?"

"Are you crazy?"

"Okay, here's the deal. I like you and I like him. But he's married, you're not, and you're giving it all up for nothing. He gets a gorgeous hottie on his arm, he gets to play outside the school yard, and he gets to relive his youth and vigor, which he then brings home to wifey, whom he can fuck to oblivion with impunity every night. But what do *you* get out of it, besides a long wait between trips to get fucked?"

"You are *so* out of your mind."

"Honey, people talk. I'm amazed they haven't cracked down on him yet. So you'd better reorder your priorities. When he takes you along, don't fuck him unless he gives you something in return. Like some really expensive gift. Or like money."

"Like per hour?" she'd sneered. "Like a hooker?"

"No, like a businesswoman who values her assets and what her time is worth."

"God, you are *so* off the mark, you'd be dead if I had a knife."

"Think about it."

"Not going to happen."

He had sauntered away, giving her a meaningful look over his shoulder, the son of a bitch.

At that moment, it had been two months since their last trip. Two months since she'd had sex with the boss every day, twice a day for a week. They'd snuck it in everywhere: a quickie in the morning, a blow job in the men's room during lunch, a midnight tryst. And he'd gone back to his nice suburban home, his really nice suburban wife, and his urban executive position: guy on top.

It *was* insane for her to give up so much in return for just a trip out of town every now and then.

She'd hated Zach for pointing it out, and was wary of him after that exchange. But Zach wasn't done yet.

A month later, she accompanied her boss on a trip to the Midwest—a big trip with the big guns, because they were in danger of losing the account.

A test for her, perhaps? Could she stay away from her boss, knowing that management was right in the next room, and he was down the hall?

"God, I can't stand not having you," he'd whispered in her ear as they grabbed a cab to the client's headquarters the next day. "I can't stand that they're all looking at your tits; they all want to fuck you." He ran his hand up her thigh, between her legs, into her naked cunt, knowing she wouldn't be wearing panties. "It's been too long." He probed deeper, and she groaned.

"I know. I want it, too. But we can't take the chance here."

"Then somewhere else. Another hotel. Just an hour. Just so I can suck your tits. That's all I want. An hour of tit fucking."

What's in it for me? What's that hour worth to me?

"We're almost there," she warned.

He pressed deeper, his whisper thick with arousal. "I want the scent of your sex on my hands. I need it."

"You can't do this ten minutes before your presentation. Please, Bill, don't," she hissed.

"Then don't tempt me," he said abrasively, sliding away his hand.

What? It was *her* fault that he couldn't control himself?

"Then don't bring me on trips unless you're willing to pay for the privilege," she shot back without thinking.

"Pay for it?" He looked stunned. "You've been giving it away, for God's sake. Pay for *what?*"

Bingo, Zach.

This was not the great secret love of her life. This was just a guy who'd lucked into easy, no-demands sex with a naive twentysome-thing who had stupidly believed he cared about her.

"For *me*," she said tersely, so he knew she meant it. "From now on. *If* I decide I want to go any further with this relationship."

"Shit to effing hell. Forget *that*."

"Fine." It didn't even hurt to say that. Because she realized she wasn't that easy or that gullible after all.

And Jillian wasn't easy this night in London either, when she met her lover for dinner, dressed exquisitely in Chanel.

He was with a man named Oliver Baynard, an English bil-lionaire he was courting to partner in a major business deal. He introduced her as his companion and they had a leisurely dinner together, full of good conversation, humor, and easy companion-ship.

At the end, her lover murmured discreetly, "Would you mind if Oliver joined us?"

"Join us how?" she asked sweetly, smiling at Oliver.

"He prefers to watch rather than be a participant."

She looked at her lover from under her lashes. This was the

time *not* to be easy. "I'm agreeable, if you agree to additional compensation."

He looked faintly annoyed. "Which would be?"

She didn't want to give a sum in front of company; that would be crass. She sensed he thought she ought to accommodate this sexual extra as a favor to him, but that wasn't possible if she were to maintain her standards. She folded her napkin, leaned forward so that only he could hear, and murmured, "Double."

Her lover gave her a hooded look, which told her that she was on thin ice—that this was important and that she ought not to have brought money into it, and that her having done so would make things difficult for her if they proceeded.

But she knew he wanted Oliver in that room watching them fuck. And she was there to please her lover—no matter what it cost him.

"Done," he said reluctantly and stood up.

"Oliver," she said warmly, holding out her hands. "I can't wait for the rest of the evening's events."

"Nor I," he said gallantly, taking her arm.

"I won't disappoint you," she whispered, snuggling against him.

"I'm certain you won't."

The minute they entered the hotel room, she ensconced their voyeur in an overstuffed chair inches from the bed, where he could see everything. Then she stripped for him, sinuously shucking her expensive clothes and kicking them lightly to the other side of the room with a bare foot.

She fondled her naked body for Oliver, stroking her nipples, her breasts, her buttocks, between her legs, sinuously belly dancing for his pleasure until she finally sank onto the bed, propped herself up on her elbows, and splayed her legs to reveal every detail of her shorn cleft to him.

As Baynard fondled his penis, her naked lover climbed into bed with her and turned to showcase his hard shaft in the lamplight for Oliver to admire, before he lifted her legs, tilted them over her shoulders, and drove deep and emphatically into her cunt.

He was a stone god that night, his penis massive and vigorous between her legs, spewing orgasm after orgasm in every possible position before he collapsed onto the bed.

"Oliver?" she asked with a playful tweak of her lover's wilting shaft.

"Do him," Oliver rasped.

She grasped her lover's penis, erected it with consummate skill, and pumped him until he oozed his last drops of semen. She looked at Oliver from under her lashes, coated her nipples with her lover's cream, and Oliver ejaculated, hard and hot all over his expensive suit.

"We'll call the valet," she said huskily. "Just take off your pants and come here beside me."

She wasn't exhausted, but Oliver was, and so was her depleted lover. She stared at the ceiling. Tomorrow an insane amount of bonus money would be transferred into her bank account, a test of her true worth to her lover. She could almost count the dollars as she counted orgasms, and she didn't know which was more pleasurable.

She loved sex, and she loved the substantial sums she earned by pleasuring her exclusive clientele. Maybe Oliver would eventually become one of them. He was a very cultured man, very nice-looking, with a hefty enough package to attract her. If voyeurism was his thing, she could accommodate that—and that nice, thick penis that was elongating deliciously even as she watched.

"Suck it off," Oliver said huskily, watching her.

"I'd love to." She went to work, vacuuming him into her mouth and sucking on him with gusto.

Her lover propped himself on an elbow to watch while he stroked her heaving buttocks. A moment later he was on top of her, lifting her rump so he could enter her from behind. And then it was all pumping and sucking, and they both came nearly simultaneously, her lover in her cunt and his guest in her mouth.

"If he agrees to partner with me, this will be worth every dollar," her lover rasped in her ear before he toppled off of her.

She called in the valet at 3:00 A.M. with instructions for him to return with pressed suits, washed underwear, and shined shoes by seven. She ordered breakfast to be delivered at six-thirty. She allowed Oliver to watch her bathe and let him ejaculate onto her nipples and watch as she pleasured herself by swirling his cream all over her hard nipples.

She sent him off with the memory of her feeding him tea and scones while sitting naked on his lap and shimmying against his burgeoning erection. At which point she just had to have his spunk for breakfast, which she proceeded to suck from him with dainty cat laps of her tongue until he swooned and spewed and gave himself up utterly to her greedy mouth.

After, she dressed him with much coy playfulness, saw that he finished breakfast, and *then* her job was done.

Because these high-powered, high-testosterone men wouldn't be caught dead trolling for prostitutes, a sleek, sensual, naked, and willing woman like her could command massive sums of money for her exclusive companionship, her body, her adoration, and her time.

But it had taken Jillian a long time to come to grips with that. It started just after that client rescue trip to the Midwest when Bill, her boss and former lover, caught her alone one evening when they were working late.

"I can't believe you meant what you said to me when we were in Denver."

"I meant it." She'd given a lot of thought to what she'd say if he should approach her again, and how serious she'd be about her demand for compensation. It was a scary thing to take office sex to that hard-line level. But their sex wasn't casual anymore, and he was forever married, and that made all the difference.

"You want me to pay you for sex, is what you're saying." He clearly couldn't believe it.

"I deserve some compensation for my companionship and my time," she said, keeping her voice neutral and firm. She deserved it, she wanted it, and it occurred to her suddenly that this could possibly be her way to secure that future where she'd never be poor and hungry ever again.

"And the thing between us, the incredible sex—that's not enough?"

"It should be enough for you to make certain you have a way to exclusively continue to fuck me."

"You're selling yourself? Go to hell." He wheeled away.

"I'm offering certain things that are available to you only from me," she corrected, mastering her temper. "If you think someone else can fill that . . . need, by all means, take advantage of that."

That might have been a bluff. She felt as if she were taking baby steps toward something, but she didn't know quite what it was. It *sounded* like she was prostituting herself, but there was some difference between that and what she was asking. She didn't quite know what it was—but sex was a commodity, and every bit as salable as anything else.

Only Bill wasn't buying. His outraged morality instantly blocked out the fact that he'd cheated on his wife. He was furious because she held the whip hand, and her body was now off-limits unless he wanted it badly enough to accede to her demands.

She felt a surge of sensual power. How badly *did* a man want her body? That was the question. And how much was he willing to pay—and for what?

Bill made it very plain that he wasn't willing to pay for anything, as if that somehow would change her mind. But it only firmed up her resolve. There were too many memories in the way, anyway. She had no future here, either way. Her only recourse was to find another job.

"Learn a lesson from this," Zach told her. "I mean, everyone's sleeping with everybody else, and nobody's thinking about the fallout."

"Oh, yeah? Who're you sleeping with?"

"What if I said Bill?"

"Ha." She didn't believe him. But . . . maybe. What if all his good advice had been rooted in jealousy?

Before she even started looking for a new job, she got a phone call.

"Is this Jillian?"

"This is."

"I was referred to you by Bill Nagel."

She clutched the receiver, her heart pounding. If Bill had betrayed her—

"I wonder if you'd join me for a drink tonight to discuss a business proposition."

This phone call was really when and how it began. Arthur Server—perhaps his real name, perhaps not—was a closeted member of the board of directors of a major *Fortune* 500 corporation. He needed a female companion for a trip overseas, and he was willing to pay top dollar for her company and her discretion.

It required that she quit her job, which was not a problem. The fee was twice her year's salary. The job required that she look and dress the part, and Arthur paid for that, too—the makeover, the clothes, the first-class ticket to Europe, the luxury four-star hotels, the dinners, the plays, the sightseeing.

There was no sex, there was just his delightful companionship on a whirlwind trip to Europe, during which he conducted business with affiliates, showcased her at half a dozen business dinners, and made sure that she was happy and entertained.

"It's almost too much, Arthur," she said one night during dinner, after he had given her a tiny perfect diamond set in eighteen-carat gold on a long, thin gold chain. "It doesn't need to be this much."

"I think it does," he said, "precisely because you don't expect it. I can afford it, and it's my pleasure."

This was the kind of man she needed to target and attract. The man who could afford it, afford *her,* and she needed to make herself into a sexual object of desire who was worth the money.

Arthur was so pleased with her, he passed her on to another executive, who in turn recommended her to another friend. That was the beginning. She offered discreet companionship based on trust, mutual attraction, exclusivity, discretion, and choice.

Her twin sister knew nothing about her choices. Justine was as straight an arrow as they came. She was the logical one, the just-the-facts one, the resourceful one who'd kept things together during their horrible abusive childhood when, every day, Jillian felt as if they'd fall apart.

That lasted until the night their mother gave birth to her third child, when social services unexpectedly stepped in. Jillian often wondered if Justine had called them because she was too young and overwhelmed to cope with a newborn baby, and to take care of her bedridden mother, alcohol-sodden father, and emotionally distraught twin sister.

They'd all been separated and had grown up in different foster homes, their baby sister adopted out days after she was taken and long gone from their lives, if not their memories.

Now she and Justine lived separate lives, in touch weekly by phone, by text, and dinner out once or twice a month, each of them having chosen a different path to security and certainty. Justine dealt in the clear certainties of science, and Jillian on an erotic path to big money and living in luxury.

Her cover story, that she was a body parts model, explained the huge sums of money she earned and why she was constantly traveling. But it didn't explain her insistence on giving Justine a one-time "lock box" tour of her apartment, showing her the secret panel in her closet that hid the safe where her valuables were stored: her computer and her cell phones.

"And I'm giving you the key."

"Why?" Justine had asked. "You're acting like you're some kind of secret agent or something."

Jillian hadn't replied, but later, over dinner, she'd said, "If I ever invoke the code, you have to take it seriously. You have to go to my apartment."

"Why to your apartment?" Justine had wanted to know.

"Because I always leave you a message before I go on a trip. Just in case."

"In case of what?"

"I'm always flying off somewhere. What if the plane crashes on my way overseas?"

Their childhood fail-safe was a code that meant she was in trouble and she needed the security of knowing someone had her back.

Jill never mentioned it again, because both of them knew, no matter what happened, Justine would never fail her.

Several hours later, Jillian was sucking off her lover's hard-on fifteen thousand feet over the English Channel. She obediently swallowed as he ejaculated in thick, heaving spurts, and then drew her up between his legs so she could cradle his penis between her breasts.

"We don't have much time. Sit," he demanded.

But for some reason, Jillian just wasn't feeling it and was regretting her subtle suggestion for more alone time.

"I have a better idea." An *easier* idea. She moved down his body to the sweet spot beneath his scrotum and began sucking ferociously. Hearing a movement behind her, she withdrew slightly, slanting her head just enough to see the pilot when he said, "Twenty minutes ETA, sir."

"Get up here. You heard him. Twenty minutes. I want naked cunt *now*."

She hoisted herself up reluctantly and mounted him. One thing she didn't play around with was obeying her lover's commands.

"This was *such* a good idea," she murmured as she rocked and undulated against his shaft.

"A *really* good idea," he panted.

"I feel that way, too." Though she didn't.

He grasped her breasts and heaved his hips upward. "The hell with that. *Feel* this." Orgasm one. "Don't move." She couldn't. He slowly rolled her over onto her back.

"Still hot and bone hard," she whispered as she spread her legs to accommodate him.

He thrust into her violently, her hips angling upward to give him access to her pleasure point. Orgasm two erupted.

He took her like a piston, exploding into her, and thrusting through his cum and her orgasm. He didn't need to do anything differently when he was mad with lust to possess her. It was the one thing she could use to her advantage.

He took her every way he could think of as the jet descended and prepped for landing. He never noticed her waning enthusiasm as he spewed his last drops of semen into her.

"It's not enough," he rasped as he collapsed on top of her, his thousand-dollar suit in total disarray all over the cabin.

"I'm not going anywhere," she whispered.

"Don't wash off my cum."

"Nor you, mine," she murmured coyly, robotically. The dialogue never changed.

"Stay naked till I finish my business and then we'll fuck our way back to London."

She gave it a moment's thought. "I'd love nothing more than to wallow in your cream, but isn't there a second meeting, tonight?"

"Shit, hell, fuck—I forgot."

"Then . . ."

"Till then," he whispered, slipping his fingers between her legs and feeling her semen-soaked cunt. "I'll take this"—he held up his hand and inhaled—"with me."

Jillian stood on the tiny balcony on the fifth floor of an exclusive hotel in Montmartre the next morning and let the incomparable sights and sounds of Paris wash over her.

This made everything worth it—her aching body, her well-used cunt, her lover-lies, the endless fucking after his meeting, with selected invitees.

If she was weary, sore, or tired of the game, she only had to remember the money. She only had to soak in a tub this morning, then fly back with him to London, and this trip would conclude with a fat deposit to her bank account.

Her lover was attending yet another meeting this morning with the same business associates she'd entertained the night before. There had been no morning delight today. But meantime, there was coffee waiting, a hot breakfast, and a soothing tub, all at his behest. He could be thoughtful sometimes.

This moment, with him gone and Paris at her feet, was perfect. She did care for him, *a little*. She found she always had some feelings for the men she traveled with regularly. There had to be some spark of attraction, of affection, or she wouldn't have chosen them. She loved having the variety, but especially loved having the choice.

That made all the difference; it *was* the difference. She chose her lovers and never had to settle because of the money.

She idly flipped on the TV to CNN and sat down to have breakfast. A nibble on a croissant. A sip of black coffee, always reviving. God, she felt bruised. It couldn't be that she was too old for all the acrobatics. Not yet.

She examined her legs. The faint black-and-blue marks on her thighs where her lover had grasped her could be hidden with makeup. He didn't need to see anything else. It was her job to preserve all illusions, including her naked perfection.

The newscaster's voice permeated her thoughts: ". . . word comes this morning of the death . . . Oliver Baynard . . . security . . . contracts . . ."

Her head shot up. Oliver? The Oliver who had been in her room, in her bed, two nights before? Her body went cold, and she raised the volume.

His picture was on the screen. *That* Oliver, the potential partner who liked watching, who preferred jacking off on her soap-slicked nipples to fucking her, who loved a blow job better than boning.

The Oliver with whom her lover was negotiating a business deal?

". . . sources are reporting the death of Oliver Baynard, the British billionaire entrepreneur, in an automobile accident early this morning. Police believe Baynard was returning to his estate in Shenbridge when his limousine took a turn too fast and shot across the median into an oncoming car. According to witnesses who arrived on the scene later, the limousine was engulfed in flames . . ."

The camera cut to an eyewitness.

Jillian froze. No. She had to be seeing things. Maybe.

"There was nothing to be done," the man was saying, his voice shaking as the camera zoomed in. "It was all on fire—you'd have been horribly burned if you'd tried . . ."

He wore a hat, low on his forehead. He stood just beside the interviewer, his shoulders hunched, his hands stuffed into his pockets. She knew him, anyway. It was his voice. The mouth. The glimpse of him she just caught from an angle on the floor on her knees was enough. Ellicott's private pilot was right there on the screen, his voice pitched just a bit higher, his speech more colloquial. He said he had only just been told who was in the car. He said what a shame it was. He said he wished he could have done something.

Jillian sat very still, a chill washing over her. The fact that a companion was sometimes privy to business secrets was not always a good thing. She knew that her lover Ellicott had been negotiating a major security contract from the British government. She knew that Oliver Baynard had had the inside track and her lover had hoped to convince Oliver to partner with his firm and take their merger to the global marketplace.

She didn't know what Baynard had decided.

Or perhaps now she did. But *why* would she even think that Baynard's unexpected death had anything to do with a potential multibillion-dollar business deal—or his rejection of it?

It *had* to be just an unfortunate accident.

Their pilot was in England because Ellicott had sent him there yesterday afternoon. On business.

Purely a coincidental accident.

Not something to make a mountain out of. Scotland Yard would investigate every angle, talk to every conceivable witness. The death of Oliver Baynard was no small thing. They'd ferret out any and every connection. Including Ellicott. If there was anything suspicious about the crash, they'd find it.

No, no—wait a minute. That would impact her lover, and subsequently *her* life. No. She had no reason to think . . . it was just her imagination; that chill of suspicion in her gut wasn't real.

But when she left for the airport very early that morning in a chauffeured limousine, she still wasn't sure. And when the pilot appeared to welcome her on board as if nothing had happened, she instantly knew she'd made a big mistake. She didn't imagine that look between Ellicott and the pilot.

She'd always been aware that Ellicott was a cold-blooded bastard. And it was possible that she might be only one of a handful of his associates who knew of his meeting with Baynard, who could place him with Baynard two nights before his death *and* could connect him to one of the alleged witnesses.

More than possible. Probable.

Maybe he'd thought she'd never see a newspaper or turn on a TV in the wake of all that sex. Or that she wouldn't recognize the pilot.

Maybe Ellicott was a gambler, but a man could only trust his instincts—and his whore—so much.

She had no choice but to get on that jet and fly with him back to London as if nothing had happened.

He acted as if nothing had happened, and she wondered, as she slipped out of her clothes and onto his erection, whether she *had* imagined the look.

The sex was intense. The flight—and the orgasms—seemed to go on and on, spiraling out of control. Or was it the plane? Swaying right and left, nosing subtly downward, tilting dangerously. Her lover pulled abruptly away from her, diving for security. She scrambled after him, pawing on her clothes and grasping for her cell. She pushed herself behind a seat and texted off one word on her cell before grasping the seat, preparing for the moment of impact.

Chapter Two

Justine Durant wouldn't have said her life was monotonous, but this was one of those days she wished she did something more glamorous than researching the neurobiological causes of addiction for a living.

Like her twin sister. Jet-set Jillian, flitting all over the world, baring parts of her perfect body to be photographed for this or that skin cream, perfume, bathing suit, designer shoes, high-end jewelry. She got to see exotic places, meet erotic one-time-only men, earn obscene paychecks that kept her in a luxurious Park Avenue apartment.

Who would have thought their lives would diverge so completely?

Justine kicked off her shoes the minute she opened the door to her spacious studio apartment. At least she wasn't cramped, at least she had a remodeled kitchen and a fabulous view from a perfect little balcony overlooking the Hudson River. She had a growing nest egg in the bank, and she loved her job.

Except for some reason, it had all gotten to her today.

Bureaucracy. Rules. Procedures. Endless, stupid, sanctimonious university lab supervisors who shot you down when maybe—just once—a little faith might have given credence to an otherwise amorphous theory.

But that was over now. She was dead tired and just wanted to sleep. She left the lights off, let her clothes drop on the floor, navigated over to her bed, and just sank into the duvet.

Bliss.

From this vantage point, she could see out the window to just the tops of the buildings across the river. Their lights twinkling like stars. The running river, the calming thought, soothed away problems and pulled her into sleep.

And then somewhere in her mind or her dreams, she heard the musical sting that meant *something*—she wasn't awake enough to comprehend just what . . .

But as the sound rippled across her consciousness, she groggily reached for the light.

Her cell. She groped for it on the side table and flipped it open. Who'd be texting her at 2:00 A.M.?

A truncated text message was sharp against the screen: *justine . . . t . . .*

Justine shot upright, flipping on the light and holding the screen up to view it more clearly. *Justine t.* Her heart started pounding. No. No. Jilly would never use the old code unless . . . no. Not Jilly. Just a mistake. Just—it was three in the morning, for God's sake—it's a joke. An error.

She heard herself panting as she waited for more of the message to materialize. But there was only *justine t.*

Just in time. The I-need-you-help-me-get-here-yesterday-you're-the-only-one-I-trust fail-safe code.

Justine caught her breath. As far as she knew, Jill was on a modeling assignment in England.

What time was it in London?

How the hell could she do anything for Jillian if she was in London, anyway?

Justine felt panicked and helpless. For Jillian to use the code, she had to be in some awful mess. They'd come up with the code when they were kids in separate foster homes. It signaled when things became so untenable that they needed to hole up somewhere and solve a problem together.

In all the years since, they'd lived such vastly different lives in the same city, seeing each other once a month religiously. They were in constant contact but never impinged on each other's life.

That was just the way it was, the way Jillian wanted it. Justine never questioned it.

Now she wished to hell she had.

But she never could constrain her twin, not even when they were children, so how could she help her now?

Justine was so panicked, she wasn't thinking straight. Jillian had been clear about it: if she coded Justine, it meant she was to go to Jillian's apartment.

In case, Jilly had said, of something like a plane crash.

Justine dove for the remote and flipped on CNN and watched for ten minutes. No major disasters. Some billionaire had died in some car crash in the English countryside, but not Jillian.

But still—*Justine t . . .*

Jillian hadn't even finished typing the code, a play on Justine's name: *justine time*—just in time. But how could Jilly possibly get in trouble on a modeling assignment?

It was a dumb question. Even Justine's logical mind could come up with half a dozen possibilities: someone had attacked her, kidnapped her, taken her hostage, put her in jail, hurt her— killed her?

It wasn't possible. She would feel it, know it deep in her soul where their twin connection lived. No, Jilly was alive. She *had* to be alive. Justine held still for a long, fulminating moment and felt nothing. No darkness. No emptiness. No sense that Jillian was not alive.

Justine fought her rising fears. She could call Scotland Yard. If anything had happened, they would know.

But Jillian's instructions were plain. Go to Jilly's apartment. See what this message business was about and *then* contact Scotland Yard.

She took a deep breath and tried to make a plan.

She should call into work first. She rubbed her forehead. She'd leave a voice mail, so she wouldn't have to deal with explanations, and take an emergency leave of absence to give her breathing room.

Okay. Call the university. Get dressed. Go to the apartment. They were logical steps that put her back in control.

———

Jillian's apartment was in a large prewar building with a cadre of longtime residents who didn't care who you were. You could be as anonymous as you wished to everyone but the doorman.

Luckily, the doorman thought Justine was Jilly. They had the same long, glossy, coal-black hair, jeweled blue eyes, and oval face. Had he looked closer he'd have seen that Justine's nose was longer, her mouth wider, her body more rounded. So with his dismissive wave of recognition, she hurried up to Jillian's apartment.

Justine didn't feel any less panicked upstairs. Sneaking by the doorman had only heightened her fear of discovery. Her hands shook and her body shivered as she mentally pushed away every disastrous scenario that could have precipitated Jilly's ominous text.

Her only course was to try to make sense out of Jilly saying she always left a message for Justine when she was out of town.

Jilly had bought this two-bedroom apartment about six years before because it had an unusually large number of closets. All were stuffed with designer clothes, half of which, Justine suspected, Jilly never wore.

Jilly loved to shop. Really, Jilly loved the fact that she was making so much more money than her brainy twin.

Justine felt like an intruder as she entered the long hallway that led to the living room. One plug-in night-light bathed the space in an otherworldly glow and made it all the more eerie to be there alone in the wee hours of the morning.

It felt so wrong, rooting around Jill's apartment, prying into her things. *Please Lord, make the message obvious*, Justine prayed.

It would *have* to be obvious. If Jilly always left her a message, it would have to be easy. On a desk, maybe, or propped up somewhere.

It was only 5:00 A.M. No hurry. No time constraints. And no other task but to figure out what Jilly meant for her to find.

Justine stared out the big, old-fashioned picture window in the living room. Dawn colored the skyscrapers in the distance, lifting from deep blue to pink and gold high over the rooftops. Everything was so quiet, the city just waking up, oblivious to the fact that her sister could be in dire trouble.

The apartment itself was minimalist, almost as if no one lived there. There was nothing on the kitchen counter, no pictures, no sentimental keepsakes anywhere. Everything was pristinely clean—not a speck of dust, nor personality.

Justine peered into the guest bedroom, which was furnished with a bed, dresser, and desk. It was furniture you'd rent to stage a house or something.

This wasn't like Jilly, not at all. Except for the closets, which were crammed with clothes. *That* was Jilly.

Jilly's bedroom was much larger, and there was actually a trace of her personality in the antique walnut bed, the lush bedding, the ornate Victorian dresser, and the reading lamp on one side of the bed. There was even an upholstered rocker by the window to take in the view.

And there was something propped on the luxurious pile of pillows against the headboard.

Justine froze, licked her lips, and waited a minute before bending over to pick up the object.

A hotel key was tucked into a holder that contained a foldout map. On the front, a picture of Jilly—naked, prone, her curves barely covered in black satin, and the words,

> *Impeccable and incomparable*
> *Discreet and discriminating*
> *Subtle, skilled, sophisticated, seductive . . .*

And on the reverse side, against the same luscious black satin background, the words, *If you dare . . .*

Justine felt faint, but somehow had to calm her shaking hands and unfold what was inside the key insert. Because everything would come clear in that moment, and it wouldn't be as bad as it looked. At least that was what she told herself.

The key holder had a slip pocket, with Jillian's card on its outward face and the underside, with the coy invitation *If you dare . . .* that folded back against the pocket. The foldout was a map of Manhattan, and on the reverse side was the usual list of theaters and restaurants near the hotel.

Okay, this isn't so bad.

Justine studied the map.

There were big numbers in blue circles—obvious points of interest, such as the Empire State Building and the United Nations. Justine wrote down the numbers: 7, 5, 3, 2, 1, 4.

Was it a code? Alphabetically it made no sense, but the numbers couldn't be random, since the 6 didn't follow suit.

A computer password was all Justine could come up with. But there was no computer in sight. Maybe Jilly's laptop was locked behind that panel she had made such a fuss of showing Justine. Why all the subterfuge, Justine wondered as she made her way toward the panel.

The laptop was right there, in the safe behind the secret panel—the key for which she'd automatically put on her key ring along with Jilly's apartment keys so long ago.

Justine took the laptop and a handful of cell phones out and tossed them on the bed. She sank into the nearby rocking chair and opened the laptop. She powered it up, just brushing the touch pad and a file flashed on the screen.

With her name on it.

Justine started shaking again. This could not be good. Not paired with that blatantly sexual hotel key.

She moved the cursor and clicked.

Slowly, a densely written letter appeared.

Justine. This is the time for plain speaking. If you're reading this, I'm in trouble. You have to help me. And I have to tell you the truth: I'm not a model. I'm an exclusive traveling companion to wealthy men who want a beautiful, intelligent, sensual (with all that entails) woman to accompany them on their business trips.

*Someone with whom they connect and feel safe, admired, strong,
sexy, virile, and in control. I am that woman. I want to stress that
this is my choice, that I choose the men I travel with, and they pay
me extremely well for my time and talent.*

*But because these are all highly placed executives, I'm some-
times aware of confidential information that, were I to reveal it,
would be disastrous for my clients—and for me. I've always known
that was the danger of being a companion, but the rewards have
been well worth my discretion and my clients' trust.*

*I don't even know now if something I know is the reason why
I coded you. But I do know that you're the only one who can help
me. And I am begging you, please, please find me, wherever I am.
Never give up, keep looking—do whatever you have to do.*

Jilly.

Justine's body rocked with shock. Like she held a bomb in her
hands that would explode if she made the smallest movement. Jillian is a—*what?*

A whore.

The word reverberated in her brain. *This* was how Jilly had
chosen to exorcise their godforsaken childhood?

Justine's tears burst out of nowhere, anguish torn from deep
inside her.

She didn't know how long she sat there sobbing, but when she
finally wiped away the last of her tears, the sun was streaming in
the window with near-blinding intensity.

What am I going to do?

Justine looked back at the laptop. There was *more.* Jillian's letter
had faded and three words were juxtaposed against a black satin
background:

If you dare . . .

It looked like a website.

Justine bit her lip, steeled herself, and clicked on the phrase.

Black tie only.

She clicked on the tie icon.

> *Impeccable, impressive, indulgent, intriguing, incomparable*
> *Discreet and discriminating*
> *Subtle, skilled, sophisticated, selective, seductive*

Another icon, another click. The next page displayed the picture of Jillian, sleek and seductive with her knowing smile and sensuous curves.

And her name: *Jillian Dare.*

She clicked on Jillian's name.

How may I contact you?

She clicked on the question. Immediately a page came up with an invitation to e-mail Jillian and a discreet back button on the lower right-hand corner. She clicked on it, and the program booted back to the first page: *If you dare . . .*

Jilly was soliciting for sex? Justine could barely breathe.

Stop, she told herself. *This isn't about Jillian's choices. This is about Jilly in trouble.*

> *"Find me. Help me.*
> *Whatever you have to do."*

Justine closed her eyes to ward off the replay of those words in her mind.

Quick photographic shots of their childhood flashed before her—the desperation, the alcohol, the drugs, the abusive parents, Jilly in tears, herself stoic, beatings, verbal abuse, starvation, nights locked in closets or tied to a bed, eking out spending money by babysitting, walking dogs, begging for a quarter, whatever she had to do to protect Jill. Her father, blindingly beating on her, demanding every last penny she begged in order to slake his thirst.

Of course Jilly wanted money—lots of it—as quickly as she could get her hands on it.

Justine took some deep breaths. She drank some coffee. She picked up the hotel key and looked at it. It was the same picture as on the website.

She pressed "enter" on the keyboard, and the screen went blank. Jillian Dare and the letter disappeared and a dialogue box appeared demanding a password.

Of course. Jilly had rigged it for one-time viewing, and now she had what she needed. Now to configure the password. The circled numbers on the map had to be the clue.

Jeez, Jillian. I'm hardly Nancy Drew.

She typed the numbers in varying combinations.

Nothing. She tried variations of Jillian's name and the numbers, again in every sequence she could think of.

Nothing.

Maybe this wasn't some kind of password after all. Jillian wouldn't have made it this difficult, not if she wanted Justine to be able to access information that would help her.

She stared at the circled numbers on the map: 7, 5, 3, 2, 1, 4.

Did the numbers seem familiar? She played around with them: 1, 2, 3, 4, 5, 7; 5, 4, 3, 1, 2, 7; 1, 2, 7, 5, 3, 4—wait!

The numbers 7, 2, 4, 1, 3, 5 . . .

That's it!

The address of the hellhole. The prison of their childhood. The bedlam of their nightmares. Their haunted childhood. The ghost of their baby sister. The heartrending decision of the abused and forlorn eleven-year-old she'd been to break up her only family.

The hell from which guilt and the need for penance plagued her in equal measure.

All Jilly's secrets were contained under that one string of numbers that reminded her daily of why she made the choices she had.

She typed in the numbers, hit "enter"—

And nothing happened.

Tears welled up in her eyes. Damn, damn, and damn.

Jilly was in trouble, her morals already gone to hell, and Justine couldn't even get the address right of the hell in her heart?

She felt the same overwhelming emotion she had when she'd made that phone call all those years ago.

Slow down. You're not thinking clearly. That's the address. Nobody else knows it.

Jilly knew that. They never talked about those years, their unknown sister, or their parents who had died of their excesses—in their mother's case, tragically, by their father's hand.

Focus. The address . . . 724 135th—it hit her—*West!*

Jillian must have left that part out so no one could crack the password without knowing it was an address on the West Side of Manhattan.

She typed in 724W135—hit "enter" . . .

And there it all was: all the files, cataloged by names, cross-referenced with cell numbers, every detail from the responses to the arrangements, the tone in which Jillian dealt with her customers. It was all accessible only with that password. All her fees and services were even laid out so there could be no question about what a client got for his money.

The letters to her gentlemen reminded them sweetly that she regarded their interaction as a relationship, that she didn't want the necessity of mentioning payment to put an insurmountable wall between them, stemming their attraction. It was best to deal with it at the outset so her gentlemen could make their own decisions before approaching Jillian for one of her famous get-to-know-you "dinners."

The money was staggering, more than Justine could conceive of for just a few hours with Jillian Dare.

And the rates climbed even higher for each succeeding hour, day, night, overnight, weekday overnight, full weekend, or month. In addition, if there were travel, she expected first-class accommodations, the hotel's premier suite, and every accessory to be the finest, from champagne to restaurants to limousine service. And a spending allowance was a tacit given.

Beyond that, if the client wished to show his appreciation in other ways, Jillian even provided discreet suggestions.

In return, her gentlemen understood that they were getting a beautiful, selective, discreet companion with unparalleled, worldly sophistication. ". . . in me, you will find refined beauty, and a slender, athletically toned, and curvaceously feminine body," the document claimed. She characterized herself as an outstanding courtesan who rendered her clients incoherent with sensual pleasure in their private hours together.

Justine just sat and stared at the screen, her heart pounding wildly.

Who *was* that person who flaunted her body in blatant sexual solicitation? Had Jillian always sought the easy way out? Justine didn't know anymore. She didn't know this sister who'd chosen years of sexual submission to feed a thirst that couldn't be quenched and a bottomless bank account that would never be filled.

All that jet-setting. All those well-known men. Why would men of wealth, taste, and refinement need to pay for a traveling companion—and for sex?

How does she do it? How can she do it? Justine couldn't fathom it.

Based on Jillian's online calendar, when she wasn't traveling, she lived in a world of late hours and ceaseless partying. If she slowed down, Justine thought, she would have to take stock. She'd have to be aware of what she was doing—and she'd be appalled.

Wouldn't she?

What could Jillian expect Justine to do that didn't expose her? If Justine told the truth—to the police, to Scotland Yard—if she took the step of reporting Jillian missing, it would mushroom out from there. The tabloids would grab hold of it and have a field day, gleefully destroy lives, businesses, and families.

But Justine knew that Jill was in enough trouble to reveal her secret life to her twin.

It wasn't as if she had any resources regarding Jill. She didn't know any of Jillian's friends or acquaintances. She didn't know if Jillian even *had* any friends.

It struck Justine hard and painfully that she knew nothing about Jillian other than her lighthearted tales of traveling, her comic descriptions of photo shoots in foreign countries, and the mishaps that stemmed from all the different cultural norms.

It had all sounded legitimate. Now and again Jillian had even shown her ads, pointing out hands holding skin care cream, an ear adorned with a gorgeous diamond earring, a wrist with a thick gold bracelet, flowing hair in a shampoo ad.

"That's me," she'd crow, and Justine had had no reason to believe it wasn't.

But advertising was all smoke and mirrors anyway, wasn't it? And so was Jillian it seemed.

Right at this moment, staring at the website at the Jillian she didn't know, Justine had no idea what to do.

The breadth of the lie was just too stunning to grasp. The sex. The men. The money. The delicacy of dealing with a clientele that was exquisitely particular about how they spent that money, on whom, and for what. These highly sexed, supernova men who sought super value for the money they expended—and that was manifested not only outwardly—like beauty, style, manners, and personality, but also by intangibles like trust, connection, rapport, compliance, adaptability, submissiveness, obedience.

Jillian had profiled every client, down to what he wore, what he liked to eat, drink, how he liked to play, and what her particular talents were worth to him. She had set certain nonnegotiable rates for the nonvarying items: the dinner, the get-to-know-you, the compatibility overnight, all of which were listed in her files. But then there were the intangibles. The *extras*. The things like the limos, the hotel suites, the pin money, the diamonds—they were the rewards for the premium services she was willing to provide.

Those were detailed as well so that Jillian had a bulletproof reference for every man she'd ever dealt with: his weaknesses, his vulnerabilities, his special needs, so that she could unerringly play to that client.

Clever Jillian. Justine's first glance at Jill's bookkeeping records was proof of that.

Justine couldn't even compute those amounts. She knew too much already. There were too many secrets, too many lies. And she knew Jillian was too deep into this life to ever give it up. That much money was a narcotic, and Jilly was obviously addicted.

How am I ever going to find her, let alone help her?

She knew that she could *not* contact Jilly's friends and ask questions. She couldn't report her twin missing either, because she didn't know for certain that Jilly *was* missing. Being in trouble wasn't necessarily missing. It might just mean that Jillian had dropped out of sight until whatever this trouble was blew over. And Justine certainly didn't want anyone to know.

But Jillian meant for her to know all her secrets—there had to be a reason for that. Justine just needed time to process this insane turn of events and she'd figure out where to start.

Coffee. Coffee was always a good first step. Did Jilly even have a coffeepot? Anything in the fridge? Anything in this sterile apartment that could have been a metaphor for the way Jilly had chosen to live her life?

Don't think about it right now. Think about coffee.

And then what?

I should have known, I should have taken care of her.

Justine went into the kitchen and rummaged through the cabinets. There actually was a coffeemaker, and by some miracle, coffee in the freezer and creamer in the cabinet. It was more than Justine expected.

But there was nothing in the fridge except cold water. And a healthy helping of guilt and blame. *I should have known*, Justine thought.

She never should have trusted Jilly. She'd always been more emotionally scarred and *way* more determined to obliterate the privations of their childhood. Justine should have *known*. A twin should have felt it, sensed it, shared it.

It explained so much, even why, in this luxurious apartment, Jilly had pared everything down to essentials.

And it explained nothing, she thought as she poured the coffee, tears stinging her eyes. Jilly didn't live here—the persona of Jillian Dare did. And Jillian Dare was most emphatically *not* her sister.

Stop crying . . . you can't help her if you're crying.

She took deep breaths. She drank her coffee and wandered back into the bedroom. She picked up the hotel room key and examined it. Again.

And the circles around the numbers on the map—the past always caught up to you when you least expected it.

And Jillian's words, etched into her heart . . .

"Find me, wherever I am . . . whatever you have to do."

Justine thought hard. Was the key card inside the envelope just the clue to Jillian's password, or was she meant to actually go to the hotel as well?

She didn't know, but she just wouldn't leave any possible clue unexamined.

She needed a plan. She needed to avoid questions. Just for now, she'd *be* Jillian. Not that she was that much like Jillian except superficially, but if she was dressed like Jillian, wore her hair the same way, and did her makeup so she looked like the picture on the key holder, no one would doubt for a moment she wasn't Jillian.

God, she hoped there was something more to be learned in a super-expensive, super-exclusive hotel room.

Justine licked her lips, larded with more lip gloss than she normally wore, and pushed her way into the elegant lobby. No one said a word. No one stopped her. The desk clerk nodded as she passed, as if he knew her.

She almost collapsed when the elevator door closed and she emerged on shaking legs into the long, carpeted hallway on the tenth floor.

Jilly's room, 1001, was tucked away around a corner—for privacy, no doubt. Corner rooms with expansive city views were all about appearances.

She shoved the card into the slot, her heart racing. The light turned green, and she pushed her way into the room.

"Well, hell—it's about damned time." The male voice was deep, imperious, and impatient. "I hope to hell you're Jillian, because otherwise I've dropped a boatload of money paying for a room I'm not going to use."

———

"Whatever you have to do."

Justine froze. This was a complication she hadn't expected: a strange man in Jilly's hotel room. And it wasn't hard to guess why— damn, oh, damn, why had she chosen to come here dressed like Jill?

If she hadn't, he would just have gone away, and Jillian would eventually have reaped the consequences of rejecting him. She wondered if he'd even *believe* that she wasn't Jill.

He'd removed his jacket, unknotted his tie, and settled himself onto the sofa with a financial report. He had a broad, open face, maybe in his late forties or early fifties, and was tall and broad. Large hands. Nice mouth. It was too quick an assessment—but for what? Sexability?

"I . . ." Did she want to mindlessly step right into Jillian's stilettos? To *be* Jillian, with all that implied? Was that what she was thinking when she'd decided to take the *If you dare* challenge and come to the hotel?

Would she really sacrifice that much for Jillian to save her when she didn't even know what she was saving her from?

When push came to shove, Justine could "do" Jillian easier than Jillian could impersonate *her*.

Her blood ran cold.

"You're the only one . . . please . . . whatever you have to do."

She didn't have time to sift through the consequences of this mad idea. She had just wanted to avoid questions, to put herself in Jill's shoes so she could find her twin.

Justine felt her panic rising. She was alone in a hotel room with a strange man. He spent boatloads of money and he expected . . .

Her guest was waiting for an answer. It felt like an hour had passed instead of mere seconds.

"I—I'm not Jillian," she said finally.

"That's a joke, right?"

"I'm . . ." She stopped as she considered how the conversation would sound: I'm her twin sister. He'd say, Oh, yeah, is that how you get out of your obligations? You don't like the guy, you pretend to be a twin?

It could get really ugly from there, especially since it involved money *and* sex. Did she want to risk that?

Or take the risk and *be* Jillian?

She gathered her wits. The endgame was clear, and logically, at this moment, she didn't feel she had a choice. This guy had spent big money for Jillian's time.

She'd have to play it through and play down the sex, and get out of this as gracefully as she could.

There was no other option. She needed time to get a handle on what had happened to Jillian, and maybe the only way to do that *was* to be Jillian, and hope to hear a name, place, or assignation she'd last arranged.

It was a tenuous and dangerous plan at best.

"Forgive me," she began again. "A family matter is distracting me today. Of course I'm Jillian." She said it so easily, so calmly. She couldn't believe how calm she was now that she'd resolved to *be* Jillian.

"Well, okay, then. What's the first order of business? You talked about getting to know each other."

Thank goodness this was a first meeting. She had no idea how to answer him, but he probably wouldn't know the difference.

"What's there to get to know?" he added a little aggressively. She shrugged out of her jacket and hung it in the closet just to give herself something to do. "I need a beautiful woman to accompany me on an upcoming business trip. You're a beautiful woman. And I meet all your requirements."

Right. It was just that simple: hand over your money and it's hands on from there. *Oh, Jillian . . . how could you . . . be this person?*

"Of course, on the surface, it does seem that simple," she said finally, slowly, feeling her way as she drew up a chair. "But—" What would Jilly say? In her letter, she'd talked about connection, trust, choice—were those starting points?

"I feel we're starting a relationship here," she went on carefully, picking her points from what she'd read on the website. "We have to get to know each other, like each other, and trust each other. I don't see this as a one-off arrangement."

That was good. He liked that. "Sure. I get that."

"It's not as simple as you handing me an airline ticket and me climbing into bed with you. I need to be certain I'm the kind of woman who meets your needs for this trip and beyond."

Would he be that patient? Probably not. She went on, "And that we're compatible on other levels besides sex. Your business associates"—she paused to think—"need to perceive me as something more than just some prostitute you hired for the trip. And I *am*, and should be, more than that."

"Right. Right."

Oh, God, she'd already exhausted every point in Jillian's playbook. "Perhaps we should have lunch and you can tell me something about yourself before there's any talk of afternoon delight."

"That's fine."

"Shall I call for a reservation?" Things would be 100 percent easier if they were not in the room. And maybe she could sneak a look at the register and find out his name.

"Can't we eat here?"

Shit. "Whatever makes you most comfortable. Let's look at the menu, shall we?" It was a delaying tactic but it wasn't going to work for long. He looked as if he wanted to eat *her*.

He was a relatively simple guy from the looks of it. He ordered steak, potatoes, and beer. She ordered pasta with seafood; it was easy to fork up—or not. She wasn't that hungry.

"So." She settled back into the chair, keeping her distance.

"When do we get to the sex?"

Well, he knew what he wanted. "First, let's talk. Tell me about yourself. You *are* married?"

"Does it matter?"

"No. And I know we discussed the trip in general terms"—she was feeling around here, hoping it was true—"but would you fill me in on the details? You said, a week?"

"You going to take notes?"

"We didn't discuss the when and the how," she said, hoping that was true, too. She was scared out of her three-inch heels that she would make an egregious mistake. "Shall we now?"

"Going to L.A., first class all the way. Got a big meeting there, need to entertain clients, that kind of thing—I told you all this. We're staying at the Biarritz Hotel in Studio City. We leave on the twenty-fifth and return the first of the month."

"That sounds lovely." Did it? *Oh, boy. Moving on.* How did Jillian get paid for her services? Jillian most assuredly would ascertain that the agreed-upon money was already in place somewhere.

I can do that. For Jilly. She waited a beat and then asked delicately, "And the other arrangements?"

He frowned. "I took care of everything we agreed upon exactly the way you specified."

"Thank you. I don't like asking and won't mention it again. Now we can relax and really get to know each other."

What was she promising, really? To commit herself full bore to this stranger the way Jillian might if she felt the connection and wished to proceed with the arrangement?

He seemed wary. He'd laid out his money, probably a substantial sum, and now he wanted what he thought he'd paid for.

But all he was getting was lunch.

He wasn't someone she *needed* to deal with to impersonate Jilly. She should just say she didn't feel the connection, they wouldn't suit, and offer to refund his money so he could seek out someone else.

The waiter knocked discreetly, rolled in the lunch cart, set up the service, and then left with a generous tip.

"I am hungry," he growled.

"As am I."

"Not for steak and potatoes, Ms. Jillian."

"No, I know that," Justine murmured, uncovering her pasta. This guy was as blunt as a club. "Everything in good time."

"What about you?" he asked after a while. "Why do you do . . . this?"

"It pays well," she answered without thinking. *No, no, no. Be Jillian.* She amended her hasty statement, "But more than that, it gives me a chance to meet nice people, go interesting places, and develop fascinating and lasting relationships. My clients often become good friends. So, why not *this?*"

He finished his steak, and she picked at her pasta. He drank his beer, she sipped the glass of wine he ordered and then prolonged things still further by taking coffee. There wasn't much conversation. She needed time to think, to assess all the angles of taking on Jillian's life.

She was doing a lousy job, anyway. Jillian would have known exactly how to make her guest comfortable. Justine couldn't find five words to say that wouldn't give her away. She debated how far she wanted to take this when she was so not feeling the love.

She wanted to end it now.

But if she were Jillian, she wouldn't end it now. She would try him out, give him every opportunity to prove they were compatible. She would want the big payout. She might even want the sex. Her guest obviously did.

How different could it be from a one-night bar bang? Justine wasn't naive or inexperienced. She'd had her share of one-night stands and a black book full of give-and-go guys in her life.

But this was a whole other level, with his expectations rising and filling the room like a hot air balloon.

He had paid for Jillian's time and he wanted sex with Jillian. Justine didn't see any way to get out of it other than walking out the door.

And Jillian *Dare* wouldn't blow off a client that cavalierly. She'd blow him, period. Whereas Justine Durant couldn't afford to take him on, even though she was as good as trapped in the room.

Note to self: next time—public meeting place.

She couldn't believe she was thinking there was going to be a next time.

Justine wasn't really going to let him fuck her. Jillian sure would. Her imprimatur was stamped all over him: she'd vetted him; he had the key and an invitation, and by the very little Jillian had written in her confession, it seemed implicit that it was exactly what she would do.

So since she was impersonating Jillian, Justine didn't have to consider her own conscience, her own morality. She could step outside herself, the way Jilly must when she entertained these clients. She could just let him do her.

"You ready for the sex part yet?"

She smiled tenuously. "Are you?"

"Come sit on my lap, and you'll see."

Maybe that was the way to ease into it. Let him kiss her, play with his penis, make sure he was protected, and see where it led. Maybe it wouldn't be all that bad.

No. The way to approach it was that it would be *good*. That was how Jilly would play it. Everything was good—big and hard and perfect and pleasurable.

All Justine had to do was step off the cliff.

She pushed the lunch cart out of the way and delicately settled herself onto his lap. She wriggled her bottom against him, settling herself more tightly against his iron-hard shaft.

"You like that," he murmured.

What would Jilly say to arouse him further? "I adore a thick, hard penis like yours."

"I like a woman who appreciates a good, hard penis."

"How good is it?"

"Why don't you try it and see?"

Yes. No. This must be standard operating procedure for Jill.

"I'm always ready for some good, hot cock."

He lifted her skirt, feeling for her cunt; his breath caught as he found her—through her delicate silk panties—shaved bare, open, and unexpectedly wet.

She reached for his pants, zipping him out as he explored her between her legs, and she grasped his penis tightly.

"Tell me what you want now. You can keep feeling up my cunt or you can fuck it."

This wasn't her. Never in her life would she have uttered those words.

"I want both," he muttered thickly as he inserted his fingers deep into her.

Justine squeezed him harder. "Well, I have him now. And what I'm going to do to him"—she wriggled away from his hands and bent over and rounded the thick tip of his penis with her teeth and pressed lightly into his skin—"is I'm going to *eat* him."

Where was this coming from? Maybe she was trying to divert him from the main event.

She wet her mouth and took him again. It was easier to give a blow job than let him take her altogether. And she knew he wouldn't protest.

"I want, I want . . ." he moaned, his fingers moving convulsively.

She licked him up and down, saturating his shaft with hot saliva and taking him in her mouth with deep, rhythmic pulls.

He came almost instantly, thank heaven, flooding semen into her mouth as she pulled at the tender slit at his tip until he pushed her away. "No more, no more, no . . . more . . . more."

"More?" She licked him like a lollipop.

"No—yes."

"Yum," she murmured huskily, taking another swipe at him.

"Not yet."

"Then I'll just hold him, keep him hot and hard for me."

"Yeah." His breathing became progressively more shallow. "God, you're good . . ."

"You, too," she whispered. "You're incredible."

It wasn't so difficult—what Jillian would do, what Jillian would say. And when he eased Justine to the floor, covertly donned a condom, and mounted her, it wasn't even that difficult to fake her orgasm.

She could do this, she thought, as he lay panting on top of her. *I can be Jillian. I can find out why she'd sent the code and what kind of awful trouble she's in.*

If this was what a companion did, it wasn't much different than bringing home a horny guy from a bar. And it was far more comfortable with control in *her* hands.

Jilly's hands.

She could almost see why Jilly had made this choice.

It wasn't difficult to do. Not at all. And she'd negotiate the rest later.

Chapter Three

Omigod—*what have I done?*

When she came to her senses afterward, when she really looked at the five-thousand-dollar check he'd written her for incidentals, Justine felt desperate to call the whole thing off.

Except she was nearly naked and she couldn't just race out the door.

His name was Randolph Brill. Randy. He was middle-aged and rolling in dough.

I am Jilly, she is me.

It didn't take me a half hour to shed every doubt, every compunction, every inhibition, all sense of who I am and my own morality, and become someone who . . .

Justine didn't want to define the *what* of the someone *who*. That someone wasn't *her*. The practical, logical Justine had, in the aftermath of the sex, frantically tried to invent a reason not to go with Randy to L.A. for that week.

It was callous of her, but while he was still naked and erect, she tried to figure out a way to get out of the trip. She knew she had a window of about two minutes while he was still ripe with pleasure from his climax.

Right then, she murmured as sweetly as she could manage, "I really enjoyed that. It's obvious we're sexually compatible, and that's very important to me." She paused a moment to swirl her fingers over his penis. "And I promise we'll have lovely trips together, if you truly do desire my company. If it were any other week, I'd love to take this trip with you to L.A., but I"—how to phrase it?—"regretfully have to withdraw my offer to accompany you this time."

He started to protest and she licked the tip of his penis. "I really have to take care of those family matters I mentioned. But you know, when I think how close I was to actually missing the pleasure of your company today—it would have been such a loss for both of us."

He didn't miss a beat, he seemed so determined to have her—no, to have Jilly. "Then aren't you glad you didn't? And won't you be sorry if you don't come with me? Give me the weekend at least," he coaxed her. "That's the most important part of the trip for me. It's when I'm entertaining the business associates I want you to meet."

What did he mean by the *I want you to meet* part? It didn't matter. If she were in L.A., even for a weekend, and anything arose pertaining to Jilly, she'd be trapped. She wouldn't be anywhere near getting to Jillian soon enough. And what if Jillian had traveled with any of those *business associates,* and Justine, impersonating Jilly, didn't recognize them?

"Same money," Randy added silkily. "Just for the weekend."

What could a week of Jillian's company cost him? He'd already paid a fair amount for this get-to-know-him session.

She said nothing while she frantically assessed the risk of being that far away from Manhattan *and* how much further she was willing to go with this impersonation. It was not a win-win for her. She'd already gone too far. And he probably felt she was trying to up the ante.

"I'll fly you there and back, private jet, limousines. Penthouse hotel room. Spending money. The works."

A weekend fully funded, the same money as Jillian was paid for a week's commitment, with all those indefinable extras—it was probably the norm, and Jillian would have leaped at it. Given that, there was no conceivable reason Justine could invent to get out of it.

Even "family matters."

"Maybe," Randy suggested, still in that cajoling tone, "being away from *family matters* for a little bit of time will give you a new perspective. It *is* only a weekend. I'll blow off my associates and we'll fuck the whole weekend, if that's what you want."

God, he was relentless. He seemed to even enjoy the chase.

"I'll come," she murmured finally, fatalistically. It didn't obligate her to anything, she thought. *Just say yes so he'll go.*

When he left, she sank onto the bed and stared at the check until her eyes glazed over.

I am sitting in a hotel room half naked. I just gave a blow job to, and had sex with, a stranger. And I promised to go to L.A. with him to help him entertain some associates he wants me to meet.

Am I nuts?

Or were the sex and money so easy and so seductive a saint would have capitulated, she wondered later as she showered.

She couldn't scrub away his scent. Or maybe it was redolent only in her conscience.

She'd learned a hard truth that afternoon: Saint Justine was not immune to the lure of the money or its luxurious perks. Saint Justine the martyr had said *yes*.

And then she couldn't help thinking she'd made a mess of everything. What did Justine Durant know about the dicey business of being a high-end traveling companion? And how much more did she want to know?

She only had a few days until the trip to Los Angeles with Randy, and who knew what Jillian might have scheduled in the interim. After all, she couldn't have known she would accept Randy's invitation, although odds were she would not have refused it.

But in the meantime, Jillian might have arranged half a dozen other get-to-know-you "dates."

Why did I do this?

It was the imponderable of the day. Because having no idea of Jillian's true occupation was no excuse for Justine to fall into the morass of her real life. But on the other hand, her body was not some holy temple. She'd had her share of one-off sex, so there was no purity of purpose in her feelings of guilt.

So if she thought impersonating Jilly was the way to find Jilly, then that was what she'd do. And she wouldn't feel guilty about anything she might have to do in the process.

She stared at herself in the bathroom mirror as she dressed. Her self seemed like a stranger even with all the rationalizations. With her hair pulled back, and her blue eyes glazed over, she didn't look anything like the glamorous Jilly right now—or feel like her, even though she'd just had reasonably pleasant sex with a man she didn't know.

That was standard operating procedure for Jillian.

It scared Justine that she got how Jilly could do it, even how she herself could do it, but not why it was worth a lot of money to some men.

Like Randy. With whom she had promised to go to L.A.

Justine also still wasn't sure she was on the right track.

She was assuming that Jill would want everything to appear as normal as possible until Justine could find her and help her. Because if Justine sounded the alarm, stuff would hit the fan, and she'd lose the advantage of being under the radar.

She felt like she was operating on guts and gumption right now, and the guilt-inducing question of what Jillian would want her to do was killing her.

She sat down at the desk near the window and took a pad and pen from the drawer. It was a luxurious room, even in its appointments, like the expensive pen she held in her hand, but it wasn't so overdone that Jillian's clients would think she was gouging them. They probably felt it was just the place for a clandestine meeting of two like-minded adults looking for an exciting, private encounter.

Jillian knew exactly what she was doing. So what could Justine infer now about how Jilly operated?

She started writing:

The client paid for the room and didn't balk at the price.

Everything was prepaid—a tacit agreement to whatever the client had contracted for.

Regardless of how it was sugarcoated, it was all about sex.

And Jillian was very well paid for her appearance, her body, her time, and her bedroom expertise. Justine could fake the appearance and the body; the bedroom expertise not so much.

She still didn't have a clue what to do next.

Maybe she should treat it like an experiment. Gather the known facts. Theorize probabilities based on the facts. Experiment to come to a conclusion.

She needed to reread that letter and to go back into Jillian's computer files to see if there was anything she missed.

She didn't have to push *being Jillian* any further than this. She needed to take control. She controlled nothing right now except that she was the only one who knew Jillian was in trouble.

She had to call her HR department and reconfirm her emergency leave of absence. If they argued, she'd resign and deal with the fallout later.

She'd go back to square one. She'd go home, pack up some stuff, and stay at Jillian's apartment for the time being to try to parse things out.

She had to warm up that apartment, though, if she were going to stay there. By the time Justine finished packing, she'd tossed a couple of afghans and quilts into a suitcase.

She took her cell, her BlackBerry, her laptop, and a couple of the medical journals she was in the midst of reading. Any distraction to keep from thinking about this afternoon.

Like how she was going to bargain for the emergency time off she needed if she didn't even know how much time she needed.

But she didn't care. Jillian's message seemed more urgent than ever now that she was actually in Jill's apartment, arranging things, putting food in the fridge, changing the sheets, tossing a quilt over the footboard, hanging up her clothes in the six inches of space she eked out in the bedroom closet.

She didn't bring much, clotheswise: jeans and tees mainly. Whatever else she needed, she could pull from Jillian's closet.

What she really needed was time.

She had tonight at least. She'd bought take-out and diet tea. She brought her meal, Jillian's laptop, and her own, into the bedroom. She booted up Jillian's computer and read the confession again, word by word, syllable by syllable.

It stunned her that she knew next to nothing about her own twin; Jillian kept so much hidden.

It left Justine with only that elusive, duplicitous letter begging for help and the truth of a long and convoluted lie. Justine now saw that she had pretty much volunteered to be Jillian's cunt.

Someone would discover she wasn't, sooner than later, if she kept up the charade. Someone would recognize that it wasn't Jillian's body, voice, or personality. Something tiny and intangible would give her away.

But now that she'd begun, Justine had only two choices: tell the truth or keep up the pretense. Neither way guaranteed she could help her sister. Either choice could be a disaster for both of them.

Right at this moment, staring at Jillian's web page, Justine still had no answers.

It got her nowhere except back to her original, ill-conceived idea of pretending to be Jillian. Given her experience with Randy, Justine didn't think that cover would last more than thirty seconds if she ever encountered anyone who had previously booked Jillian's services.

Jillian's services. God, it sounded so—pornographic. The whole thing *was* like a bad porn movie. But the question remained, how far was *Justine* willing to go, since she'd gone that far already?

Did the fact that she was out of her mind with worry and panic count as an excuse not to go to L.A.?

Or was it too late? Once you stepped off a cliff, you couldn't arrange a do-over. And she'd nose-dived into the Grand Canyon.

Her head felt like it was going to split open. She still had to deal with the problem of her job; she was on the brink of self-destructing her career.

She told them she had a family emergency and couldn't give

a time frame as to when she'd return. No, she couldn't say if it would be a week or a month. Yes, her assistant could take over. Yes, she was willing to take a suspension in pay. Yes, she'd notify them when her plans were more concrete.

She leaned back against the pillows wearily. All she'd done was fudge around every truth, including this afternoon with Randy.

Jillian, those were not clues as to what's going on with you.

A buzzer jolted her awake, and a sharp, distinctive disembodied male voice demanded, "Jillian! Are you up there? Are you back? Did you remember the booth party tonight? Don't hide. I know you were due back this morning, so I'm coming up."

Panic. Ungodly, *what am I going to do, that person will know instantly I'm not Jill?* heart attack–worthy panic.

She had thirty seconds and only one solution: *don't* be Jill.

Scratch that—maybe this person knew where Jill was. Maybe I'll find out something. I have to be Jilly. Say nothing definitive—make him give the answers. Who the hell could it be? Oh, shit—what the hell is a booth party?

And then there was the ominous scratch of a key in the lock and the door opening.

He had a key?

"Jillian!"

She had no choice, she had to fake it now. Justine shoved the computer under one of the pillows, opened the bedroom door, and sauntered out, yawning. "Oh, crap, it's you. I was napping, for God's sake. Your voice could wake the dead."

Her visitor let out a deep breath. "Jesus God, you scared me half to death, I thought maybe you hadn't got back."

"Why would you think that?" Justine headed toward the kitchen to reactivate the coffeepot, and her guest followed.

"Some billionaire died in a car crash. I don't know. I just thought . . . maybe . . . the guy who died, wasn't he the one your guy was involved with? Wasn't there some business deal on the table in London?"

Justine played for time, trying to wrangle some coherent

response from so little information. "Well, if there was, it's not possible now. God, I'm so tired."

"I thought you said——"

Justine jumped on a distraction. "Would you cut me some slack? I'm brain-dead and not even in this time zone right now. I even made coffee, that's how out of it I am."

"You? Coffee?"

She'd been afraid of that, of not knowing Jillian's habits and making a huge faux pas that would make someone instantly suspicious.

"Let it go," she muttered, slanting a covert glance at him. He was tall, sleek, and well dressed. His features were heavy, his eyebrows thick, and his mouth a little petulant.

"Tell me everything, then. Tell me how it went with Ellicott."

Phew. She knew enough to be able to answer even in generalities. "He was pleased. He was relatively easy and very generous."

"And that English guy, the one who died?"

"I wasn't involved with him," she covered.

"Well, thank God. There was some ruckus about the circumstances of his death. Ellicott allegedly vanished, and I just wondered——"

She made a sound, buying time to figure out how to play that information. "That had to have been when I was on my way home. I heard nothing about it, and every arrangement was completed, so I don't really care." Was that Jillian enough? She thought so.

"God," he said. "So. You really made coffee?"

"Jesus, I've been traveling forever it seems like. I've been back here maybe five hours, I'm jet-lagged beyond belief, I'm not even coherent. I need *something*. Especially when people come barging into my home with no warning and want to drag me out again at night."

That truly sounded like Jilly. And this friend, this confidant, unless he was supplying her with uppers, he could be pussy-whipped inside of thirty seconds.

He'd thrown up his hands. "Okay, okay. I get it. You're tired."

"He wore me out," she added, trying to sound petulant. "Did

you think it was all business all day long? He was on me and inside me every free minute and he got in a bonus bang on the way to the airport."

"God, you lead the most obscenely glamorous life," her guest muttered. "He was humping cunt even on the way to sending you home?"

"Couldn't keep his groping hands off my beautiful body," Justine said airily. Making up the sex stuff was easy; it distracted her guest, who obviously got off on Jillian's sexual adventures, and it made her sound that much more like Jillian.

"How?"

Justine smiled a smug Jillian smile. "I made him kneel and thrust. He needed to get down on his knees to me anyway. He needed a lesson in humility. Then I let him plug me hard until we parked at Departures, and even then, he wanted to keep fucking me. But time was up and he knew that would cost and it would wreck up his evening plans. So I left him all deliciously creamy and hungry for more."

Her guest moaned. "Is he any good?"

"Good enough," she said. "What matters is, *I'm* good." Oh, would Jillian ever say something like that.

"God, you are. And you need to be thanking me yet again for putting you on the wealthy wankers' path to fantasy and prosperity."

"Thank you," she murmured, hiding behind her coffee cup.

"Thank you, Zach almighty," he prompted.

Zach—Justine searched her memory. Zach. Many years ago at the ad agency there had been a Zach. But she couldn't dredge up a single memory that indicated Jilly and long-ago Zach were still friends. They hadn't been lovers. But he was obviously a big part of Jilly's life—Jilly's sex life, too—if he knew the details of her dates and had her key.

"I owe everything to you, Zach almighty," she repeated obediently.

"That's my girl. Now, about tonight—"

Justine rubbed her hand over her eyes, pretending weariness.

"Zach, my darling, I know you gave me every exhaustive detail about tonight probably a week ago. Please have mercy and refresh my memory."

"It's no big deal. Just a few gentlemen who are interested in meeting you but I didn't think a private meeting was warranted right now. So I arranged a booth party for them at the product launch. Red-carpet glam. You don't have to give up any cunt tonight unless you want to. They know the rules. Look all you want, but don't touch."

"I like a big fat wallet almost as much as a big fat penis," Justine murmured. "Where is this event?"

"We're celebrating the launch and drinking vodka shots all night at Sweet Cheeks."

Justine stretched languorously, giving herself a minute to parse out clues from that brief description. *We're celebrating* could mean more than just Jillian and he. Like, maybe he still was in advertising, and this was an event to promote a new brand that was an agency client.

That seemed probable. But what the hell was a booth party?

"Just dress up. I'll send the limo at nine and then all you have to do is flaunt those luscious sweet cheeks."

"I live to follow your direction," Justine said sarcastically, as Jilly would have, she thought. "How bare down where is acceptable for a product launch?"

"You know exactly how to launch yourself," Zach said with an insinuating smirk. "And you do it so well," he added as he opened the door. "Limo. Nine."

Jillian knew what to do. Justine had a vague idea as she closed the door behind Zach and leaned against it in relief.

First hurdle passed.

But what did Jillian do so well?

I love to flaunt my naked body.

And if it was for a group of potential customers, well, that answered *that* question.

The only one remaining was, could she do it? *Would* she do it?

What could I possibly learn tonight that would help me help Jilly?

She knew the answer was *nothing*, that this evening would be an exercise in vanity and futility and just put her deeper into the sexual vortex that was Jilly's life.

She climbed back into the bed and went back to the computer, looking over the lists of names, the sordid details about strange men she didn't want to know.

There was nothing about Zach.

Who the hell was he? And why should she listen to him?

Jilly owed *everything* to Zach, he'd said. What was everything? It sounded to Justine like Zach was pimping for Jilly. Obviously there was some kind of quid pro quo going on. He seemed to be her confidant. He probably was her pimp. She owed him.

Which meant Justine couldn't upset that delicate balance by refusing to deal with him. It would raise suspicious anyway, and she was walking a wire-thin tightrope as it was.

Zach knew Jillian—that was another downside. Any slip—and she'd almost made one this evening—any *further* slip, and he'd call her out. She needed to convince him.

Or tell him the truth.

Assuming he knew Jillian even had a twin, that is. If Jilly had kept her secret life that separate from her family, chances were none of her acquaintances knew about Justine. And if Zach didn't know, would he believe her if she told him?

Probably not. Oh, God, how more convoluted could this get? The simple solution was just to leave.

And then what? Zach would probably scour the city to find Jillian. If they were so inextricably connected that he had the key to her apartment and he knew about her "dates," he had to be getting something from it. Sex? A cut of the money she earned?

She should just pack up and go. It was the sane thing to do. But instead she spent ten minutes checking deaths and accident reports in the United States and Britain. Still nothing, and she was so tired, she let herself drift off to sleep.

She woke suddenly with a jolt, remembering where she was: in Jillian's bed, surrounded by her computer and a jumble of cell phones, with Zach waiting at some nightclub for her to appear.

And she—no, Jillian—was half an hour late already.

I have to get out of here. She'd put everything back in the safe and go.

She was steps away from getting out the door when she heard the key in the lock and the door burst open.

Zach. "Jesus. What the hell—what are you doing?"

"Not going to your party," Justine snapped. "I'm leaving."

He grasped her arm. "You're going to the party."

"No, you contracted for Jillian to go to the party. I'm not Jillian."

He stared at her with glittering eyes and shook his head. "Sure, sure, sure. I've heard that before. You're Justine, the mythical twin, who appears when Jillian gets stressed or doesn't want to spread her legs. Forget it—you've run your course on that big fat lie."

She wrenched her arm away.

"You idiot, I *am* Justine. I'm Jill's twin. Look around you. Did you ever see Jill drink coffee? Read a book? Decorate with quilts?"

"Actually, I know you've got a store of *Justine* stuff in your closet." He leered at her. "You can't fool me, Jill"—he started walking toward her—"it doesn't work. I don't know why you keep trying." He backed her up toward Jillian's bedroom. "So get fucking dressed so we can get this frigging fuckfest on the road." He pushed her into the bedroom. "Wear that naked silver crepe thing and your tits and cunt. That's all you need tonight." He slammed the door. *"DO IT."*

The dress was the thinnest fluid silver-shot crepe and revealed every nuance and curve of her body.

She looked like Jillian in that dress. It fit her so snugly, she couldn't wear a stitch of undergarments beneath it. She left her hair down, smoked up her eyes, and found some glittery earrings and a bracelet. She left her neck and the deep plunge between her breasts bare. She slid on a pair of strappy silver sandals, and then wondered how familiar Zach was with Jillian's body, feet included.

Dear God. Don't overthink it. He didn't believe there was a Justine anyway, so she didn't need to take into account every little difference.

She stared at herself in the mirror. *Not me, this is not me.*

And yet it was. They were two sides of the same coin, she and Jill. Justine saw Jillian in her shadowed blue eyes, her oval face, her creamy skin, and even in her careful preparations to protect herself in case the evening turned into something more than just a booth party.

She saw herself merging with Jill, becoming Jill even while she knew she was Justine, but a Justine who was micrometers away from her sister in needs, yearnings, and desires.

Justine had chosen to deny them, Jilly to pursue them.

She felt like a fraud.

And she felt like a queen. The allure of seeing herself dressed up was both discomfiting and seductive.

She almost believed Jilly had meant for her to take over her hedonistic life, to live it, dissect it, and somehow make it right, make it better to save her.

Or was she meant to fully embrace it?

Zach knocked impatiently on the bedroom door. "Let's go, Jill." *"Whatever you have to do."*

She didn't want to do this. Zach didn't believe her. Maybe no one would. Maybe the choice had been made for her.

She opened the door slowly, and with the knowledge of what it meant to be Jill and fully aware of all she'd be required to do, she entered Jillian's world.

Chapter Four

All clubs seemed the same to her. They were dimly lit, played pulsing tribal music, and starred wall-to-wall people trying to dance, make conversation, or squeeze in sex somehow in the corners.

Sweet Cheeks was no exception, except the promo was primo. A huge wall displaying the product backed the red carpet into the club as limos drove up and dropped off B- and C-list celebrities. The corporate guys and the agency guys. The party girls. Drinks were passed down the line to those queued to get inside. The flashbulbs, the paparazzi, the shouted questions, the posing and posturing.

Justine's limo inched forward; it was one in a long line. She felt a surge of excitement as the crowd cheered.

She also felt cold with anticipation and dread. She hated the way Zach sat across from her with such proprietary certainty.

This is not my normal life, she thought. *I'm on a stage, it's all an illusion. I'm too real to carry it off.*

The limo drew up to the velvet cord stanchions. The door opened and Zach exited first, giving her his hand. She felt a sudden wave of pure panic. *What am I doing?*

Zach knew the importance of how things looked. He made certain that she gracefully emerged from the limo, and he displayed her to the cameras before he took her arm and led her down the carpet.

Questions here, questions there—Zach answered them all briefly, and then presented Justine to the hungry horde. "Zach Leshan, account executive, Apple Agency. And the amazing Jillian Dare."

The photographers were all over her, snapping her body every which way she could pose. Every few steps, another photographer, another camera hungry for form-hugging, sexily dressed bodies. Always the bodies, always the boobs, never the faces.

Finally Zach got her inside the cavern of the club, where bars were set up on either side, big Plexiglas icelike bars that served vodka on the rocks by yet another sexy body to the milling crowd.

"This way," Zach whispered, drawing her through the dancing throng to a curtained VIP section. It was lined with booths which, in the dim light, she could just see were occupied. It was all about drinking, dancing on tables, making out, and making a fool of yourself. And see-me, sample-me sex.

There was no backing down now.

Their booth was in a secluded corner and her guests were already there, two of them already deep into their vodka shots and peering anxiously out into the crowd.

"Here we are," Zach called out over the music, and gave Justine a little push forward so she approached the booth ahead of him.

She got the lay of things almost immediately. Two of the men were clients, most likely, happy party guys; the third, not so much. He was too sober for an event like this, and while he had a glass in hand, it didn't look as if he had drunk very much.

Zach leaned into the booth. "So this is Marty Gandel"—who was a really handsome man, even though he was losing his hair—"and Ralph Baines"—who was tall, swarthy, and had a harsh-looking face and quirking lips that formed an "O" as his gaze swept over her—"and that is Doug Rawls."

He was tall, lean, and elegant, with unruly black hair and a sardonic expression etched into the deep lines on his face.

All he had to do was look at her and Justine knew Doug Rawls was trouble. His ice blue eyes saw everything, even saw through her. He knew everything about her instantly, and he hated everything, particularly her. She would sleep with him in a minute, no questions asked; he knew it and had rejected the idea in that same minute.

She wasn't so far from Jillian after all.

"I hope you can make some room for me," she cooed to Marty and Ralph. Immediately, Ralph slid out of the booth so she could wriggle her way in next to Marty, who draped his arm around her.

So it was going to be a kiss and cuddle party. Did Jillian the scrupulous do this kind of thing on the side, despite the money she demanded? But Justine could tell these men had that kind of money anyway. They were awestruck by her body, her availability, her I'd-love-to-fuck-you aura.

They ordered drinks, Ralph asked her to dance, while Marty avidly watched and Doug Rawls frowned.

Ralph clearly couldn't wait to press her body tight against his while they writhed to the beat. He was hot and burning hard for her, and the more she undulated, the more he just rubbed her belly against his jutting erection. When the set was over, she covertly stroked his penis to give him that extra something he was so avid for.

She wasn't as out of breath as Ralph when she took her place next to Marty, who whispered in her ear, "I need some tongue."

"I barely know you," she whispered back.

"We could get bare and remedy that."

"I'll take the kiss," she retorted, lifting her mouth to his and letting him sink into her. His mouth was hot on hers, and his hand draped over her shoulder, seeking her breast.

I'm going under, she thought in amazement as he compressed her nipple between his fingers. She felt the urge to reach for him. It had already been too long. She felt like doing him right there, right then.

What am I thinking? I can't.

Or did Zach intend for her to?

She pulled away slowly. "Nice."

"Just the beginning," Marty murmured, his fingers still surrounding her nipple. "Nice responsive tit, too. Feel it, Ralph."

They acted like she was a blow-up doll they just could hand back and forth. Just what was the deal with Zach and these men?

Those men. Not Rawls, who just sat there with that disapproving look on his face. *Dear God, let him go find somewhere else to root.*

"Excuse me?" she said sharply, tearing her gaze away from Doug Rawls.

"It'd be easier if you just showed us your tits," Marty said.

"Really?" Jillian did things like this?

"Sure. Then we could sip and sup all night and you could just sit back and enjoy."

The image was offensive and arousing all at once. Surely Jillian didn't give away sex when she could charge the earth for it. There had to be some kind of agreement. But maybe, at private parties, because she needed it, lived for it, couldn't go a day without it, she just gave in.

Justine watched Doug Rawls from the corner of her eyes. His face was impassive, his steady blue gaze contemptuous. He made her furious; the way he looked at her made her want to go over the edge. Just to see how he'd react.

She gave him a hard, lancing look, and then she jumped.

"That sounds delicious," she murmured coyly. "Come on, help me with the straps of my gown. And then you can just take your time with my nipples."

They did more than help—they felt, they fondled, they played with her breasts until finally Rawls levered himself up from the table in disgust and stalked away.

"Hard-ass," Marty said as he nuzzled Justine's ear. "I don't know why he even came. How would you like to come?"

"How would you?" she countered, sliding her hand down to his throbbing penis, and then giving Ralph a deep kiss. "Your penis feels like it's more than ready for a thorough milking."

"Only if I can fondle you," Ralph said.

Whatever you have to do.

She closed her eyes and nodded, unzipping Marty's pants and grasping him tightly.

No wonder Zach had hidden them away. She'd tumbled into standard operating procedure at these events—the coy flirt, the shrouded strip, the covert sex, however much you could get away with in a public place. No one particularly noticed she was naked from the waist down the whole night, or that Ralph was stroking and sucking her nipple, or that Marty was kissing her while she held on tight to his still-erect penis.

All of that would be taken care of, wiped away as if it had never happened, and later spoken about in code by those in the know. The great time, the incredible music, the excellent food, the fabulous women, sensuous, wild, and willing, and right in your booth for the taking.

I am Jillian and she is me.

It was too seductive, this world of saturating sex. Justine felt like her body was primed for a night of unending lust, but there came a point where all urges were satisfied, the body sated, and it was time to give it up and go home.

The breaking point at Sweet Cheeks was around four in the morning, when people began straggling out of the club.

By then, Marty was asleep on the bench, and Ralph was slumped on the floor. Zach was nowhere to be found, as Justine discovered when she finally pulled up her dress and went looking for him.

She didn't have any money, or any sense, for that matter, if she really stopped to think about what she had done.

She couldn't even look at herself in the restroom mirror as she cleaned up.

It wasn't me. It was Jillian, what Jillian would do. Dear God, what was I thinking?

Someone took her arm as she emerged from the ladies' room.

Doug Rawls, his expression still impassive, speaking words that for a moment were incomprehensible to her. "You're coming with me."

"I'm *what?*"

"You did your club girl thing; now it's time for something different."

"*You're* different?"

"You know it," he said, propelling her toward the entrance.

"Can't you just give me some money for a cab?" Really, what was the point?

"I don't think so."

Justine was too tired to argue. It wasn't as if he were dangerous. Zach would not have paired Jillian with anyone questionable, she was fairly certain of that. Although Marty and Ralph, well, they'd just been two raunchy guys let loose in the candy store of her body.

And now Mr. sees-all-knows-all. He was the kind of guy who could grab a cab even if it were full and the driver would swear it was empty and open the door for him.

She leaned her head back against the hard leather seat and closed her eyes. "Whatever, I'm too tired."

"I'm sure all that breast-feeding wore you out."

She clamped down on a quick response. "You're just in town for the event, right?"

"No, actually I'm an acquaintance of Marty's, just came along for the ride."

"And now you want your turn to ride me," Justine muttered with a touch of bitterness.

He hesitated a moment before he said, "So to speak."

She made a sound. She didn't want anything else to be about sex tonight. Particularly with him. Especially with him. He'd had his chance to fuck with her in the club. She didn't see why he was fucking with her now.

She didn't have to acquiesce to anything or anyone—not him, not Zach, not even Jillian. She didn't have to say yes to anything or anyone else ever again.

Especially, particularly him.

But it was too easy to be easy, and too hard to say no after.

"Where are we going?"

"To my hotel."

"Out of towner, are you? That's good. Leaving when?"

"Probably not fast enough for you," he said grimly. "But that's the way it is, Jillian. And you knew it the minute Zach introduced us."

She didn't acknowledge that comment at all. She felt dank and used from all that sucking and hand fucking. A shower would be nice. A soft bed. A longtime lover. But those didn't exist anymore, either in her world or Jillian's.

And what had she learned of Jillian?

Nothing. Just that fast fucks were about as filling as fast food. *Not.*

And expensive hotels didn't make the man. They just made things more difficult. Why had she agreed to come with him?

Well, "agreed" wasn't quite the word. She was railroaded in a weak moment. But it didn't matter—she was going to sleep, no matter what he wanted, said, or did.

They were silent in the elevator, silent down the hall, silent as he opened the door to his two-room suite. It startled her into further silence because Doug Rawls was the very definition of a man who would be Jillian's gentleman client.

"In the bedroom."

"Now, listen—"

He bent his head and gave her a long, level look. "In the bedroom, Jillian."

"Fine." She stalked into the bedroom and looked at him defiantly.

"Good. Now take off the dress."

"I don't think so."

"Take—off—the—dress." That was the CEO on a rampage tone of voice, dangerously quiet and menacing. He meant to get his way.

She slipped the straps off her shoulders, still holding his gaze, and let them drop. The dress slowly slid down her body and pooled at her feet.

She heard the faint catch of his breath. She felt herself pulse with arousal at the look in his eyes, and she wished she hadn't done anything sexual with anyone ever in her life so she wouldn't disappoint him.

It was the strangest feeling, born of a certainty about him that she didn't know she even possessed. Her whole body unfurled in subtle recognition. Her nipples hardened under his gaze that saw everything, from the tips of her toes to her shorn pubic vee, the curve of her hips, the lift of her breasts, the slope of shoulders and neck, her touseled hair, her defiant eyes.

All he'd said was, *Take off the dress.*

NO!

But she was Jillian, was she not? What would Jillian do when confronted by those eyes and that man who was slowly stripping off his clothes, slowly revealing his long, lean body and the iron length of his thick penis.

Jillian wouldn't turn down that penis. Jillian would climb into his bed and onto him in a heartbeat. That, or she'd flaunt her naked body and make him crawl to *her*. And she was Jillian, was she not? And bound to act exactly how Jillian would act, to lust for the man Jillian would lust for, to fuck him the way Jillian would fuck him.

Justine turned, threw a look over her shoulder and climbed into his bed, sandals and all, and braced herself up on her knees. She sank down onto her buttocks, with one leg bent under her and the other bracing her body, so her legs were spread and her bare cleft was visible.

She could have sworn his penis elongated even more. If he came near, she'd bite into him and devour him. And he would come. The Jillian in her knew it, felt it, tasted it.

She ran her tongue over her lips, waiting, holding his eyes. She could outwait eternity if it took that long for him to come into bed.

He said her name, his voice rough. "Jillian."

Not *her* name. Her persona, her character. The naked woman in his bed lusting for his penis. "I *hate* waiting," she murmured with just a touch of irritation in her voice.

She spread her legs wider and stroked her cleft lightly as she fixed him with a smoldering look. "Don't make me wait."

He erupted then, moved to the side of the bed, grasped her legs, and pulled her toward him. The gesture was so abrupt that she fell flat on her back, her body canted against his, her legs braced on his chest, before she even comprehended what he was doing.

But he knew exactly what he was doing. She was positioned at the precise angle of penetration for maximum depth. Without foreplay and without another word, he thrust his penis hard between her legs and planted himself deep in her.

She levered herself up to watch. His hips undulated to reach deeper inside her as he hefted her buttocks farther off the bed, jamming himself even tighter against her hips.

She couldn't see his penis at all, he was that deep inside her.

"Don't move." It was his CEO voice again.

She had never felt more naked than at this moment, with his penis so purposefully rooted and his body rocking against hers. She had never felt such a hunger to possess someone. He couldn't rut deep enough to satisfy her burning lust for him. No, not for him—for his penis, for the pleasure and the evanescent orgasms that kept Jillian constantly seeking and never satisfied.

She felt his controlled shudder. He needed that final possession of her, the hard, piniouning thrust that he couldn't hold back.

He pulled her bottom so she was nearly off the bed, the heft of his penis the one thing connecting her to anything. And then he drove into her again and again with hard, slick, hot thrusts. She heard herself groan, deep, guttural ohs—*oh, oh, oh, oh, oh*—her body jolting and convulsing as her orgasm hit.

Another *ohhhhhhhhhh* as his orgasm gushed out in a rush of hot cream.

She wanted to bathe in it, to coat her nipples with it, and rub it all over her body. This was no party trick like in the club, to titillate and excite. This was real. This was something she couldn't define but felt all-consuming and inexorable.

When Doug abruptly withdrew from her, she pulled him onto her body so that he covered her as she wrapped herself around him and inhaled his scent. His penis stayed rigid with vibrating urgency as they lay locked together in the aftermath.

Had Jilly ever slept with a man like this? With *him*? A surge of pure jealousy suffused her body, nearly suffocating her. *Not him.*

"Jillian—"

But the way he said her name, Jillian couldn't have fucked him. Justine buried her head in his shoulder. This was enough, to be enfolded like this under his body, his penis pure heat against her belly.

Very subtly he shifted, sliding his hand down her back, over her buttocks, and pulling her leg over his hip so that she was open to him and they were side by side, face-to-face.

His hand was hot on her thigh as he caressed it, molding its shape, moving upward to her buttocks, pausing at her anal bud to feel and fondle as she squirmed at the luxurious feelings. It was so new to her but not unwelcome wholly because it was him.

She just let herself feel, let herself slide into the miasma of however he wanted to fondle and arouse her.

And then he was at her cunt lips from the obverse direction, slipping his fingers into her slick hole from the rear. Her body seized, just spasmed at the feeling of his fingers exploring her sex so forcefully, so thoroughly, and then his penis pumping between her legs.

His mouth covered hers, dominating her response. As he inched his way deeper, he thrust his finger into her from behind so that she was trapped by him both front and rear. She didn't know which pleasure point made her swoon more. She never wanted to move; she wanted to stay joined like this forever.

And his mouth was hot, rough, almost involuntary, as if he couldn't help it.

She wrapped her arms around him and just held on. She had never felt so open to a man. She had no idea she could take in so much of a man's passion.

Her body stretched and undulated against him. She couldn't get away. She was bound, front and back, at the mercy of his indomitable sex, his questing fingers boring deeper into places she wasn't aware could arouse such intensity.

He was as hot as a blowtorch, blasting into her, and alternately biting her lips and kissing her deeply.

It was almost too much—his possessiveness, his experienced fingers, his perfect kisses, her volcanic response to his sex. She was molten in his hands, her orgasm explosively shooting up in red flame and pouring out like lava.

He came a moment later, hard and forceful, still deep in her mouth, deep in her body, and all over her.

He whispered again, barely a breath, "Jillian."

A whisper. "Jillian."

Jillian. Jillian's sex. Jillian's man whenever she returned and he contacted her again. The thought caught her, in the backwash of all that pleasure, like a kick in the gut.

Don't assume he's not yours. Not ever.

He held her tightly, still in possession of her body, and she dozed off. After a while, she became aware of a change—of an emptiness—his penis was gone, and yet she felt invaded.

"Shhh. I'm just . . ." He kissed her. "My penis knows your cunt intimately; now I know your cunt thoroughly."

His fingers thrust into her, feeling her, kissing her, simultaneously fondling her anal bud with his other hand.

"Any way I can open up your body," he breathed against her mouth, "any way I can fuck you." He nipped her lip. "Every way I can ram my penis into you"—a deep, tongue-drugging kiss—"I am going to fuck you." Another kiss, hot and possessive as his fingers explored her, as he pumped her from the reverse position and maneuvered his body to bore his penis into her.

He came fast, just the way she liked it when a penis couldn't contain its lust for her.

"It's not enough," he growled in the aftermath. "I want more."

"There's more," she whispered. So much more—his erection never wavered. He kept his fingers anchored in her anal opening so that he was always inside her.

He kissed her for hours after. Long, arousing kisses as she played with his penis, then kissed it, nibbled it, swallowed it, and pulled his cum from its luscious head into her mouth.

He ate her, too, sucking at her pleasure point like it was whipped cream. He took her doggy-style, sitting, standing, on the desk. He took her with curtains open, in front of the window, in the bathroom, the tub, on the sofa, on the floor.

Hours and hours of fucking, hot, voluptuous fucking.

"You don't have anywhere else to go." It was a statement, not a question.

Not today she didn't, maybe not tomorrow, but she had her

other life, Jillian's life, and it would intrude with her upcoming weekend with Randy.

Don't think about Randy.

"You went away." They were on the bed, entangled in each other, his penis back between her legs. They were facing each other, both of his hands working her from the rear—the one, his fingers rooting in her anus, and the other, fondling her cunt lips beneath.

"I'm here." Her nipples were bulbous with the need to be sucked as only he could suck them—with that cat-lapping lick that sent her into a purling orgasmic trance. "I just don't know what day it is."

"Does it matter?"

Their bodies, slick with semen and raw carnal need, felt bonded. Her lips were swollen from his kisses. She felt as if he owned her body. No, it didn't matter. "No," she whispered. "Fuck me."

He moved, undulating his hips to bore deeper inside her.

"I like it hard," she breathed.

He kissed her. "I know how hard you like it. I know everything about your body."

"Good." She kissed him. "I'd live naked with you."

"Then we'd be fucking every minute of the day."

"Is there something wrong with my fucking your penis all day long?"

"I like having a permanent erection."

They kissed again. He whispered something against her lips. She thought she heard, "God, I can't get enough of your cunt." But it was too soon for him to admit anything like that. Too soon, after only a one-night, all-night fuck.

His body tensed. "I'm creaming for you."

She caught her breath as he convulsed. "I love how much you cream for me," she whispered, taking a kiss.

"I'm not done." He was still hard with his ravenous greed for her body.

He took her again, his fingers invading her in the rear, anchoring her body and her building orgasm. His mouth seduced her, licking and sucking until she tipped over into a slow orgasmic slide.

She wanted nothing else, ever.

Words were superfluous; she just wanted to stay coupled with him for—for as long as possible.

Chapter Five

Later she sat on his penis while he played with her nipples—compressing them, licking them with his hot tongue, sucking them.

The lights were bright, and since they were sitting right in front of the floor-to-ceiling window, anyone could see them, but she didn't care. Anywhere he wanted to fuck her was fine by her. His penis was rooted in her, hot and hard—she cared about nothing else.

I'm infatuated with him. They weren't even having intercourse *every* hour of the day. There were quiet moments of just touching, of him holding her vulva, of her caressing his balls, of quiet kisses and tacit exploration of each other's body. It was then that he discovered the secret of her nipples. Then when he finally penetrated her, she understood how much she loved him filling her from behind.

Two days and nights went by, full of uninhibited sex, no questions asked, no thought of anything else. It was like time had stopped.

They ordered room service twice, both times licking and sucking liquids and syrups off each other.

They didn't need coffee to keep them awake—desire was their caffeine, their bottomless well of ravenous need.

Justine discovered things about herself in that time, not only what she liked and how much she liked it, but also that she could surrender wholly to a stranger without a qualm, and that she was as much of an exhibitionist as *anyone* she knew.

She lay on her belly with him on top of her, his penis rumpusing for some back-door action. She teased his penis by undulating her bottom, and stretched her hands back to spread her ass cheeks to entice him.

He grasped her hands and pushed her cheeks farther apart. She felt him nudging her bud, and then the thick penetration of his penis spread her small opening to accommodate his heft.

He paused there with his penis barely penetrating her; she went breathless with the urgency of her passion for him there.

He pulled himself out abruptly and inserted himself again, pulling and pushing, letting her feel the turgid ridge of his penis as he deliberately slipped in and out of her.

In and out—her body convulsed. In and out—he braced himself with one arm and began pumping her cunt with his fingers until she collapsed, sobbing, her body thrumming with impossible pleasure.

And then she ate him, sucking his penis like a straw until she took every last drop from his body.

He collapsed onto her and they slept.

Day three began with him penetrating her from behind as she came awake, she staying still until she realized he was inside her, and then her body responded almost apart from her brain.

"I like morning penis."

"He doesn't like to waste time."

"I don't like to waste a nice, juicy penis."

"Neither does he."

After a bone-melting orgasm, they spent a long time in front of the window, kissing and fondling each other.

She went down on him again, first with her mouth and then pumping him vigorously and sucking until he shot hard into her throat.

When it was her turn, he held her in front of him at the window, spread her cunt lips, and pleasured her by hand. Then he pulled her down to the floor, mounted her, and rode her to orgasmic oblivion yet again, while he spewed what was left in him into the backwash of her pleasure.

He collapsed and rolled over onto the floor.

"I think there's nothing left."

"I don't believe that." For one thing, he was still hard and pulsing. She grasped his penis with her hand. "I *definitely* don't believe that."

They lay still for a long time, Justine forcibly restraining herself from asking questions—from *wanting* answers—about the future.

At some point he would have to leave, she thought, closing her eyes, trying to block out the reality.

And she definitely had to go. In two days, she had committed to flying out to Los Angeles for Jillian's date with a man she barely knew but fucked. It was no different from this date. Except it was. If she kept her mind on Randy now, *Doug's* leaving her, whenever, would be easier to take.

Forget that. Don't think. Don't project. Don't assume.

Just lose yourself in this miasma of sex and semen. *Nothing outside of that matters right now.*

Justine awakened hours later to the closing scene of a bad porn movie. She lay on the bed, discreetly shrouded by the sheets. The curtains were partially drawn across the window where they fucked for all to see. In the filtered light of the bedside lamp, she saw Doug talking on his cell, staring through the part in the curtains, and in the last stages of dressing.

Something in her caved. *It's over.*

She levered herself onto one elbow, and when she saw the wad of bills on the nightstand, she almost stopped breathing. *Please, no—*

He turned, almost as if he sensed she was awake. "I have to go. You can stay, have breakfast—checkout is at one. Zach will come get you."

Zach?

She sat up and swung her legs over the bed. They were too shaky to stand on yet. It was just past 10:00 A.M., and she didn't understand how Zach fit in. "You spoke to Zach?"

He didn't need to confirm it. She knew.

Her disappointment bubbled up. "What did he say?" She didn't even know why she asked. It was the kind of question that could reveal things she didn't want to know. Was her gut feeling right on the money, and all it boiled down to was whatever dollar amount Zach had charged this guy for two nights of fucking?

"That you're one hard-core bitch in heat." He reached for his jacket. "He was right. And you were worth every cent."

She froze and then slowly got up from the bed, so full of fury that she could barely speak. "I could say the same about you." She scooped up a handful of bills. "In fact, let me pay *you* for your services, you bastard." She threw the money at him. "Worth every *dollar*," she sneered. "You're one high-flying son of a bitch—fucking you wasn't worth what you paid. Zach should have asked for more."

He said nothing in response, and she felt her anger rising, contrasting to the look in his eyes, the look saying he knew everything about her, the truth and the lies.

She grabbed the rest of the money. "Don't *ever* approach Zach again." She shoved past him toward the bathroom. "Don't ever come near *me* again. Don't—"

He grabbed her wrist as she started to wind up. "Right, and if I threw more money at you, all your scruples would add up to how much and where."

"Try it. See how far your money goes."

"It's going right down your hot hole." He was unzipping his trousers even as he held her tight. "Get on the bed."

She jammed the money down his waistband.

"I have it on good authority my penis is well worth it." He pulled her over to the bed and pushed her down onto the mattress. "On your belly, cunt lady—I still have an hour on the clock, and I intend to use your body for every minute of it."

He stayed fully dressed. He didn't care—his anger was as volcanic as hers, and she couldn't combat it. She hated that he didn't strip while she was buck naked. Only his penis was bare as he pulled it from his pants, hauled her bottom up, and rammed himself into her furiously.

She lost track of everything but the feeling of him drumming himself into her again and again, almost as if he wanted to imprint himself on her, in her.

She hated him, *hated* him. He sprawled on top of her, holding her wrists and canting his body at the knees to give him purchase to pound her body unrelentingly.

Her ripe, moist body that took every inch of him without a fight belied every word she'd thrown at him.

Her orgasm came thick and slow, seeping down her legs and triggered a hard, rocketing grenade of pleasure.

He let it eddy away, holding himself in check, and then, slipping one arm around her waist, he lifted her so she sat on his thighs. She didn't know how he balanced her there, keeping himself embedded, still hard and roiling with anger. One move and she might cripple him. One moan of pleasure and she might seduce him.

The feel of his hands skimming up and down her body was alluring enough after such a cataclysmic orgasm. She needed no more from him, *wanted* no more. And yet, with all his banked fury, he kept giving. His hands seduced her as he concentrated on her nipples, stroking and squeezing them. His touch was like a breath—hard and soft, hard and soft.

He pulled her hands down to feel the point of their joining and his penis pulsing deep inside her. The way his manipulated her nipples made her writhe with pleasure. As he felt the moment of give, he compressed both nipples and sent her into orgasm.

He poured himself into her then. He slowly lowered her to the bed and lowered himself to cover her. He withdrew the heat, the hardness, the pleasure from her body and took it back for his own.

"When and where," he whispered. "You'll come whenever I wave the money, you insatiable bitch."

God, she didn't think she could hate him more than she already did. She rolled over onto her back. "I'll never come for you again," she hissed. "You'll never see me naked ever again."

She jumped up off the bed, squeezing out all memory of the pleasure still hot between her legs because otherwise she'd die.

"*Ever.*" She stalked into the bathroom, slammed the door behind her, and collapsed onto the toilet seat, shaking, appalled by her anger, shamed at how much she had given him, and feeling degraded by how much she'd let him take away from her.

That was *not* Jillian talking. There was nothing of Jillian in that tirade. It was all Justine—her sex, her greed, her need.

Oh, God. Not so far from Jillian after all.

And *him* . . .

I will kill Zach. I can't let him control Jilly like this.

Sex was too much of a trap, especially when she didn't know how to navigate the waters. She was a naive nymph at worst and shark bait at best.

And one lone shark had just eaten away her flesh and left her bones for the picking.

I need to get back home. I need—she closed her eyes and felt tears seep out—*to get ready for Randy.* Nice, middle-of-the-road, uncomplicated Randy.

She heard the door close rather emphatically. He was gone—finally.

Justine hopped in the shower, hoping to wash him away and forget Zach.

When she came out, scrubbed raw, the wad of bills was still on the nightstand.

Goddamn.

She sank onto the bed and started counting it. Ten thousand dollars, most of it in thousand-dollar bills, the rest in hundreds and fifties.

The bastard. I have no choice. I can't leave that much money here.

She left a hundred-dollar tip on the pillow for the maid.

The money also meant she didn't have to wait for Zach.

Zach was incensed that she'd gone off without telling him. He'd barged into the apartment that afternoon, flaming with righteous rage.

"Oh, for God's sake," Justine yawned, instantly out of patience at his theatrics. Just like Jilly would be. She was dressed like Jilly, too, in a tight tee and jeans. She was barefoot, with her hair bundled up carelessly, devoid of makeup, her inner companion at rest as she sat cross-legged on the sofa with her computer, searching the morning reports of the missing again.

She'd needed some rest. Doug Rawls had worked her body hard, and she still felt him all over. The scent and sense of the weight of his body on hers, the insensate pleasure—the insult.

But that was not for Zach to know.

"We have business to conclude," Zach growled.

"How much do I owe you?" she asked flatly, thinking it was the best way to find out what their arrangement was. There was probably a dollar menu somewhere detailing every date Zach managed, with charges dependent on the wealth and status of each client.

"I charged *him* ten," Zach said with a pout. "So two grand for me."

No, he didn't deserve that much—not for Rawls, not for what he'd done and made her feel. Jilly wouldn't have let Zach get away with that.

"I don't think so, Zach. All you did was make the date, frankly. I did all the work."

"I got him there," Zach muttered defensively. "I got him interested enough to pay that kind of money."

"A thousand on this one," Justine said firmly. "You can't really go to him and collect."

"Maybe I will."

"Maybe you won't."

"Christ, we sound like five-year-olds. Fine. A thousand. But only with details."

Justine took the folded bill out of her pocket and tossed it at him.

"You're so sure of yourself," Zach sneered. "When you're *on*."

"That's why you love me," Justine said, a predictable response.

"Tell me more. About him."

"Nonstop fucking for two days. Everywhere in the room, every way you can think of, even right in front of the windows—"

"God—why didn't you tell me? I could have . . . Was it good?"

"Floor-to-ceiling windows," Justine elaborated. "Like him. Floor-to-ceiling."

Zach groaned. "I was *so* right about him. The other two—not so much. They were there for the freebies. But they hooked Rawls all right. He wanted those nipples."

Justine made a sound. "He got those nipples." And more, too much more.

As she talked with Zach, she still couldn't figure out why Jillian let him pimp for her. Jillian *Dare*, by the accounts on her laptop, had more than enough business to satisfy her monetary and sexual needs.

"I need to know more," Zach prompted her.

Maybe she just loved watching Zach get off on the details the way he thought Jilly did.

"The minute we got to the room, he made me strip off my dress. I wore heels and nothing else. Just him. I wore his penis between my legs, and I wore him out. That's what you want to know, really. He couldn't keep his hands off me, and he couldn't get enough. He plugged my cunt night and day. And when time was up, he wanted more. His penis never let down. His desire never let up. I handled him like I handle them all.

"His penis was long, thick, and hard as steel. I couldn't empty him no matter how hard I tried. And I *tried*. I'm not so sure how it's going to go with raunchy Randy this weekend, I'm so sapped."

She watched Zach trying to switch gears as fast as she had to comprehend how Randy tagged on to the porned-up description of Doug Rawls's sexual prowess.

His eyes widened as he remembered. "Did you really contract with him?"

"I really did. Not for a week, though. He's paying full freight for the weekend—to meet his friends. You know what that means."

"Can you handle it? You sure you're not too fucked out?"

Handle *what*? "Me? Need you ask?" So blasé, so like Jilly. Even if she was boneless and collapsed on the floor she'd say she could go on. Maybe she *was* boneless and collapsed on some floor some-where. Maybe she was unconscious, or a hostage, or dead.

Justine shook off the thoughts.

"Zach—"

He slanted her a wary look.

"Don't ever solicit Rawls again."

"Huh? Wait a minute. You said this guy has a pistol-packing penis. Why not?"

"I never want to see him again."

"That doesn't make any sense. You just said he fucked you hard to heaven. You enjoyed it. You got your money. Really *good* money. What's the problem?"

"Just my preference."

"You'd fuck Randy sooner than Rawls?"

"Probably."

"You'll change your mind after this weekend."

She made a *whatever* gesture.

"Fine. In the meantime, don't forget the ball. It's the day after you return from L.A."

Justine sighed. Maybe Zach was Jilly's social secretary as well as her pimp.

"What ball?" she muttered.

"The fabulous, one-and-only Crystal Ball."

Justine closed her eyes. "Right." The blurring merry-go-round of Jillian's life was never-ending.

"I got you a fabulous mask, to-die-for shoes, and special jewelry to enhance certain body parts. It's going to be totally out there."

Jewelry to enhance body parts? Masks? "I can't wait," Justine murmured in Jilly's bored tone. "How many have I attended over the years?"

"Each one more over the top than the last," Zach interpolated. "You always say it's the best one-night party in town, and you always get more clients than—come *on*, you're not bored, are you?"

"Maybe I am," Justine said languidly. "I mean, being naked all the time diminishes the libido after a while, don't you think?"

"Don't even say that out loud. Obviously this Rawls guy really got to you."

"No, he got to my cunt. He got everything he paid for and more. I was stark naked for nearly three days, and he used my cunt every way he could get himself in. Isn't that enough?"

Zach threw up his hands. "Fine, you get the money."

God, he was easy. Or he just didn't want to lose his clandestine income stream.

"You're absolutely right. My girls worked hard. So I'm going to rest and pamper myself before I get on that plane with Randy tomorrow. If I have any appointments scheduled, cancel them."

Zach pulled out his BlackBerry. "I think there's a get-to-know-you dinner tonight."

"Tell him I'm under the weather."

"I could tell him you're under Randy."

Justine rolled her eyes. "Is he a big deal, this guy? Are we talking major money, long-term services, what?"

Zach punched up the information. "He's from the Midwest, CEO of an extrusion company. I think he's safely in the hundreds-of-millions range. He contracted for the five-hour dinner and already paid. He's in his early fifties, and it's his first companion experience."

"Cancel him," she said suddenly, her voice sharp. Dinner with Mr. Midwest CEO wouldn't get her any closer to finding Jill.

Zach looked at her quizzically. "What? He prepaid. You really can't back out."

"I can do whatever I want," Justine said firmly. "Cancel him. I'll refund the money. He'll find someone else to try him on."

"Do you know how much money we——"

Justine bolted up from the sofa. "I know how much money *I* would make. I'm beginning to wonder just what's in this partnership for me if I have no control over my life. Cancel him, damn it"—she loved watching Zach back down—"and then get the hell out and leave me alone."

———

No amount of willpower dislodged the memories. It was the hardest part of all that wide-open, uninhibited, body-devouring sex. Justine couldn't forget it, excise it, suppress it.

Worse, she thought, as she tossed and turned in Jillian's bed, she wanted *more*. She hated herself for that, and she wasn't sure what "more" even meant. More as Jillian? More as herself?

Justine was still at the same crossroads: if she reported Jillian missing, it would be a tabloid frenzy, not only for her clients, but also for Jill herself and by extension Justine.

If she didn't—well, she'd only complicated things further by her inability to convince Zach she was Justine. It also didn't help that she let her own suppressed sexuality drive her ill-considered choices.

She was no closer to finding Jillian, and every hour that passed dropped like a stone on her conscience.

Jillian lived a high-speed life—one sexual encounter after another—while everything in Justine's life was wait and see. Read the data. Formulate the theory. Set up the experiment. See what develops. Try another tack.

It was time to try another tack.

She'd already scoured the missed phone calls on Jillian's cells, but the numbers meant nothing to her, and calling back might put her in contact with someone who knew Jillian carnally—or not—and that'd require explanations she didn't have the talent to invent.

She didn't need more traps than she was tripping over already. She needed to disappear and work this thing out.

Blow off Randy. Blow off everything.

Zach wouldn't be a problem. He wouldn't search for Justine if "Jillian" disappeared. She didn't need anything but Jillian's and her computers. She could just pack them up and go.

She felt the sudden urgency to get out of Jilly's apartment. She grabbed her bag, her jacket, opened the door, and—

"Going somewhere?"

Zach was a guard dog, too? "What the hell are you doing?"

"Making sure you keep your commitments."

"I keep my dates," Justine said through gritted teeth. "Now go away."

"You're acting weird. I'm staying right here until the Crystal Ball. I'll sleep in the damned hallway if I have to."

"Jesus, Zach—"

"It's a lot of money."

"You mean there's money for *you* on the table somewhere," Justine said furiously. She leveled a hard look at him. "Let me guess. You guaranteed I'd attend the ball."

He didn't deny it. "And your weekend with Randy."

Did Zach get a percentage of *everything*?

The weight of it all pulled on her conscience. Time was her enemy now, she felt it keenly, even though it had been but days since that awful text message.

It was obvious Zach would keep her on a tight leash, at least until she'd fulfilled these two commitments.

Justine couldn't disappear—not yet.

"Indeed, Randy," Justine murmured caustically.

"I hate when you get like this," Zach said petulantly.

"Like what?"

"Like this isn't a business. Like you could care less about the money and all the expensive perks that come with it. Plus all the sex your incredible cunt can handle. Women envy you. *I* envy you, for God's sake."

"You're getting paid for that," Justine snapped snidely. "Just leave me alone."

She slammed the door on him.

"I'm not leaving!" he shouted.

"I don't care!" she shouted back. She threw down her jacket and stamped into Jillian's bedroom, swung the briefcase with the computers onto the bed, and opened the window. There was no way out.

It was the money, she thought, climbing into bed. The huge, eye-popping sums of money that those high-testosterone executives just loved to lavish on adoring women—and their willing bodies.

Even Justine found it all tempting. It was too easy to be Jillian and too easy to understand why Jillian might hand the practicalities to Zach so she could just concentrate on living the life.

She'd known Zach a long time. He was someone she trusted, someone who'd crack the whip if she slacked off. As he just had.

She'd only skimmed over the vast sums of money detailed in Jillian's computer files. She ought to check that Randy had kept up his end of the bargain. It was something to do, at any rate.

She took Jill's computer from the briefcase and booted it up just as Zach barged through the door.

Shit. She'd forgotten he had a key.

"Why aren't you packing?"

"I'm not leaving until tomorrow."

"You always lay everything out the day before."

"Fine." Justine emphatically closed the laptop. "I'll lay things out." God, this guy was intrusive, domineering, and—scared.

"That's like, today. Now."

She could see he was working himself up. If she begged off, he had a lot to lose. She kept coming back to that.

She had no choice about the weekend with Randy. Zach was here to ensure that she got on that private plane Randy was sending for her.

If she tried to sneak away, he'd follow her, and she would lose her one advantage—that Zach didn't believe Jillian had a twin.

What was one more sex-sodden weekend? Sure, it delayed her still further but she'd already fucked Randy. She could deal with him and all the luxurious extras. Her best strategy now was to stop arousing Zach's suspicions.

She hopped off the bed and gathered up her briefcase and the laptop to make room. Don't make it obvious, don't make him suspicious.

"I'll pack tonight." She swiped a look at his expression.

"*We'll* pack tonight," she amended. "Why don't you start. I'll be back in a minute."

She didn't like the distrustful look he gave her. She had to reassure him somehow while she deep-sixed Jillian's laptop.

She went on instinct. "Then we'll do the rest together."

———

Randy lived up to every part of their agreement. A limo came for her the next morning at seven and drove her and Zach, at his insistence, to the airport. He watched as she boarded an executive jet with every amenity, including a cabin attendant solely to provide her comfort, and he waved her off as the plane taxied down the runway.

The plane delivered her to LAX, where another limo waited to take her to the hotel. She only had to breathe her name to the front desk and a bellhop materialized to take her luggage, and she was whisked by private elevator up to the Sky Suite.

And sweet it was. It had three rooms—bedroom, living room, media room—and three huge bathrooms. The closets were as big as Jilly's living room. She even had her own maid to oversee her wardrobe and personal needs, and a makeup artist and hairdresser on call.

And—the cherry on top—her own ten-thousand-dollar gift card to spend *however* she wished.

But first, she needed a bath. The maid readied it for her, and while she soaked herself in expensive oils, the maid unpacked, set aside what needed refreshing, hung everything else in the closet, and, when Justine was finished, wrapped her in a soft robe and said, "Would madame like a massage now?"

"A massage?"

"It is all arranged; you have only to ask."

"Then, yes, I would."

"Excellent." The maid disappeared and in two minutes, two men carrying a table appeared. They set up in the bedroom and waited her pleasure.

Well, she had no compunction about her nudity now, so she shucked the robe and climbed onto the table, belly down. She was covered with a light blanket as soft, watery music began to play.

The first stage was a relaxing full-body massage with fragrant oils. The second masseur took over afterward for a deep-tissue massage, complemented by a foot massage performed by the first masseur simultaneously.

By the time they were done, she felt as if she were floating. If this was the kind of treatment Jillian usually commanded, Justine could see why it was so seductive. But the real question was what tonight would bring when she accompanied Randy later.

And what she suspected he really meant by these friends who were so anxious to meet Jilly.

When Justine went to dress, she found another surprise—a white column of matte jersey hanging in the closet with a note attached: *Wear this tonight.*

She couldn't wear much else. The dress fit her like a glove. There was no margin for error in this dress, with its deep, plunging back that grazed her crease and framed the curve of her bottom, the deep slit up the right side, the high neck with the revealing opening at her breasts, and the diamond necklace collar. It was as smooth as a vanilla milkshake. It was the kind of dress that covered everything and *revealed* everything.

Like her nipples, two taut points against the fabric.

"I like the diamonds," she murmured, surveying herself in the three-way mirror in the walk-in closet and just barely speaking to the maid who had helped her inch into the dress.

"The dress is quite stunning," the maid said. "Mr. Randy will be very pleased. I'll let him know you're ready."

Justine hadn't seen him all day, so her luxurious pampering seemed almost like a dream. Maybe he'd watched the whole thing, maybe he got off on that.

But, she thought reprovingly as she stared at herself in the mirror, she'd admit there was no reason to be here other than to let him throw money and perks at her feet.

It was all about the money. And the power of sex.

Justine felt weak for a moment.

I'm doing Jilly no good here. And I'm fooling myself if I'm pretending I don't know why Randy brought me here.

She looked down at her nipples, so obvious under the matte jersey. She turned sideways. Her stomach was flat, her rear end enticingly curvy, her nipples pointy, every body part erotically clothed to make Randy's point: this gorgeous naked-under-her-dress creature was his to fuck—and offer to his friends.

If I were smart, I would devise a way to deal with this before I'm play-ing musical penises.

Randy showed up at six o'clock, in a tux with flowers for her. He gave her a chaste kiss, took a long, hard, sexual look at her body, and an approving predatory gleam shone in his eyes.

"It's been a very successful week," he told her. "This weekend will cap the whole thing, and you're going to seal the deal."

"I hope so," Justine said. "How exactly do I do that?"

"Oh, you know."

Justine had an inkling—and an idea. "Maybe I should make some preparations."

"Do whatever you want. Just make sure my friends are happy."

"They will be," she murmured.

It was an interesting idea, one calculated to lessen physical con-tact rather than invite it. She rang for the maid, gave her whis-pered instructions, and then turned her attention back to Randy. "So how will this evening go?"

"Not nearly fast enough," he growled, eyeing her nipples and licking his lips. "Dinner first, and then you'll be asked what you'd like to do. And we all know what that is."

"I see," Justine said. Yes, she saw what Jilly inevitably saw. She was three thousand miles away from anything and anyone she knew. Zach was not looking over her shoulder. Any other memo-ries were negligible, and the money was way more than Rawls had paid.

Oh, God—DON'T bring up his name.

Just get this done, she thought stoically. It's only a weekend. It might even just be one night, just to seal the deal.

———

There were four guests at the five-course dinner. Justine decided not to concentrate on names and faces. She saw them as avatars to whom she addressed polite questions and with whom she made erotic-lite conversation. They all knew what was coming; it was just a question of how and when she would direct the event.

Randy ordered drinks and a tableful of food, most of which would not be eaten. Everyone's attention focused on Justine. She kept her demeanor elegant and reserved as a prelude to the uninhibited courtesan who would magically appear later.

"You are perfect," Randy whispered in her ear at one point. "I can't wait to get you alone."

"Alone will be very crowded for a while."

"What are you planning?"

"You'll find out," Justine whispered.

They ate, they drank, they danced in the hotel's club lounge. Justine took turns with each of them as they slid their hands all over her.

She knew this scene, and she suppressed the memory of where it had led that night at the nightclub. But this was a different story altogether. She'd make certain of it.

At 1:00 A.M. she whispered to each avatar individually, "I think we should have a nightcap in my room."

No one said no to that.

As they entered the suite, Justine led the way to the bedroom. There, with a light bathing it, was a massage table, slightly wider than usual, beside the king-size bed. A silver tray held a silver bowl filled with condoms. And on the dresser, a bar setup was stocked with wine, scotch, bourbon, ice, club soda, and beer.

"Help yourselves," Randy invited them.

"And then make yourself comfortable on the bed," Justine added. "Don't hesitate to take off your clothes."

She watched with amusement as they got drinks and hesitantly took off their jackets and ties but not much more.

After they were settled with drinks in or on the edge of

the bed, she continued with a touch of coyness. "I thought we might play a little game of the masseur and the voyeur. I need a nice massage tonight. So those of you who are so moved may each take a turn massaging my naked body while everyone else watches. Nothing is forbidden. You may massage me anywhere you wish. You may strip or stayed clothed. You may masturbate— or penetrate." She looked around at their faces, which were slightly dumbstruck. "And if you feel the need to express your excitement, I invite you to make use of the condoms and my cunt."

She glanced at Randy, who was salivating. But he wouldn't take the first turn; he'd wait, excellent businessman that he was.

She reached up and unfastened the necklace that held her dress in place. The bodice dropped sinuously to her hips. "Who would like to get his hands on me?"

She slipped out of the dress and levered herself onto the massage table, naked except for her stilettos. No takers. They were all openmouthed and a little stunned.

She posed for them, showing off her body, her shorn cleft, her nipples. "I really need that massage," she exhorted them. "Won't one of you relieve me?"

"Take on two of us," a voice said.

"Sure. How?"

"He likes tits, I like ass."

"I've got tits, I've got ass," she murmured. "Right here."

Now the game was on. The one at her breast was an insatiable sucker. The one squeezing and caressing her bottom, encouraged by her exotic hip movements, started exploring her nakedness more deeply.

"I want in that cunt," he growled.

"Condom," Justine directed him coolly.

His quick strip broke the ice as he shrouded his penis, gave a short, sharp thrust, penetrated, and had a five-stroke orgasm.

The others lined up so they could both see every detail of everyone else's fucking and have a turn.

It went on for another couple of hours. On the fifth go-round, the condoms ran out, just as she'd planned.

"Aw, man, just one more quick fuck."

"No condom, no cunt," Justine said firmly. "That's my rule."

They were all naked as dawn broke, and Justine was still prone on the massage table. The others were sprawled on the bed, surrounded by their thousand-dollar suits and a pile of used condoms. The room reeked of sex and booze. It was five in the morning, and no one wanted to leave.

"Get more condoms," one of them slurred.

"Yeah. Coffee and cunt. Breakfast." The voices petered out. They all fell asleep, worn to the nub.

Justine eased herself up into a sitting position. She was achy from the all-night pummeling. But the deal was sealed. That would be the end of Randy.

"Hey," a voice said from behind her. She turned to see Randy emerging from the bathroom.

"Hi." There wasn't much to say. He'd gotten everything he'd paid for and more.

"Best damned party ever," Randy mumbled. "Don't ask why I was in there."

"I can guess," Justine said caustically. "I need a shower. I need some sleep."

"What about a nonobligatory breakfast bang for the guys?"

Justine stared at him. "That was four hours of nonstop fucking once they warmed up."

"That was genius, by the way," Randy muttered. "The masseur and the voyeur. Genius."

"I'm so glad," Justine murmured, not without irony. "Now—shower and sleep."

"Right. Use the guest bathroom. You can sleep in the media room. I think these guys are going to be out of it for most of the morning."

"Good. Then tell them I went home already."

"You sure loved banging them. You sure you wouldn't want—"

"A shower and some sleep."

"Okay."

She threw him a bone, pausing at the door. "Besides, if anyone gets any extra goodies, it should be you."

She should have known it was too generous an offer and that Randy would take her up on it. Her body was his until that plane landed in New York.

He was smug with triumph—his business associates had all signed on the dotted line, and they wanted Jillian to come with him the next time he was in town.

"We'll see how my schedule looks," Justine temporized as they took a break to have some lunch.

When there was no sex involved, the trip was rather wonderful. She'd had every luxury, all the clothes he'd bought, the best food, money to spend, and a diamond necklace as a gift of gratitude. Randy was actually a nice date when he wasn't salivating over her nipples.

"You are the best money I've spent in years," he whispered in her ear as he fondled her. "Those guys were blown away."

"I'm glad." She had tempered his enthusiasm. She was on automatic pilot now. The plane would land soon, and it would all be over.

She couldn't wait. She needed to hold him at arm's length until they landed. "I should get dressed."

"No, you should stay on my lap and let me play. Dress when we land."

"How about *I* play until we land?" she countered, grabbing his balls. "We still have a half hour before we touch down."

He groaned.

"And who knows," she added, unzipping his pants and rooting for his penis, "we might be held up."

She held him up and began the task of pumping him dry. This was the perfect solution, and if he thought she was chomping on his manhood because it was so irresistible, well then, she was a better actress than she thought.

That's what the whole thing was about, anyway. Acting. Faking. Money. Sex. Jillian. Making him happy.

There was no holdup. They rolled into the hangar right on schedule, but there was no time for her to dress before the pilot came back and the ground crew swarmed the plane.

They all saw Randy tucking away his thoroughly worked-over penis, and her on her knees between his knees.

A perfect end to her odyssey in L.A.

Chapter Six

Justine lay staring at the ceiling, thinking that twenty-four hours earlier she'd been naked on her back, enticing a roomful of strangers whose names she didn't know, didn't want to know, and whom she would never see again.

Given Jillian's m.o., that wasn't likely, however. They'd probably all contact her for private parties—today.

Did Jilly *ever* take a vacation?

But why should she, when fucking came with all those perks? If you charted the hours Jilly lay on her back versus the hours she had free to luxuriate, sightsee, shop, and enjoy all the extras that went along with the ride, she probably was on vacation more than she was on call.

Justine buried her head in the pillows.

I'm not Jillian. That should be my mantra. I am not Jillian, I just play her in real life.

I'm finding it way too easy to play her in real life.

NO. Never admit that. Never.

Focus on what's real: getting a handle on Jillian's text. She had had a plan before discovering man meat.

She pushed the thought of a particular someone firmly away. She couldn't believe she could be seduced into this life faster than randy Randy got into her.

It was a rather powerful position for a woman, naked and flat on her back, her body worshipped and desired by all the penises in the room.

She couldn't stop thinking about sex now. It didn't help that she'd started sleeping naked or that the silk sheets were slick against her hot skin. Her body squirmed at the thought of a penis between her legs.

Enough!

She ripped the top sheet away and jumped out of bed. A cold shower. Some hot coffee. And then—Jillian. It was time to focus on Jilly's problem, instead of all this fantasizing.

Jilly was still in trouble. And for the short amount of time that Justine had walked in her high heels, she'd gotten no clue about what the trouble was or how to help.

Zach gave her half a day's rest before the buzz of the intercom woke her up. "Are you there?"

She answered with an irritated "I'm here."

"Good. I need to know these things."

The problem was Zach *didn't* need to know, and yet there he was, buzzing around like a gnat, bustling into Jillian's kitchen with take-out. It was Jilly's usual fare and he unpacked and assembled it on the coffee table.

"Sit," he directed her. "Talk."

It was time to spin fairy tales for the boy who still inhabited a world between adolescent curiosity and grown-up lust.

She wanted to say again who she really was, but she knew that train had long gone. She was on her own with this one. Zach was not her ally, nor was he Jillian's.

Just eat and talk and give Zach what he wants.

So she described the flight, the hotel, the perks, the dress, the condoms, and the swamp of sex.

"They watched everything. I wouldn't let them do it any other way. There was one moment when two of them were humping to get off, so I took each of them in one hand while the third one was fucking me and I blew them all off. Three thick streams of cum spewing all over me."

Zach almost came listening to her.

"And then we did it all again," she went on, modulating her tone to a coy disdain. "And again, and again—I think Randy got what he wanted."

"Did you?"

She gave him a languorous, sleepy-eyed look. "Let's see. A boatload of money, a private jet to and from L.A., a mansion-size hotel suite, spa pampering, great food, fabulous clothes, a diamond necklace, a gift card for an amazing amount of money, not so amazing sex—nooo, I didn't get what I wanted at all."

Zach groaned. "I can't stand how insanely fabulous your life is."

"Isn't it," Justine murmured drily. Because when she added it all up, it did seem insane—why wouldn't anyone want to live that life?

"So," she added, picking her way delicately to gauge Zach's reaction, "because Randy and his friends just about wore me out, I'm taking tonight off. I don't care if anyone else has paid for my time. I *need* some downtime."

"You never take time off," Zach said. "And you're not backing out of going to the ball."

"Why do I have to go?"

"You just have to."

"You're too insistent, Zach. Yeah, yeah, I know all about the potential clients. But there's more to it, isn't there?" Justine had a feeling that maybe something was up that Jillian didn't know about.

"You're cohosting, for one thing. Which you seem to have forgotten."

She sighed. "I remember. What else have you cooked up?"

"You'll see."

"Zach." There was definitely a Jillian warning note in her voice.

"You'll see. Meantime, you did have a date set up for tonight."

She felt very weary suddenly. "Did I?"

"He's coming to town, just wants the company."

"Have I had him before?"

Zach consulted his BlackBerry. "No. He took the dinner meet."

"Do I have to?" she muttered with no enthusiasm and caught Zach's sharp look.

She couldn't back down now. She had to keep this date, keep up the impersonation. She threw up her hands. "Fine. Upload the details to my cell. I'm going back to sleep."

She consulted Zach's notes a little later. Mr. Jarvis was in town on business. He wanted an elegant and well-mannered dinner date, trusting that an experienced companion would know what was wanted.

Sex was wanted. Always.

Money was already on the table, with a deposit prepaid.

Mr. Jarvis met her in the lobby of his hotel. He was tall with thinning hair, a sharply featured face, and he had the air of knowing exactly what he wanted.

Justine had dressed the part—the fluid designer dress wrapped tightly around her body to show her curves. She wore strappy heels, a very small, metallic shoulder bag with a magnetic closure, barely any jewelry, and she had her hair twisted into a classic top-knot.

Mr. Jarvis took her arm and discreetly slipped an envelope into her open bag.

"So," she murmured. "Mr. Jarvis."

"I think I want to dine in my room," Mr. Jarvis said.

"I'd be delighted," Justine responded.

His room was contemporary, sleek and masculine. The bed was king-size, and Mr. Jarvis wasted no time getting her on her back.

He wanted cunt, period. It took just a pull on the sash, and her wrap dress fell open to reveal her nude body beneath.

"Do I please you?"

"Just lie down and spread your legs. That's all I need from you."

He barely bothered to undress, just whipped out his thin, rigid penis, shrouded it, and proceeded to work it into her body purposefully. She wrapped her legs around him and let him go at it. She intermittently made appropriate noises and wriggled her hips, wishing she were someplace else, with someone else.

Like . . .

Her breath caught. *Do not NOT think about him.*

Her nipples hardened and her body liquefied. The room had floor-to-ceiling windows. If only . . .

He drove into her. *Yes.*

Short, furious thrusts. Yes.

He rode her hard, and she wanted it over with—*now.*

He licked her nipples. *Please don't.*

He thrust in, she heaved upward, and he shuddered with his sudden orgasm as he sucked at her breast.

This was the other side of the life Jilly had chosen—the men she didn't want but had no choice about servicing.

Because she always chose the money.

And Mr. Jarvis would take his pound of naked flesh and wrest every dollar out of her body. Justine was certain of it.

The next morning she was finally back at Jillian's apartment, with a substantial amount of cash in hand.

It was never enough for Jillian. It was clear to Justine after walking nearly a week in Jillian's four-hundred-dollar shoes. Jillian needed the rush, the excitement, the men, all of it. She was wholly submerged in the culture, in the need and the desire to captivate and copulate.

Justine would just have to come to terms with that.

After she found Jilly.

After she relinquished her tenuous hold on the companionate life.

The ball was a place to vanish. There would be crowds of people, music, drink, aphrodisiacs, sex. One could easily get lost in the crowd, choose a partner, and go behind closed doors.

But Zach was always on her tail, trailing her like a shadow. She wondered if he had a life beyond the one Jilly created for him after every encounter.

"So you wouldn't do Jarvis again?" Zach asked.

"Good God, no. I thought one of the benefits of this whole thing was that I choose."

"You do have a choice, yes. You chose not to see Rawls or Jarvis again."

Justine bit her lip. Rawls was the last name she wanted to hear right now, especially after the memories of their coupling had flooded her last night. "Right."

"Was Jarvis that bad?"

"Jarvis got right to the point. He dined on me, soup to nuts."

"But he paid up front."

"Yes, he did."

"Penis not so hot, huh?"

She nodded.

"Okay. Cross him off the list. The ball's the important thing. You know how Pemble is about his once-yearly."

"Oh, yes. We all have to toe the line." Or at least it sounded like that to her from Zach's tone of voice. She wanted to ask him if he ever got tired of being immersed in someone else's sexual stew, if he had somebody himself.

But Justine asked none of that. She felt strangely wrung out, and divorced from the Justine who had offered herself to Jill's clients. Men like Jarvis made you feel like that. As high end as he wanted his companion to be, he still truly believed that her function was solely sex on demand.

On the other hand, it was pure hypocrisy to pretend it was anything else. Respect and choice really didn't enter into it. They were illusions, fostered by Jilly to make it feel like there was another, more altruistic rationale for selling herself.

She was just as subject to external demands as personal ones. She must attend this ball. She must meet the friends of her clients. She must lay herself bare to any and all who wanted her and give herself willingly with commensurate energy and desire.

She must . . . and at the moment, Justine didn't know which "she" she meant.

She must be crazy.

"I really need some sleep," she said finally.

"You're acting weird," Zach said. "You're never tired. The ball is tonight, don't forget."

She couldn't stop herself from yawning, though she tried. Right now, the differences between her and Jill were in laser focus, and Zach had picked on them like ticks on a hound.

"Never tired?" Justine forced herself to say, gearing up to spank him again. "Let's see where *I've* been for the past week: sex with good old Randy on our get-to-know-you at the hotel; partying down with your vodka guys the same night; a two-day bang binge with Rawls; an overnight with Randy in L.A. with an all-night fuckfest with five vigorous penises; nonstop penis pumping from L.A. to New York afterward; one night with Mr. Jarvis, who made me feel like dirt. And now the ball? Oh—there's *no* reason why I should be tired, or need some *rest*. I'm raring to go right now. Pull down your pants."

"Oh, shut up," Zach growled.

"Maybe all this partying has caught up with me," Justine went on inexorably. "I'm just feeling a little jaded today. Mr. Jarvis can do that to you."

"Fine. Just be *on* for the ball, and don't give me that twin shit as an excuse again."

"I'm always *on* and ready to jerk you off, you jerk."

"I'm leaving." He was huffy now.

"Good," she muttered, sinking back onto the couch. He took more effort than sex sometimes. But she had a six-hour respite from Zach *and* sex. Just time enough to contemplate her folly in taking Jill's place. It had only been a week, but she couldn't afford to lose any more time. The deeper in she got, the worse her ultimate exposure would be. She'd dodged that bullet so far, but her luck could run out at the Crystal Ball.

Someone there would know she wasn't Jilly; someone would catch on.

She closed her eyes for a long moment and just shut down. Had she had even five minutes to herself without Zach or sex intruding?

She needed time to think, to take the facts, assess what she knew, and plan what to do next.

The facts first. Jillian had gone to London—on a modeling

assignment, she'd told Justine. Now she knew it was to accompany . . . wait—what was his name? Zach had said it just four or five days ago.

But no problem—she'd just go back to the computer, the source of all knowledge about Jillian. When she booted up the database, though, a warning started flashing.

There was a stop-payment notice from one of Jillian's clients.

Justine's heart started pounding. She hadn't checked since making sure Randy deposited his payment. Mr. Jarvis had opted for cash.

The stop payment was a big one, leaving a gaping hole in Jill's balance sheet. The client was listed as C.E. And it was dated only a day or two after she'd begun inhabiting Jillian's life, after Jillian's London trip should have ended, and Jill had conceivably returned home.

C.E. had removed all that big money because—Justine couldn't think, her heart was drumming so hard—because he wasn't satisfied, and in that event the client's money was automatically refunded?

Or because he knew Jilly wouldn't be needing it?

What *was* that name? She scrolled through the database and stopped abruptly at the name *Ellicott*.

Clive Ellicott. That's it.

It was a canyon-size leap from a dissatisfied customer to his being the cause of Jillian's disappearance. But he'd been the last to see her. Either he had taken Jill to the airport, or he'd taken her someplace else for reasons Justine couldn't even begin to fathom.

And given himself a refund.

Ellicott wasn't a new client either, according to Jillian's records. She'd traveled with him at least four times for a commensurate amount of money. She was a known commodity; there were no surprises there. It made no sense for him to stop payment after this trip.

Keep calm. Don't panic.

She closed her eyes. Zach had mentioned Ellicott—and something about an accident.

It was time to do some research. Who was this Clive Ellicott?

He wasn't hard to find; he was a hotshot risk management entrepreneur who just brokered a major deal with the British government.

He was pictured right on the first page of the company website: president and chief executive officer of the Guardian Group. She stared at the image. He had a thin mustache and a haughty expression. His memorably simple face, so at odds with his sexual predilections.

She jotted down the London office phone number. It was a place to start at least.

There was also the accident Zach thought might have delayed Jillian's return.

She typed the words "Britain billionaire car crash" into a search engine, and pages and pages of references scrolled in.

She took a deep breath as she clicked the most recent entry. The article reported on the unexpected death of billionaire Oliver Baynard, CEO of Gibraltar of London, in a car accident in the English countryside.

Baynard had been bidding for a government security contract, and his company had withdrawn its proposal in the wake of Baynard's death, pending the appointment of a new CEO. The contract had subsequently been awarded to the Guardian Group of New York and London.

Ellicott's company.

So the victim and Jilly's client had been in competition for a megabucks government deal.

But Baynard's death couldn't have anything to do with Jill. She'd been with Ellicott—and presumably on her way home—when the accident happened. There was proof of that. Then there was Ellicott's payment—except that was gone now.

A computer could be hacked and reconfigured, she thought.

But why would someone stop payment?

Jilly had laid it out herself: these men wanted her not only for her perfection, her sex, but also for her trustworthiness and discretion. She'd said there were things she knew about her clients' business affairs that could conceivably be dangerous.

What about a government contract could be dangerous to Jill?

Justine should just drop everything and fly to London. Right now. She hadn't helped Jilly at all by staying here; she'd just helped herself to Jilly's sex life.

Clive Ellicott was the key. She had a phone number. He shouldn't be *that* hard to find.

But then what? That was the question she had to have answered before she even boarded a plane. If she were smart, she would make that reservation now, though, and get out before Zach came to get her.

As if Zach would even let her out of his sight.

An enigma, this relationship, and only Jilly could answer all her questions about it. Zach was back within hours, as if he had a premonition that she might disappear.

She could tell Zach sensed something that made him edgy. He knew something was off, he just didn't know what, and he didn't believe in a twin.

She had to be more careful with him until the ball. Lean on him more, the way Jilly probably did. Just for a few more hours until she could make her escape at the damned ball.

Let him help you with the dress, with the enhancements. The sexual observations. But don't let him ride roughshod over you.

Justine could do that. Just another night in Jillian's shoes, a few more hours till she made her escape. And then it would be over—she'd be in London, where no one knew her, and she could confront the mysterious Ellicott and get some answers.

She researched the Crystal Ball, too. The host, Pemble, was a social butterfly who delighted in outré parties on odd nights to which everyone who was anyone came, if they dared.

The Crystal Ball was the most infamous of his parties—the naked party. The one, he said, where one could most be one's real self. The guests wore masks, enhancements if they so desired, but they were required to enter the mirrored and glassed ballroom naked. The floors and ceilings were one-way mirrors so that a guest could look up to see everything, or look down to admire their naked reflections.

The ball was famous for hookups, hookahs, and hookers. Only the most daring, most desirable were invited—or they crashed to be seen and written about.

The narrow satin panels hanging throughout were a nice touch. They caressed a guest's body in passing; they were tactile, mysterious, and sexy.

And, as Justine discovered when she and Zach arrived, warm air blew under the panels, making them dance. It was at just the right temperature to enfold the bodies swirling among the panels, pairing up, separating, already conjugating. Nothing was forbidden, and everything was encouraged.

There was no way to know if you knew anybody, and that was the point: seduction irrespective of personality.

But still, there were some who were known, by their shape, their hair, the way they walked, or just by an unmistakable aura they projected.

Jillian was one of those. Apparently.

People greeted her like old friends, and Justine found a safe harbor in nodding or lifting her glass to them.

But that wouldn't last. They would expect her to acknowledge them by name, and then . . . and then the game would be over.

The house seemed to go on forever. It was Pemble's circus and, as far as he was concerned, the party was the event of the season. He greeted Justine—Jillian—with a hug as she and Zach entered the hallway anteroom.

"Jillian, my heart, my love. I'd know you anywhere. Hurry, take off your clothes. I can't wait to get started."

"All right," Justine hissed to Zach. "What does he mean by *that*?"

"I didn't want to tell you before we got here," Zach said reluctantly. "He invited *her*, too."

Her who? Zach had dropped that piece of information like a bomb, like he expected a reaction at the news.

"Of course he did," she snapped, feeling her way. "Why should I care?"

Zach gave her a strange look. "If I remember your last encounter, you were going to take *her* down, big time."

"I forgot all about it," Justine retorted dismissively.

"Well, Pemble didn't, and he lured her here with the carrot of a mud fight with you."

Justine went explosively silent for a long moment. Her reaction was real, a combination of the anger Jilly would have felt and her own fear of being trapped in a confrontation that was meaningless to her and could lead to exposing her impersonation among the premier gossipmongers and tabloid tattlers of the city.

"I see," she murmured finally with as much sangfroid as she could manage. "And why would Pemble think I'd even consent to something like that?"

"Because the judge—and the prize—is Zoltan Brisco."

That was supposed to mean something to her. "I see," she repeated.

Who the hell was this mysterious *her*?

"Come on." Zach tugged at her still clothed elbow. "Get undressed. We have a party to start."

She hated the disrobing part. It was one thing to be alone with a client, and quite another to face a roomful of strangers eyeing her speculatively.

Zach had chosen the satin slip dress she wore. "So easy to shrug off," he'd said as he ran his hands all over the material. He had also provided the glittery, golden mask, the matching strap heels, and the golden thrall collar around her neck.

Zach, naked, was unimpressive. A penis not in the throes of lust was a limp and pallid thing—particularly his. She wondered if he was even capable of a hard-on.

Hate, hate, hate—she slipped off the dress—*I hate this.*

Zach took her hand, swiped two flutes of champagne, and with jazz playing softly in the background, led her into the first circle of hell.

Everywhere, bodies stood close, talking, drinking, kissing. The warm air had a thick, sweet scent, and the room filled with the drone of voices and laughter.

There were rooms and anterooms, all shrouded in the flowing satin panels. Waiters with trays of drinks and finger food milled about, as much to keep the appetite at bay as to use for sexual purposes.

Bodies swirled around her, in a do-si-do of sensory exhibitionism and tacit sex.

Where was *she*, Justine thought, the woman she was meant to fight.

Justine drank more champagne and gave herself up to the crowd, talking to people Jilly knew, pretending she knew them, too, thrusting herself into the moment and hoping no one noticed the truth.

The masks helped. Everywhere, masked faces looked toward the mirrors to catch a glimpse.

And all that time, Zach didn't say another word about *her* or about Zoltan Brisco.

Until they were descending to the secret lower level, the exclusive province of a chosen few.

"Are you ready?" Zach asked. "This is the main event. She's waiting."

Justine waited a calculated moment. "Let her wait."

Zach shook his head. "The Principessa hates to wait; you know that."

The Principessa? The name meant nothing to her. "And the Principessa is the queen of what country that we're all so terrified to make her wait?"

Zach gave her a sour look. "You know how she is."

"So, she'll have a tantrum? I frankly don't care. I've been dragooned into this, and I'm not happy either."

"Pemble's the ringmaster, you know that. He tosses all the balls in the air, knowing everyone else will work to keep them there, just to amuse him."

It was a perfect description of the party.

And Jillian—Justine as Jillian—was the main event.

She muttered a curse under her breath. It was another damned situation where she must push her impersonation of Jilly to the limit.

How could Jilly believe any of this was her choice—except it *was* her choice to debase herself like this.

She quelled a shuddering breath. The Principessa. What the hell was a Principessa? And a Zoltan Brisco? Obviously there was some kind of rivalry between Jilly and this Principessa, and they both wanted the same man.

Zach and Justine stood on the first step down toward the lower level. Beyond, they could hear a low murmur of voices, feel the warm, circulating air. When Justine looked up, she could see guests mixing and mingling from below.

This is Jilly's life. This is where she goes, what she craves, what she lives for.

It was time—the naked competition with her rival. Down in the depths was Pemble's reality show, manufactured out of decadence, dust, and diamonds, with all his guests primed for the fight.

Who was the Principessa?

Justine hated being at such a disadvantage, and her nudity didn't help matters either. Naked men were not so beautiful. They were thinner, more vulnerable. Their penises retracted, their bodies exposed on a different level. But they acted like gods and were avid voyeurs of the naked female flesh grappling in the mud.

Zach knew all this. Zach was the puppetmaster, and Jilly was always jumping when he pulled the strings.

But why?

Zach tugged at her arm. "Come on. Brisco is waiting."

Justine girded herself. *I am Jilly. This is what Jilly would do. I can't slip out of character. Not now. Not with so much at stake and so many people here who know Jill.*

She followed Zach down the narrow stairwell that ended at a slightly ajar wooden door.

This was it—the room of secret vices, secret sex, and secrets altogether.

Zach pushed the door open to reveal a vast, dim space that was quite obviously the real basement of the town house, which had been remodeled to retain its original elements. There were certain telling details: the discriminating lighting, the nooks and crannies carefully etched out, stone benches for the voyeurs' comfort and pleasure, the carpet-strewn concrete floor—and in the center, down three shallow steps, was a pit, filled now with a chocolatey-looking substance. Around it, guests were lolling with drinks, talking, kissing, fondling each other.

There was something pagan about the scene. The focus of all their attention was on one man who was reclining on one of the stone benches in the center, directly opposite the door.

He was massive and muscular, his body tanned and toned. He was magnetic—it was the only word for him. He didn't need to move for anyone to see that he could command an army. He wasn't handsome but his face was arresting, with high-carved cheekbones, smoldering eyes, and ink-black hair.

The judge. The prize. Or at least that was what Justine deduced. She also gathered that sometime Jilly and the mysterious Principessa had both desired this man, fought over this man, or competed for him sexually—why else would Pemble arrange this secret mud bath as the centerpiece of the ball?

There's no way she could get out of it. She had to somehow get herself into that pit and wrestle Jilly's foe.

Who was her enemy? She suddenly felt a dark force aimed at her, as if the Principessa were hovering, waiting, knowing somehow she wasn't Jill and that the Principessa had the advantage.

Who, among the masked, slender, busty women milling around, was the dreaded Principessa?

The moment Pemble saw Justine, he came forward with both hands. "Come say hello to Zoltan."

She looked at Zach, and followed Pemble across the room until she was face-to-face with the charismatic Zoltan.

She palmed her hands and bowed slightly. It would have to do—respectful but noncommittal. She hated not knowing what Zoltan was, who he was, and who her adversary was.

"Ah, the Principessa is here, too," Pemble said.

And there she was, standing tall across the width of the pit, blond, slender, masked, and wearing a gauzy cape she held out like bat wings as she posed.

She didn't look much different from any of the other naked blond women at the party.

They stared at each other across the pit, and then the Principessa moved around the pit to formally greet Zoltan.

Her bow was nearly to her knees in supplication.

I'll kill Zach, I will kill him.

The Principessa rose, and they were eye-to-eye through their obscuring masks.

The Principessa shot Justine a look of contempt. "Take your mask off. I want to see you face-to-face."

"I would never hide from you," Justine snapped back, ripping off her mask.

Now they were naked on every count, and Justine was shocked to see that the Principessa was much younger than she. Young and very self-assured.

"Zoltan is mine," the Principessa spat.

Fine, I don't want him—wait, maybe I do—because the moment the Principessa claimed him, his penis shot to attention.

Which made Justine stand at attention.

She slanted a look at the Principessa.

"Mine," the Principessa repeated.

Jilly wouldn't let her get away with that, Justine thought. She took a covert look at Zoltan's stallion of a penis, so alluring in and of itself.

"I don't think so," she murmured, grasping the Principessa's arm and catching her off balance so that she stumbled into the pit.

She levered herself upward in return and lunged at Justine, pulling her into the mud.

The mud was cold and wet. And in some obscure way, it was sexy.

It got into their hair, all over their bodies, and between their legs. They threw it at the other, rubbed each other's face in it, each other's ass cheeks and mounds with it.

They pulled each other down into it and wrestled, slipping and sliding while the audience hooted and rooted for their favorite.

The Principessa never let up. She was full of feints and dirty tricks, and Justine didn't know how to counter her moves. Only her growing irritation that this bimbo could possibly defeat her kept her swinging.

They scrabbled around the pit, looking for chances to pull the other down, while every now and again, Justine caught the eyes of the masked strangers roaming around the pit, all of them alight with salacious hunger for this overt brand of sexual violence.

Once she thought she saw a familiar unmasked face—a face that it took her a full five minutes of grasping, pulling, shoving, and flopping to remember.

How could that be? She'd only seen the one online photo of Clive Ellicott not hours ago. He was in London. She must be mistaken. Her imagination was in overdrive, and the man she saw was not who she thought—he couldn't be.

She lunged at the Principessa with an untoward surge of strength and barreled her down into the mud, straddling her writhing body.

Justine felt an insensate satisfaction at besting the younger woman, and a pouring of desire when she looked into the hot, dark gaze of Zoltan Brisco.

He motioned to her, and she levered herself off of the Principessa's prone body, rising from the pit like a goddess of the sea.

She toppled forward onto her belly as the Principessa grabbed her legs, pulled her down, climbed on top of her, and pulled her head back by her hair.

"Now then," she growled as Justine futilely tried to wriggle out from under her.

The crowd clapped and howled. With her head in that taut, untenable position, Justine scanned the crowd, looking for a sympathetic eye—not one in this fickle crowd. They liked winners. They liked a good fight. They liked dirty girl-on-girl violence and naked bodies.

She felt dizzy—surely seeing things again—when another unmasked face in the crowd looked familiar. It was just an instantaneous impression of Doug Rawls edging his way through the crowd, and then it was gone, as the Principessa pulled her hair, demanding she give up.

She was suddenly aware of everything—the feeling of the thick dry mud all over her, the lust of the crowd, the hallucinatory visions of Rawls and Ellicott—neither of whom ought to have been there—the roaring approval of Zach, the rapacious sexual appetite of Zoltan cupping and stroking himself.

What am I doing here?

She barely heard the Principessa grunt in her ear, "Give up, give up."

Justine was tempted. She felt dirty, weary, and sexless, but she was aware that the tension had soared to sultry levels. The guests were aroused; they all wanted her flesh.

She could *not* let the Principessa win.

She gathered her wits, her strength, and her guile, letting herself go limp. And then, with one mighty move, she heaved herself up and unseated the Principessa hard onto her butt, to the approving roar of the crowd.

God, how she ached. Her head, her muscles, her eyes. She had to end this somehow, even though the Principessa now was out for blood. She had to do what Jilly would do. Triumph.

Justine watched impassively as the Principessa slowly got to her feet and they faced each other, wary, watchful, each of them propelled by a contained fury and a desire to win.

"You will not—" the Principessa growled just as Justine leaped, grabbing the Principessa's arms. Kicking her ankles, she mashed the Principessa back down into the mud.

"Enough! I want them both."

Zoltan.

Everyone clapped; it was the just decision.

She and the Principessa slowly got to their feet as Zoltan came forward with his hands—and his penis—outstretched. "I want you both—now."

The Principessa took his hand with no hesitation. Justine forced herself to grasp it, and he helped them both step out of the pit.

"Come." He led the way to the rear of the basement, where a

panel slid open on the far side to reveal another pit, this one filled with suede-covered foam.

"The next test," Zoltan murmured, sinking onto the foam and displaying his formidable body. "Pleasure me."

The Principessa's eyes flashed as she elbowed Justine out of the way, got to her knees, and took his penis in her mouth.

Zoltan pointed to Justine. "You . . ."

What would Jilly do? The guests were all around her, whispering, clapping as Zoltan's body bucked. His burning gaze never left Justine's face. "You . . ."

There was no room for her on the bed, which was pocked with dried mud as the Principessa continued.

It was a curiously sexless scene, and Justine felt momentarily at a loss.

"I want *both*!" Zoltan roared. Someone pushed Justine forward, onto her knees, and Zoltan pulled her close to his face, to his lips, and he began plundering her mouth.

His orgasm came fast, his body jerking under the force of it, and falling limp as it faded. But he sustained the kiss, and as the Principessa eased away, he maneuvered Justine's body onto his so that she covered him. He rubbed his body against hers so that caked mud smeared onto his skin, and his penis elongated once again.

"How should I fuck you today?" he murmured against her lips. "Front, rear, tongue, tits?"

"I'm not going to tell you if you can't remember," Justine retorted.

"I remember," he growled, angling his penis between her legs. "I couldn't decide."

"Why should you?" God, she wished he had. The last thing she wanted was minimally protected sex with him. But this wasn't a crowd where she could insist on anything more.

"Come with me on my yacht to Monte Carlo."

"Are you choosing?"

"I would never not invite the delicious Principessa. Her blow jobs are exquisite—as luscious as your cunt. I want cunt today."

"I want a bath," she muttered under her breath, but he heard it. The Principessa probably heard it too, because she was on them like a tiger.

"What are you saying, what does she want? She's had enough time. I want more penis, *now*." She grabbed Justine's shoulders and tried to haul her off of Zoltan's body.

A chant went up: "fight, fight, fight . . ."

Zoltan rolled Justine onto her back so that when the Principessa leaped, she landed on his back. He manuevered himself with the Principessa hanging on tight above and Justine pinned below.

This was it. The guests started clapping, the guests were restive—they were there for sex and action, and Zoltan gave it to them.

The Principessa's weight seemed negligible as he canted his hips and emphatically drove between Justine's legs.

And that was that. The Principessa held on as he thrust and rolled, drove and undulated, the crowed urging him on.

His orgasm hit hard; his whole body stiffening. He lifted himself on his hands, threw back his head, and stifled a howl as he erupted.

A moment later, he pushed away from Justine and rolled the Principessa over onto her back.

It was a covert signal for couples to form, to join them on the bed, to veer off into little cubbies and nooks to spend themselves on whatever was their pleasure.

Justine scrambled out of the pit, hopeful that was all.

"What the hell are you doing?" Zach whispered angrily.

"I have to wash. I'm all itchy." She wasn't, but maybe Zach would at least let her go to the restroom.

"He's taking you to Monte Carlo."

"I got that."

"Just stay put. I'll get everything together."

Horror shot through her. Get everything together? Like clothes and money and . . . a passport?

"I'll do it," she whispered back.

"What's wrong with you? If you don't stake your claim, he'll choose someone else."

"So?"

"So? *So?* Are you crazy? What's wrong with you?" Zach whispered.

"Zach . . ." she said desperately. She couldn't let him go to Jilly's apartment and rummage around unfettered, no matter what Jilly would do, but she didn't know how to stop him.

"We've done this a dozen times. It's a no-brainer. You know what kind of money it involves."

God, it was always about money, and what Jillian's cunt was worth.

She started to protest and realized the futility of it. Zach had a key; there was nothing to stop him from going to Jilly's apartment. She couldn't even bluff it out.

Zach would look for Jill's passport and the other things she would need. He wouldn't find them, and all Justine's lies would hit the fan.

She had to accelerate her plan—get out of there and get back to her own place, pack and leave the country, as she had intended.

Thank God, she had tucked a small purse into her coat with her cell, some money, the key to her apartment, and a credit card.

"I know what kind of money," she said finally, stifling every impulse to run. "I'll go home and pack. I need a shower."

"Wash upstairs. You know he doesn't wait. He goes when he wants to go, and you'd better be ready. You know the Principessa came prepared."

There was no way to get out of it. How much time did she have? How long would it take him to discover the missing passport and come racing back here to demand an explanation?

Faster than fast.

I'm sorry, Jilly. I'm sorry my stupid plan didn't work. I'm sorry I was careless. I failed you again.

"Doesn't she always?" she hissed in answer to Zach's comment about the Principessa. "And you left me out to dry. Fine. Do what needs to be done."

"You'd better get back in the pit before he forgets who you are. He's almost done with the Principessa."

Justine could just see him; his massive body seized, reared back, and stiffened again. He shoved himself tighter between the Principessa's legs before he released his orgasm slow and hard.

"Go," Zach commanded, pushing her toward the pit.

She scrambled onto the mattress, eyeing him covertly. But Zach didn't move until she put her hands on Zoltan's heaving flanks, and then he turned and disappeared among the groping bodies.

She jumped out of the pit before Zoltan could grab her. She caught a view out of the corner of her eye of the Principessa, now held down by two men on either side of her, shackling her wrists and her thighs, while a third heaved himself between her legs.

She saw Zoltan rage around, holding his engorged penis, searching for her, and then grab another willing body and unceremoniously shove himself into her.

Time to duck and run. She threaded her way through the crowd, avoiding the hands reaching for her. Her mask was long gone; everyone knew who she was now.

"Ladies' room. I need the ladies' room."

She felt as if the mud marked her like a scarlet letter. She felt tainted, as dirty as the mud itself. She felt like everyone was watching her. *Someone* was watching her.

"Wherever are you going?"

Pemble blocked her way, and her heart sank.

"Nature calls," she said lightly. Terror gripped again as she held back asking where a bathroom was—*Jilly* would know.

"Well, you know where the loo is," Pemble said dismissively. "Although this is not like you."

"Yes, well . . ." A feeling of dread seeped over her. What was like her? Like Jilly? How many, among those who knew Jilly, were thinking the same thing?

God, if she didn't escape this minute, she'd punch him. Where the hell was a bathroom? Where was the ground level?

So many naked bodies and the scent of lust and drugs permeated the turgid air. She felt panicked again. Someone was aware of her. She felt it like a pulse, like a breath.

She couldn't give in to the terror—or look like she was panting to get out of there. She couldn't do anything but keep saying she needed a ladies' room.

And finally, the anteroom. The coatroom attendant pointed to the adjacent powder room, which was little more than a toilet and a tiny sink.

Finally. Alone.

I have to get out of here.

She took a deep breath, opened the door, calmly asked the attendant for her coat—and ran.

Trying to catch a cab when you were naked under your coat and tottering in stilettos was futile. Her sense of urgency and dread was even worse, and the feeling that unseen eyes were watching wouldn't go away.

She stood on the dark street in the dead of night, hoping for an errant cab. It wasn't the best strategy when shadows lurked everywhere and Zach would be back any second.

Was it luck or fate that one magically cruised by?

Going back to her apartment after more than a week away made everything feel new and different.

She felt *safe* for the first time in days.

But there was no time to revel in it. She booted up her backup laptop and ran to the shower to scrub away the mud, the smell of Zoltan's sex, of all of them.

As she toweled off, she pulled up a travel website, nearly choked at the cost of a book-it-now ticket to London, and then bought an even more expensive one-way ticket, and printed the boarding pass.

Then using a website for hotels, she found an inexpensive room in the Paddington Station area. It was close to Ellicott's office and there were lots of people and mass transit.

Hide in plain sight.

She checked the conversion rate and booked a week's stay, printed the confirmation, and logged off. She checked her voice mail, finding several urgent messages from the university.

She logged back onto her browser, shot a fast e-mail off to her boss explaining nothing except that she was deeply sorry about her ongoing and unavoidable absence and that she was going to be out of the country and would be in touch soon.

She logged off, glad to have that out of the way.

But she couldn't think. She couldn't shake the feeling of dread. She had to have imagined that she'd seen Ellicott at the town house. And it couldn't possibly have been Doug Rawls prowling around the mud pit.

Don't think about it, you'll go crazy. Her flight left in three hours. All she needed was a carry-on bag, packed with a suit—pants, blouse, and heels. She'd wear jeans on the plane, sneakers, and a blazer. She'd have five outfits if she wore a sweater with her jeans. Anything else she could buy later.

She felt a screaming urgency to just vanish.

Just like Jilly.

Passport. Driver's license. Credit card. Cash. She'd get more money at an airport ATM. Crap. Even if it could be traced.

She'd never felt so panicked in her life. Jilly was missing. Zach was poking around Jill's apartment. All that sex. Zoltan's expectations. Pemble's questions. Ellicott and Rawls naked at the ball. Her sex-and-sin fall from grace.

Had she left any clue of her true identity at Jill's apartment?

She couldn't remember and didn't care. She grabbed a raincoat, jammed her laptop into her bag and urgently hailed a cab.

Even at the airport, she didn't feel safe. She'd allowed herself enough time to sit and think, but it was nearly five in the morning, and she still had to clear security.

Zach would eventually figure it out—that she wasn't lying, that there *was* a Justine. Maybe someone had already guessed. How would she square all she'd done in her name with Jilly, and with her conscience, in the end?

Don't think about it. It was in the past. She could bury it, she could forget it ever happened. She could pretend—she was good at pretending, it turned out.

She was not good at hiding her fear though. And definitely not good at planning. She was absolutely useless in a crunch. If she had an ounce of sense in her, she would have flown to London the minute she found out Jilly was there.

And she could have avoided all this upheaval in her life.

She had no life anymore. Taking an extended leave of absence on a fly-by voice mail, with an e-mail follow-up? She could say good-bye to her job, for sure.

And impersonating Jilly? Say hello to opening the door to information about herself she wished she didn't know. Her life would never be the same.

She looked at her watch. It had been about two hours since she'd left her apartment for the airport. Zach must know the truth now. She wondered what he'd do. Tell Zoltan? Pemble? The Principessa? Had his role been solely to lure her to the town house and let her nature—Jilly's nature—and her desire for Zoltan and hatred of the Principessa take its course?

Or was it all just pretense, an act?

She couldn't think straight. Zach and Jilly's relationship made no sense to her, and frankly, it almost didn't matter. She still didn't have a clue what she would do when she arrived in London.

And she missed the sex—some of the sex—already.

Oh, God.

It was impossible to sleep during the seven-hour flight to Heathrow. Her body betrayed her as she tried to get comfortable, liquefying with lust at the thought of a hefty penis all her own, to eat, to suck, to feel pulsing between her legs.

Not that, not him—she didn't want to think about *him.* Because she knew, she was certain, Rawls saw her, all mucked up, down and dirty in the mud, and under Zoltan Brisco, not hours ago at the Crystal Ball.

It *had* been him. She was sure. Doug Rawls had been naked and on the prowl around the edge of the pit as she and the Principessa fought over Zoltan. She hadn't dreamed it, imagined it, or conjured him up out of desire.

Her body went hot at the thought of him watching. He had to have seen everything. And there was no way she could erase the *everything* part. Or the sex. The random, who-cares-who-fucks-who sex—exactly the kind she'd had with him.

He was just like all the rest—a random male body with a talented penis.

Except—

She clamped down on that thought ferociously. *You can't have wishes and dreams. You wrecked that up when you dove into Jilly's secret life and embraced it.*

There were no do-overs in that life. She'd made her bed. She missed the sex. Her body creamed.

Four more hours to go.

Chapter Seven

The airport train took Justine straight to Paddington Station and the Raynour Hotel, her choice from among nearly two dozen other hotels in the area.

It was a good thing, too. The long lines to debark, the time it took to get through customs and then find her way to her destination left her exhausted after the sleepless flight.

She wanted nothing more than to rest. The desperation she'd felt in New York had dissipated like smoke the minute the plane touched down at Heathrow. Jillian Dare didn't exist here—in her—anymore. She was Justine again, the scientist, the practical one, the one in control of her life.

When she got to her room, she slid deep into a dreamless sleep that erased time, memory, and sin. She slept hard, her weariness superseding her panic, her body a deadweight of strung-out emotions.

She slept right into the next afternoon, even though that had not been her plan. So when she awakened, it was with the sudden comprehension that she was in another place, it was another day, but nothing had changed: Jilly was still missing and she still didn't have a clue how to find her.

She called for breakfast, showered, and then threw on jeans, a shirt, and a sweater just before the service cart arrived.

She had tea first, hot and revivifying sanity in a cup. She couldn't believe she'd slept through the day. Manhattan—and Jilly's sex-larded life—seemed light-years away.

But even an ocean and a continent's separation couldn't quell her conscience. What was different?

Zach finally knew she wasn't Jilly, and probably told everyone else in Jill's universe by now. Justine was also pretty sure that a man who looked very much like Clive Ellicott *had* been roaming around the mud pit at the Crystal Ball.

Except she couldn't be certain that she hadn't imagined it from her own disastrous, dizzying free fall into sex.

Guilt was a bigger trap than sin.

She'd start with Ellicott anyway. She logged onto a search engine and typed in the Guardian Group, and there he was again—Clive Ellicott, CEO. She stared at the image. She knew that face, so at odds with his sexual leanings. He *had* been at the town house.

Now Justine had a banging headache and still no answers.

Ellicott's callous looting of Jillian's bank account was the galvanizing gut punch.

Why did he do it?

Because he knew Jillian would never try to reclaim it.

It wasn't the first time she'd had this chilling thought.

She knew two things: Jillian had been with Ellicott a week earlier, and, by her own admission, Jillian was in trouble.

"Find me, wherever I am . . . whatever you have to do."

The only clue she had was Ellicott.

The futility of all she'd done hit her suddenly. She should never have tried to impersonate Jill. She should have investigated the SOS through legitimate means: called the police, reported her missing, or at the very least, hired a private detective. Something.

And she should have just told randy Randy flat out that she wasn't Jillian, because at that point, she could have proved it. Whether he'd have believed it was another thing altogether.

Would she have gone down the same path if he hadn't, made the same ill-considered choices, landed in exactly the same place she was now?

She didn't know, she didn't want to know.

She was stuck with the reality—and the memory—of her choices, and because of her carelessness, Jilly could be in even worse trouble—she could be dead.

NO! She would know, she would feel . . .

What? What would she know if she hadn't remotely guessed that Jilly had lied to her all these years and she'd never sensed any of it.

Damn. She grabbed the phone, rang the desk to ask how to dial out, and punched in the number of Ellicott's office.

"Guardian Group," the voice on the line said sweetly.

"Mr. Ellicott, please." Justine felt light-years away from being confident, but she tried to sound as assured as she could.

"Whom shall I say—?"

"Ms. Jillian Dare." *Oh, dear God.* She hadn't meant to say that, she'd meant to give her own name, to end the charade, to stop all the lies.

There was a long pause after she uttered the words, and then the voice said, "Mr. Ellicott is not available at the moment. Where may he reach you this afternoon?"

Justine hadn't expected to actually speak to him. He was in New York, wasn't he? She had to think fast. What else would get his attention besides using Jilly's name?

She thought of one thing instantly. "He may reach me at my replenished bank account," she snapped. "Otherwise—"

She didn't need to finish the threat. She had no leverage at all, and the fact that she, as Jillian, was in London was probably enough of an *otherwise* for a man like Ellicott.

If he was complicit—and it was a big *if*.

What was she thinking? Phone calls were traceable.

She hung up, her hands shaking, as the speaker was still asking questions.

She had to calm down and treat this like a scientific process, where each step opened another door until all the questions were answered.

It was inconceivable that she, who had a talent for solving the intricacies of the laws of *nature* couldn't figure out her twin's whereabouts.

At least she'd baited the enemy. She needed to know if the morsel had tantalized him. She needed to take her plan a step further and get Ellicott face-to-face, demanding to know where Jilly was.

It smacked just a little of the girl detective as she weaved theories out of dust motes. But Jillian was somewhere out there if she could text even a fragment of their childhood code.

It was time for action. She grabbed her jacket and bag and headed out the door.

Paddington Station was just steps from the hotel. According to her map, she needed to go east, toward Marble Arch. But as soon as she started off in that direction, unease washed over her. She whipped around in midblock, nearly tripping an elderly lady in the process.

"Excuse me, pardon, I'm so sorry . . ."

It had been two days since she escaped from the town house. People now knew she was not Jillian. Someone could have tracked her down by her credit card. Ellicott could have someone following her.

Even that innocuous old lady could have been watching her. Maybe it was coincidence, but maybe it was instinct. It wasn't so different from making conjectures in the lab and then digging for the proof to support the theory.

She'd made a conjecture based on limited information, and now she had to prove it. The main clues: Jillian's coded message, her letter confessing to knowing things that might be dangerous to her, and Ellicott.

Put it in those terms, and there was nothing off-limits in the name of finding Jillian.

She turned and walked in the direction of the Guardian Group's offices, a look of determination on her face.

It had turned into a foggy day, and the air was heavy with the moisture of a coming storm. There were swarms of people on their way somewhere—mostly tourists. She felt out of place, as if she were living another lie and everyone knew it.

But this was no time to seek absolution. Jill had an enemy somewhere, and Justine had to stay alert and in character.

She had no time for an attack of conscience. She'd stripped away her morals faster than she'd stripped off her clothes. Deep in her soul, she shared her twin's sensibility every bit as much as she wanted to be herself again.

She was almost there, and her heart was racing. She could see the tall, glass building two or three blocks ahead. She felt like running. She felt as if anyone she passed could be her enemy.

She quickened her pace. The simplest thing was to go to Ellicott's office and claim she had an appointment. As Jill. She had to be Jill, especially if there was any chance she might actually meet him.

Would he know the difference at first glance?

She eyed the elevator for a moment. It was time to be a heroine. She waited until she would be the only occupant of the elevator and stepped in.

The elevator doors were just closing when an arm blocked them and a tall, familiar figure stalked in, barring her way as she tried to push him aside.

He stopped her easily enough, and the doors closed. "Do you have a goddamned death wish?" He jabbed the "stop" button, and the car jerked to a halt.

She barely recognized Doug Rawls before she reacted. "Do you?" *Dear God, why him? Why now?*

She reached around him to push one button, any button, to get the elevator moving, and he grabbed her hand.

"Not going to happen. We're getting out of here."

"I have business to do. *You* can get out of here." The tension grew, compounding her utter shock, her desire, and his bulldog tenacity.

"You think?"

His eyes were like lasers. She couldn't hide from him. The

attraction bubbled up like boiling water, hot, potent, and shooting through her body like fire.

He gave her a challenging look, released the "stop" button, and punched "lobby," all while shackling her wrists.

"We're leaving—*now*—and you're coming with me."

"Why would I do that?" Every minute alone with him was fraught with memories of their two nights together. His hand mercilessly grasping her wrist reminded her of another time, another place, another kind of imprisonment. She did *not* want to remember those nights with him.

"How about to save your life?"

She had to be abrasive; she had little else to combat him.

"You don't know what you're talking about."

"Believe it or not, but I do."

"I'll scream."

"That's one thing I know I can make you do." He relinquished her wrist suddenly, stepped aside, and motioned for her to move. "Please."

She covertly looked for a way to get around him, but he grasped her arm as he blocked her way.

"Let's go."

He forced her through the lobby, telling her without words that she should just acquiesce and ask questions later.

A car waited at the curb.

"Go on."

"I'm going nowhere with you, and now I *will* make a scene."

"Get in the car."

She wrenched her arm away, pushing him off-balance.

"Come get me." She wheeled away and began to run. Thank God she was wearing jeans and sensible shoes. But Rawls wasn't running after her. *Good.*

A moment later she knew why. The car pulled up beside her, moved ahead of her, and stopped. Rawls got out and leaned against the car door, waiting.

There was nowhere to run. Especially since she didn't know where she was or which way to go.

"Get in." Rawls motioned to the open door. She gave up, and climbed into the limo as passersby clapped.

"Shit—they think this is some lovers' spat," she muttered.

"Isn't it?"

"Go to hell."

He closed the door, nodded to the driver, and the privacy window lifted as the car glided into the clog of traffic.

Being closed off magnified everything, being this close to him, feeling this aroused, and feeling this uncertain, this scared.

But those weren't Justine's feelings—they were Jill's.

Surely Justine was much more in control.

But she wasn't. She just stared helplessly out the tinted window as the limo maneuvered through traffic away from Paddington, deeper into the heart of London.

There was nothing to prove that the threat from Rawls was not greater than from Ellicott. He could be involved in Jill's trouble. Nothing indicated if he was an enemy or a friend.

"Where are we going?" she asked calmly.

"As far away from Guardian as possible."

She cringed. He knew about Guardian. Okay, now *she* was in trouble.

A week or so ago, he'd been a tireless, humping body, using her for all she was worth. Now he conceivably knew why Jillian was in trouble. He might even be Jill's enemy.

Except he thought *she* was Jill and maybe, just maybe, he was the key to everything. Maybe his contacting Zach to buy her body—Jilly's body—wasn't coincidental.

Maybe she had stumbled way too deep into something she knew nothing about, something equally as dangerous as whatever Jill was involved in, and now, between the two of them, there was no way out.

Maybe she was still asleep and this was just a bad dream.

She looked over at Doug Rawls. He was too quiet, stoically quiet, his face expressionless and his body stone still. But something about him was alert and aware.

She stared out the window. They were now in the trendier part of the city, with new construction, place-to-be-seen restaurants, and fashion-forward shops.

"I'll have your bill paid and your things brought to my hotel," he said. "No, I'm not answering any questions. Yes, I'll kiss you."

Her body twinged at the thought. "No, you won't," she snapped. "You don't have enough money for anything I have to offer."

"Maybe we can find other currency to exchange."

Bingo. He wanted something—from Jill. What on earth was Jilly involved in that some corporate bigwig was ready to barter with her?

Who was Doug Rawls, anyway? All she knew about him was that he was intimidating, relentless, and willingly paid for pleasure.

"You were at the Crystal Ball," she said suddenly, turning to look at him.

"Was I?" His deep blue gaze met hers and then moved lower to settle on her lips, watching intently as she spoke. She remembered that intensity; she remembered too much.

"Why? Why were you there?"

He answered without answering. "It's the event of the year, I'm told."

"You think?" she murmured, echoing his sarcastic statement.

"We're almost there."

"Almost where?"

"Here."

The limo had stopped in front of the most expensive hotel in London.

"Hide in plain sight," Rawls said, grasping her arm again as she made a move to open the door. "You'll wait for James, if you don't mind. Every propriety must be observed."

A nice way of saying, *don't try it*. She had never dealt with anyone so implacable. But she should have known that about him just from . . .

Don't think about that. She was in over her head. She'd felt too much with him, including the humiliation of her life—and it wasn't even *her* life.

James opened the door and waited for Justine to emerge, hovering to keep her from bolting. But then Rawls appeared beside him, and there was nowhere she could run.

"Let's go." He propelled her forward with a commanding, sexless grasp of her arm.

Into the luxe lobby they went, enveloped in marble from floor to ceiling. They headed right to a private elevator and a crowd of tourists, his tight grip on her arm warning her not to make a scene. The elevator shot to the topmost floor and the doors opened into what had to be a thousand-dollar-a-night suite. Floor-to-ceiling windows on two sides overlooked the Thames. There was a fifty-inch digital TV on the wall over a marble tile fireplace, an efficiency kitchen, a bedroom with a sitting room. Even the bathroom was luxurious with its double sink, separate shower, and whirlpool tub.

And someone—James?—was going back to her hotel to pack up her "things" to bring them here. He'd go through her "stuff"—her papers, her computer—he'd look at everything, he'd know everything.

"Make yourself comfortable."

She faced him defiantly, even though her whole body was suffused with terror. "I'm intensely *un*comfortable. I want to know why you strong-armed me."

"Nonsense. We're old . . . bedmates. No one forced you here."

"God . . ." She turned to the floor-to-ceiling windows, from which she could see Parliament, Big Ben, the curve of the river, and the stately shadow of Buckingham Palace. None of it was reassuring. She felt like she was flying over the city without a parachute, about to crash and burn.

She couldn't imagine what he'd do when he found out she wasn't Jill.

She wheeled around impatiently. "What do you want?"

"We have time to discuss things."

"What things?"

"We'll save that all until after dinner."

"No saving. No dinner. No discussion."

"Whatever," he said with a shrug. "Since you have no choice right now, there's no point arguing. When James returns . . ."

He meant after James thoroughly searched and packed her belongings—her computer—and found out the truth.

At least he couldn't pillage her computer files. She had changed her password to conform with Jillian's computer. No one knew that hellhole address of their childhood, no one knew about that sliver of their past, or that it was the touchstone by which Jilly lived her life.

She had to calm down. Rawls might think he had the upper hand, but his being here now—his preventing her from going to Ellicott's office—had to mean something.

She stared out the window. Drops of rain spattered the glass, and the sky had darkened. She had no idea what time it was. Rawls moved around behind her; it sounded as if he was making tea or coffee.

Maybe he was preoccupied enough that she could sneak out. She took a covert glance around the room. The doors of the elevator opened nearly directly into the living room, with a small foyer. The mini-kitchen and the luxurious bathroom flanked the foyer.

If she slipped into the bathroom or asked for something to eat, would that divert him enough so she could slip out?

Maybe. But the expanse between where she stood and the elevator felt like a mile.

She was trapped. She could only keep up the pretense for so long.

And when James returned . . .

What would Jilly do?

She'd bluff it out. She'd be a bitch. She'd make Doug Rawls sorry. She'd pretend she'd never even heard of Justine Durant.

She had no other strategy.

"And James will be back when?" she asked, infusing her tone with an insolence she was far from feeling.

"When he gets here. There's coffee. I've ordered dinner. Sit *down*."

She started pacing instead. The rain was coming down in sheets outside, but the windows were so insulated, she couldn't hear a thing.

Just her own breathing. And his boiling impatience.

Jilly wouldn't sit. Only Justine's knees felt like noodles and her resolve felt as firm as a bowl of oatmeal.

Rawls came around from the kitchen, sat on one of the counter stools on the living room side, folded his arms across his chest, and just watched her.

What did he see? Not the immaculate, impeccable Jill, or the cool, cooing courtesan always perfectly made up, perfectly coiffed, and perfectly embellished.

No, Justine's version of Jill wore a tee shirt under a sweater, jeans, and a blazer, with plain white sneakers and her hair up in a wild topknot.

No makeup. No élan. No attitude. There was no vestige of Jillian in her demeanor at all.

She pulled herself together. It was time to slip into the attitude, especially with him watching her with that biting skepticism.

She plowed ahead. "Good, you ordered *something*. I'm damned hungry."

"And what about the after-dinner part?" Rawls asked with deceptive gentleness.

"I have no idea what you're talking about." She pivoted toward the windows again.

"Discussing things."

"We have nothing to discuss except why you high-handedly kept me from my appointment."

"That part comes later."

"No. That part doesn't come at all," Justine snapped. "I'm leaving when James gets here."

"I don't think so."

"I guess we'll see." It was worth a try. James could walk in at any moment with a suitcase full of her deceptions. The tag on her luggage read Justine Durant. The hotel registration and the bill were all in the name of Justine Durant. Anything he found on the computer, if he could hack in, would read Justine Durant.

She turned away from him, giving herself a moment to figure out some way to deflect him.

A thought struck her. An *avatar*. Turn Justine Durant into *Jillian*'s other self.

Justine becoming Jillian, Jilly becoming Justine. It hadn't quite worked with Zach, and convincing Rawls would be doubly difficult. But it just might work.

At a minimum, she could confuse him. If he didn't believe her—well, all she needed to do was keep him off-balance.

"So, Justine . . ."

Her heart stopped for a terrifying instant. He knew already?

She turned, willing herself to a frigid calmness.

"So you know about Justine."

"I know you're not Jillian."

"I'm not Justine either."

"How come I don't believe that?"

"Believe whatever you want." Where did that cavalier tone come from? She couldn't believe she had the balls, but that was Jill. "Where's that dinner you promised me?"

Now he was off-kilter. He hadn't shocked an admission out of her, and he eyed her with just that edge of wariness that was either admiration or a steely determination to break her.

"I believe you're an exceptional liar, as every whore must be."

"You should know. You paid handsomely to prove it. I'm glad that's settled. Do you mind if I use the bathroom?"

"There is no window," he said. "In case you planned to escape. Don't lock it either or I'll break down the door."

She believed him. She grabbed her handbag, closed the door, and sank onto the edge of the tub, her knees shaking and her hands ice cold.

God, he was formidable. Now what?

Deep breath. Keep insisting you're not Justine. Keep Jilly's secrets until you uncover his.

Don't let him get to you.

She opened the door just as the elevator doors were closing. She glimpsed James inside the elevator car.

So James had come, along with dinner, and Rawls had her computer, her maintenance kit, and her luggage tag dangling from his fingers.

Nowhere did she see her suitcase.

Okay. She didn't *need* her clothes.

She ignored Rawls and sauntered over to the cart, lifting one after the other of the domed covers. The traditional fare: sausage and mashed potatoes, fish and chips, fruit and cheese.

She looked up to see him watching her again.

"Help yourself."

If she heaved a plate at him . . .

"Don't even think about it," he said, as if he could read her mind.

She peeled off a piece of cheese.

Now he knew everything—and he knew nothing. The thought empowered her. She tossed her bag on a nearby chair and pulled it next to the dinner cart. She began to pile food onto a plate, and sat back to eat.

Let him make what he wanted out of that.

He just watched her, with his disconcerting gaze never wavering.

The reckoning was coming. She felt it in the air, a combination of his utter amusement at her brazen denial and that not-to-be-acknowledged carnal awareness between them.

She ate, a taste of the sausage and the fish, a bit of fruit, anything to keep the moment at bay.

She didn't fool him either. He knew they had all night, all week and beyond, because she had nowhere to run and a lot to hide.

He let her eat and he didn't say a word. He let her wonder what he wanted, what he would ask, how she would dodge his questions.

She pushed away her plate finally, poured a half cup of tea just to prolong having to speak, and eyed him over the rim as she sipped the scalding liquid.

He lifted a brow. It was a mistake to even look at him with the magnetic pull between them so intense.

He deliberately reached across the cart to pour himself some tea with his deft hands. She knew those hands too well, the feel of them stroking, lifting, invading. She abruptly turned away.

Which gave away too much. *Shit.*

She bit her lip and forced herself to turn back, meeting his gaze as she took another sip.

The silence thickened.

He thought he could hold out longer than she could. But for her, it was so much easier not to talk, even at the cost of those erotic memories playing in an incessant loop in her mind.

Those men—Jilly's men—were all forgettable. That was why she'd made all those detailed notes about them—because they *were* so unmemorable. But Rawls? Had Jill written anything about *him*?

Justine had never thought to look.

What didn't she know about him, essentially? He was *un*forgettable, dangerous, and the stoic patience that could ride a woman to multiple orgasms overlaid a ruthlessness that she'd be suicidal to challenge.

Any which way, she didn't have a lot of choices.

Just be Jilly: aloof, aggressive, belligerent if she had to be. Defend her position—that Justine *was* her alter ego—and don't let him punch a hole in that story.

Chapter Eight

It felt more like a safety net than a strategy.

A torrent of rain poured outside now, but she couldn't tell if it was midnight or midday. Something had to give. They couldn't sit there forever.

Or maybe they could. In addition to impassive calm and impressive stamina, Rawls had the patience of a rock. He had her computer, he had the luggage tag, and he knew what he knew.

She had to convince him it wasn't what he thought he knew.

She leaned back in her chair and felt the bulk of her handbag against her back. Oh, no—all her identification was in that bag, her credit cards, her passport.

She blew out a breath. She'd just tell him Justine was her legal name, and Jillian was her nom de working girl.

The minutes ticked by and she didn't need a clock to hear them in her mind. The tension stretched to the screaming point.

Finally she reached for her bag and stood. He made no move to stop her as she stalked to the elevator doors. The instant she punched the button, the doors opened and there was James. With a sinking feeling, she sensed Rawls behind her so that she was sandwiched between them.

There had been no point to her brief rebellion at all.

Rawls unhooked her bag from her shoulder, took her arm, and pushed her back into the living room. She sank onto the closest sofa as he opened her bag and dumped the contents onto the coffee table, tossing out the relevant items—passport, driver's license, credit cards—one by one into her lap, as he read her name: "Justine Durant, Justine Durant, Justine Durant."

She said nothing.

"Where's Jillian?" His tone was deadly calm.

"You're looking at her."

"You're lying."

She shrugged.

"You're Justine Durant, whoever the hell *she* is. Where's Jillian?"

"I'm right here."

"I don't believe you."

She shrugged, gathered up her identification, put it into her bag, and then looked up at him. "Stalemate."

"The hell." There was just an edge of irritation in his tone. "Well, there's time. You're not leaving here." But that was only because he knew he'd eventually get what he wanted.

She channeled Jilly. "Whatever. I'm tired. Do I get the bedroom or the couch?"

He leaned against the kitchen wall. "You get to take off your jacket, sweater, and shirt. Then I'll decide."

That stopped her cold. He couldn't possibly think Jilly would give up anything to him after this. No, that wasn't true. Jilly wouldn't even be thinking about him the same way. He wasn't anything but a big dollar sign to her. Jilly was a player.

She wouldn't have a qualm about baring any part of her body; she always used her nudity to give her the advantage anyway.

Justine shot him a hostile look and shrugged out of her jacket and pulled off her sweater and shirt.

I am Jill.

"Take off the bra. You're not going anywhere."

She toyed for ten seconds with the idea of daring him to remove it, but then he'd have to touch her and that could be explosive.

She had no fallback position unless it was on her back. He'd seen her naked, explored every part of her body. There was nothing about her that he didn't already know.

Except that she wasn't Jill. She shrugged and unhooked her bra.

Immediately his gaze sharpened and her nipples tightened. She felt a surge of power. She threw the bra at him, followed by her jacket, sweater, and shirt.

Then she stood up, putting her hand on her hip. "I'm taking the bedroom tonight, and I'm leaving in the morning unless I hear something that makes it worth my while to stay."

"Not until you tell me where Jillian is. So sit *down*."

That tone brooked no argument; the air was so charged—with lies, with memories, with desire—she sank onto the arm of the chair, suddenly feeling hopeless.

She couldn't let him intimidate her. He had no answers, and she had little else but wit, guile, and shame to sustain her. She motioned to her upper torso. "I'll go naked if I have to, but I will get out of here."

He raised his brows slightly. "Try it."

That effectively stopped any smart-mouthed comeback.

Lust blanketed the air like a down comforter, smothering, suffocating. She could barely breathe, it was so potent. He wasn't immune to it either. She saw his body tighten, his ferocious will to suppress it.

"Where is Jillian?" His voice was icy now, freezing her and his need.

"How many ways can I answer that?"

"The truth would actually be refreshing, *Justine*."

Her flaring desire dissipated—just a little. Just enough. She felt edgy and out of control. Not Jill-like in the least. She stood up abruptly and stalked to the windows. The rain curtained her view and all she saw was the memory of him fucking her for anyone to see.

Her body twinged with the thought. Against all reason, she wanted more of that. Now.

"Justine . . ."

His voice sounded too close. She whirled around, but he was still across the room, still leaning against the wall.

Her face burned under her skin, remembering. What she *needed* to remember was the humiliating moment when she'd counted his money. Let her lesson be about the money—that big gambler's roll of bills that defined the value of her sex and services rendered.

Standing there half naked was more difficult than she thought. She didn't know what to do with her hands. She folded her arms loosely around her midriff, pushing her breasts upward and making her nipples more prominent against her pale skin.

She tilted her chin defiantly as he stared.

It lasted less than a minute. The two of them together in a room was a dangerous combination heightened by the way he roamed her body with his eyes, as if he were remembering those nights, too.

It was stupid and insipidly romantic of her to make something out of what was purely a business exchange.

Heat fused into anger. Fine, if he wanted her body, he could have her body, all of it. She kicked off her sneakers, ripped open her jeans, and shimmied out of them. Every inch of her was naked for the taking, but the price this time would be as steep as Mount Everest.

She threw her jeans at him, and the look in his eyes flared a deeper blue as he caught them. He crushed the material against his face, inhaling the very scent of her.

The air couldn't have been more explosive as she stood there, arrogantly flaunting her naked body.

She didn't need to dare him to come to her. He slowly edged his way toward her, forcing her back against the window.

"Tell me again that you're Jillian."

She felt the cold glass against her skin, and the fury in his voice that she would lie again. She knew at that very moment she couldn't lie anymore.

"I know you're not Jillian. Do you want to know how I know?" He held up her jeans. He tossed them aside and moved in on her.

"This is how I know." He cupped her cheek and then moved his hand down her neck, to her breast, squeezing her nipple for an instant, then across her belly to her hips, until his hand was between her legs, cupping her mound.

"And this is how I know . . ." He parted her labia and thrust his fingers deep inside her. He covered her mouth almost simultaneously, his tongue ruthless, his kiss so hot her knees nearly buckled.

His fingers worked her cunt and she didn't stop him, she couldn't stop him, she didn't *want* to stop him as she undulated hard against him.

She'd wanted this, she'd fantasized about him when she'd been with those other, forgettable, men in Jilly's name. She gave into his expert fingers as they thrust, pushed, reached, shooting pleasure through her body. Not yet, not yet, too soon.

But she couldn't stop, it crackled through her body like lightning, leaving aftershocks that shook her to the center of her being.

He pulled his mouth away slowly, tasting her lips, licking them, with his fingers still embedded in her, motionless.

He scrutinized her for a long moment, as if he were memorizing every detail of her face—or comparing her to someone. Justine shook her head and turned away.

It was only a matter of time now. All the passion drained out of her body, out of the air, out of him. Back to business—because that orgasm was all business. It was the one strategy he knew would work.

She pushed at his hand, still wedged between her legs, but he didn't remove it.

"You *are* Justine," he said. It was the moment of truth; realization was dawning. "Jillian's a twin."

Bluff it through. "How fun. I have a twin? Justine is my legal name, you bastard. Now let go of me."

She had the satisfaction of seeing momentary hesitation in his eyes, because it *was* possible. She had no idea how much anyone in Jilly's circle knew. Certainly she had kept her childhood secrets buried; she just as easily could have kept quiet about her siblings.

Rawls hesitated just long enough that she could wriggle away from him, grab her jeans, and put them on.

"Don't touch your other clothes. I goddamn know who you are now. That was a good on-the-fly story, Justine, but you *are* her twin." He held up his hand and brushed his fingers against his nose. "Proof certain."

She sank onto the closest sofa. Sex betrayed you every time. The scent of sex was individual, unmistakable. But she wasn't willing to give in just yet.

"Think what you want. You got what you wanted. Can I go now?"

"Where's Jillian?" He stood over her, meaning to threaten her, she thought.

"Well, since I'm her——"

He bent over her, imprisoning her against the sofa. "I think you can stop singing that song now, Justine. I've got the whole picture."

"Well then, you don't need me."

"You're wrong about that. I absolutely need you." His eyes changed suddenly, and he pushed away abruptly and settled himself beside her. "Now that we have that all settled . . ."

But nothing was settled. She felt wholly unsettled after that shattering orgasm. It lingered, invaded her space, her memories, her fantasies.

Her career as Jillian was over. It was time to go back to her sterile, everyday life where she was always in control and would never be caught dead lusting for a man like this ever again.

She wanted his penis. Now.

How on earth could she still want him when he'd just stripped away every pretense, every lie?

She didn't want *him*. She wanted the feeling, the surrender, the blinding, satiating, orgasmic release.

It could be anyone who walked through the door. Not just him. How could she want *him* again?

But against all reason, her *body* wanted him again, that little throb of arousal and pulse of memory.

Don't. Wanting more sex with him was just a naked ride to disaster. Giving into her crazy uninhibitions, giving into the feeling of total sex-starved depravity and not caring was exactly what she wanted.

Do it.

Her body warmed at the thought, becoming aware of everything: her jeans against her skin, the rain beating on the window, the moistness between her legs, his bulging erection.

Shouldn't waste a perfectly good erection.

She sat up, thrust her breasts forward, and cupped them. She brushed her taut nipples with her fingers. She got up and paced around as he watched.

He wanted her. She knew it, she felt it.

Let him look. Let him . . .

Do something.

He was hard as stone just sitting there.

"Sit down," he commanded.

"I don't want to. I want—"

"I know what you want."

Her breath caught and she finished unsteadily,"—to get out of here."

"Liar. What you want is to get my penis out of here "—he unzipped his jeans and released his jutting shaft—"and deep inside there." He gestured toward her.

Her body went hot. She wanted—right there for the taking—his penis and lots of answers, in that order. And she wanted another day of fucking every which way.

He just sat there patiently, his penis at full staff, his eyes watching her reaction. It was in her face, the hardening of her nipples. Her body was suffusing with lust.

She ached to touch him, enfold him between her breasts, to lick and suck and devour him. But she did nothing. He had to come after her this time.

She waited. He held her eyes for a long moment and then rasped, "I want my penis inside you—now." He started shucking his clothes. Simple as that. He was as long and lean as she remembered, his penis stiff and voracious with need.

"Get on the couch." He pushed her onto the nearest one and straddled her legs to remove her jeans. "Don't ever wear clothes when you're with me. I don't need impediments. I want every part of your body naked for me."

He threw the jeans behind him, spread her legs, and with a heaving thrust, he penetrated her ripe flesh.

She lifted her hips to take him deeper, with a long sigh of pleasure.

"Don't move."

"I can't move."

"Good. God, I haven't even finished fucking you, and I want more."

"Me, too," she whispered, hanging on as he started to ride her hard.

Yes, yes, yes. The sensation of him pumping into her was heaven. She must remember she wanted that penis and nothing more. Just his luscious penis.

She was right at the pleasure point, on the edge, and they came together, her orgasm spilling into his, a hot geyser of perfection.

It aroused her all over and again as she savored the slickness of his shaft rooted in her. He worked it, slowly, undulating his hips, letting her feel all of him inside her.

Another wash of pleasure streamed through her body and pooled between her legs. Words couldn't describe it, only the most primitive expressions of pleasure with his penis still hard inside her, his body covering hers.

She stretched as best she could under his welcome weight. This was only the beginning. "Don't forget every part," she whispered.

"I meant every part," he growled.

Every part—he was ready for all the other parts. He shifted her body, canted her bottom upward, nudged her opening with his penis, and then heaved and thrust his way home.

She went breathless as she felt every hot inch of him penetrating her. She loved that her body was capable of this—and that his penis could give it to her so masterfully.

"Don't stop," she whispered. She could stay like this forever with him. "Don't stop . . . I *need* more."

His stamina was unimaginable. His hands grasped her ass cheeks, felt her thighs, caressed her belly as he rutted deeper from behind.

Something had to give. His body felt explosive, and her body hummed with the overriding need to feel him come.

"Let it go," she urged him. "Let it go."

Instead he went quietly still, just stopped his rhythm, his hands tight on her bottom. And then, "Shit, damn, hell" as he pulled himself from her body and whispered tightly. "Get up—grab your bag, your clothes—now."

There was no time to think. She swooped up her jeans, her jacket, her sneakers and bag and grabbed his hand. He'd already slid into his jeans and a shirt, grabbed her computer, and packed it in a shoulder bag in the space of three minutes. He pulled her through the bedroom and into the adjoining sitting room, where he opened the walk-in closet door, yanked out a shirt rack that was screwed into the ceiling and pulled down hard on it. A narrow opening appeared behind the shirts.

Huh?

"In there, now. Then dress quickly." He squeezed into the narrow dark space behind her. It muted all sounds as he pushed the panel closed. A moment later, a narrow beam of light played across their feet—just enough so she could dress and sling her bag across her chest—and then he doused it.

"Good," he whispered. "Come."

It was something out of a spy novel. The fact that there was nothing but dead silence beyond the walls didn't erase that he'd scared her almost witless. He took her hand and they inched forward another dozen feet and stopped.

He ran a flashlight over the wall, revealing a lever that he pulled hard. A new opening appeared. He touched her shoulder and pushed the opening just an inch farther. "This lets out into the closet of the adjoining suite. Let's go."

He slipped out into the empty walk-in closet and motioned for her to follow him to the elevator. He listened for a moment at the doors and then pushed the button. The doors opened; he guided her inside, and then hit "Lobby."

"We have to get out of here fast."

"What just happened?"

"Short version: Someone's out to kill you—or us, I haven't quite figured out which—and they got past my safeguards. That's all you need to know at the moment."

"Are you joking?"

The elevator stopped and the doors slid open.

He wasn't joking as he covertly looked around. "Not hardly. They'll be onto our escape route in a minute. Shit, they've posted guards. Wait—turn your head. Now, *go*."

Thank God the lobby was crowded with new arrivals. They slipped out behind a couple emerging from another elevator and edged into the crowd.

Anyone could be after them, Justine thought with a shiver, noting the way Rawls surveyed the crowd. He flipped his cell and barked "Plan B" into the receiver. He did it so easily, Justine thought, as if this were standard operating procedure for him.

That didn't reassure her either. Doug Rawls was every bit as dangerous as any assassin.

He elbowed her to follow the crowd down an escalator to the mezzanine level, where most of the masses were headed. There was a restaurant on the floor and a bar.

"Drink? James won't be at our rendezvous point for another ten minutes."

"Yes. And explanations."

They had to take a table on the outer railing of the seating area because the bar was so crowded. It wasn't ideal, but hiding in plain sight was a reasonable strategy for the moment.

Justine ordered white wine, Rawls a beer, and she waited impatiently for him to speak.

"Isn't it obvious?" he asked finally.

"Not to me." She was still shaken—by the force of the sex, the urgency of escape, just the idea of secret rooms and hired guns.

"It ought to be. They think you're Jillian."

"Oh." Even this was about Jillian. Justine was too good at stepping into Jilly's shoes.

Was it Ellicott? But how would he know she was with Rawls?

Maybe it was a trap. And Rawls was involved, his part to corner her, seduce her, and dispose of the problem.

"You're wrong." His voice cut through her escalating fear.

"Tell me why," she snapped.

"You won't believe me. You don't believe me right now, so it doesn't matter. You're still coming with me."

"Give me one good reason."

"I'm not finished fucking you."

She ignored him. "You're saying someone wants to kill me."

"Someone wants *Jillian* out of the way. They don't know you're *not* Jillian. So whatever you were trying to do, you succeeded. But Jillian's still the target—and you're a damned idiot for having gone so public with her."

She blew out a breath. This was the stuff of fiction. But there were plot points missing. How did he know about the interconnecting secret passage between the suites? Who the hell was he *really*?

Mind-blowing sex didn't mitigate betrayals. It enabled them. Goddamn him.

She ought to just bolt, now, melt into the crowd, and disappear. She could do it.

His cell vibrated and he answered. "You there?"

Run now.

As he tossed a couple of dollars on the table, she jacked herself up and ran through the crowd, pushing aside anyone who got in her way. She went down a couple of steps into the bar, across the mezzanine—it didn't matter where she was going, as long as she could vanish in the crowd.

He wasn't one to call attention to himself. He came after her quickly, unobtrusively, stalking her like her assassin.

He was inexorable, tracking her like the slinky predator he was, and he cornered her behind an unoccupied information desk backed up against a curtained wall.

"I'm not going anywhere with you," she hissed across the podium.

"You're mistaken if you think you have a choice."

"I have a choice," she added defiantly.

"Not after you chose to impersonate Jillian. I need to know why you did it and where she is."

"Why? Tell me why and maybe I'll tell you."

He waited a long time before he finally spoke, choosing his words carefully. "Jillian was with Ellicott—and a man named Oliver Baynard two nights before he died."

He felt out her reaction. The telling point was that she didn't ask who Baynard was. "No questions?" he murmured. "Isn't that interesting?"

She knew better than to offer an explanation. "Oh, I have a question. *You.* You're the big question."

He went silent while he contemplated whether to answer or how much to say.

"I work for Baynard. The hotel—we keep the two adjoining company suites. The secret room—Mr. Baynard was always suspicious and always planned a way out if necessary. And yet, one day there was no way out and he died because of a careless accident on a deserted road. But you know all about that, don't you? And you'll tell me exactly what you know on our flight back to the States."

Back? No, she wasn't leaving London, not while Jill could still be there.

"Don't make a scene. Don't give your enemies—Jillian's enemies—anything to go on. Ellicott is in New York, as I think you know, so just come quietly."

She held his gaze. Maybe the most important thing was that Rawls knew Ellicott wasn't in London, just like he'd been aware she was even on her way to the Guardian Group's offices.

Justine suddenly felt helpless. And most important, she'd made no progress. Rawls even had to tell her that Jilly had been with Ellicott *and* Baynard.

Wait a minute—hadn't Zach worried that Jillian had been involved in the accident somehow? How much did Zach know about all this?

She'd discounted the people in Jill's life who were constants—

Zach, her regular gentlemen clients, Pemble, even the Principessa and Zoltan Brisco. She hadn't nearly mined the computer full of information. It was all in Rawls's hands now.

She had to go with him. Her identity was safe for the moment, but the danger was still real for Jill. All that would end in New York, with Zach knowing that she wasn't Jillian. Beyond that, she couldn't speculate.

Rawls knew she'd give in. And she knew it was inevitable that she couldn't outrun him now—no matter what she did.

Chapter Nine

James drove them to a small airport just outside of London, and they boarded a private plane that seated about twenty. Today it would carry just a crew of three and the two of them for the six-hour flight.

The cabin was hushed and outfitted with rich leather chairs and sofas, a privacy curtain, and walnut furnishings. There was a small bathroom in the rear, and a tiny kitchen neatly tucked in near the cockpit.

Rawls gestured for her to take a seat and buckle up as he took the chair opposite her. Moments later, the plane smoothly taxied to the runway and minutes after was in the air. Simple as that—no hang-ups, holdups, security, or searches.

God, what would she do all these hours alone with him? She felt grimy and sexless at the moment. But as the plane gained altitude and she inadvertently caught his eye, she saw that he didn't see her that way at all.

"Don't," she whispered involuntarily.

"There is no *don't* between you and me," he said drily. "There are lies and denials, but *don't*? No, *don't* doesn't exist."

She took a deep, shuddering breath. Don't look at him. Don't talk to him.

Don't suddenly raised the temperature in the cabin. *Don't* immediately rubbed against her arousal. *Don't*, in essence, was an invitation to *do*.

He knew it, too.

"I need the ladies' room," she murmured, at a loss.

"Don't lock the door."

"And where could I possibly go?"

"All the way to JFK without my penis between your legs. *Don't*." *Don't* look at his groin.

"Excuse me." She swallowed the heat in her throat and unbuckled.

"You can strip while you're at it."

She caught her breath and held her tongue—and looked at his groin.

It was bulging. Big time. *Get to the bathroom. Close the door.*

She peered at herself in the mirror. There was nothing remotely seductive there. Her eyes were huge and hollow, her face pale, and her hair an untidy mess. Everything about her translated to wrinkled and gritty.

Obviously none of that mattered now. Nothing mattered with him except the urgency of the physical and the power of greedy, lust-driven sex.

She felt it already, because he was just beyond the door, just a step away from sex.

She splashed cold water on her face, determined not to take off the few clothes she had on. Not. She had principles.

But it was no different from sex in the suite. At twenty thousand smooth-as-silk miles in the air, who would care? It would be as if it never happened, didn't count.

As long as she didn't think a minute beyond it.

The door opened.

"You're not naked." He appeared behind her, crowding her against the granite edge of the sink. "I thought I made it clear I want you naked. All the time."

His penis was there, stiff and throbbing against his jeans, pushing and prodding at her bottom, two layers away from the pleasure of penetration.

She couldn't begin to define what this insane need was between them, but she couldn't deny it. She wanted that hot, hard part of him that filled and fucked her so expertly.

Why not? He had the equipment, she had the time.

She held his hot, blue gaze as she slowly unbuttoned her jacket to reveal her naked breasts. She shimmied out of her jeans and kicked off her sneakers. She gave him a knowing look in the mirror and then turned, rubbing her body against his, coming face-to-face with him in a way that only ignited her desire.

His jeans were suddenly around his knees, his potent erection nudging into her. No words. Nothing necessary except the fastest way to get his penis into her cunt.

She hiked herself up against the cold granite, braced her legs on either side of him on the wall, grasped his shaft, and guided him to her juicy cleft.

He pushed, pausing his penis head just within the swell of her labia, and she caught her breath. She murmured an involuntary "Oh!" as she looked down at the intimate tip of his sex barely penetrating her body.

And then he gave an emphatic thrust as she took him into her body. She could feel the heat and hardness of him reaching deep inside her, owning her, there, deep between her legs and then, deep in her mouth in an all-encompassing kiss.

There was barely room to move. She angled her legs lower to tighten her cunt around his shaft and heighten the sensation. Everything fell away. Time belonged to them right now. Nothing else mattered except what she felt between her legs, how he drove her, even in this contained space, to physical overload.

In slow motion, her orgasm mounded like whipped cream, expanding until it could hold no more, liquefying in slow motion through her body and pooling hot between her legs. A moment after, his orgasm blew into hers, a long, lust-filled exhale of cream and suppressed desire.

And then, the silence. Her heart was pounding, his cum seeping from her body. His gentle mouth was on hers now, still exploring her before he moved away from her bruised lips and simultaneously eased himself from her body.

Reality slowly seeped in—the hum of the engine, the cold granite of the sink counter, her cream-saturated nudity.

He swiftly tucked himself into his jeans. "Don't think about dressing again until we land. I'm not nearly done with you."

"I hope not," Justine murmured.

Why not? They were flying so far above reality, literally and figuratively, what did it matter how many times he took her? And damn it, the minute he said he wanted more, *she* wanted more.

She stared at her reflection post-coitus. She looked so much different, her face flushed and plumped now, her eyes simmering with secret sex.

She picked up her clothes.

He was waiting when she emerged, naked and sprawled on a sofa, his penis at full staff. She tossed her clothes on a chair and knelt by the sofa. "Let me—"

"Oh, no. No, I mount you. That's how it goes right now."

"Until you throw the money on the table?" she shot back.

"Bitch." His expression hardened. "Let's just say when. In the meantime, just straddle my thighs, back to front, so I can fuck your nipples."

His voice was so cold. None of the furnace fury of before. But the irrefutable fact was, she wanted it. She couldn't avoid it.

She climbed onto his lap, spread her legs so his penis could poke out, and lay back against his muscular chest.

She pulled his penis head firmly to her belly and stroked it idly as he cupped her breasts. A swirling movement of her fingers jolted him, and his deft fingers closed around her nipples, compressing them lightly, sending a whorl of heat between her legs.

Her body moved of its own volition, her hips replicating the primitive, undulating mating dance of his not half an hour before. The pleasure was almost indescribable—she wanted more, she wanted him to stop—she wanted, she wanted. She spread her legs and bore down on his shaft, grinding hard on him, her body arching with the rhythm of his fingers.

No thoughts, no focus other than the pleasure streaming from him, her body so lust-crazed for his touch that she was oblivious to everything but the ecstasy racking her body.

Except she was hotly aware of his large hands covering her breasts like bra cups, and his semen was all over her.

She went still for a long time. It was too much for a stranger to take from her. No more sex with him. No more gut-wrenching climaxes. It was just too much.

She couldn't handle it. She couldn't do it again.

His whisper cut into her ear. "You bitch, you kept *that* from me all those days in the hotel?"

Her whole body stiffened. It was easier this way than to wish it had been different. "You got what you paid for then."

"No—I paid for your nipples, too. You kept those to yourself."

"And now you've had them," she hissed.

"I'm not done with them either," he growled. "Or with you." He spread her legs wide and felt for her cleft. He pushed her labia apart before inserting three fingers into her cunt. "Nice and moist."

He shifted his body and she found herself on her back, with him climbing over her, spreading her legs again, and nosing his penis to the entry point.

"Yes or no?"

"Yes or no what?" she retorted belligerently.

"Yes, fuck me. No, it's all over."

His face was so close to hers, his eyes burning with something she couldn't define. They had so many more hours to be together. She wanted to say no. But she couldn't say no.

"Yes," she whispered, and in a long, blasting swoop, he took her as she arched to meet the thrust. They merged into a soft, delicate torsade of pleasure that almost submerged them both.

And then they slept.

She awakened to a wet tickling between her legs. He was there, his face buried in her cleft, licking and sucking, exploring her. His tongue expertly dipped into and out of her cunt as he sucked and lapped at her.

He was adamant and precise, and he knew just how to do it. All she could do was ride his tongue and let him have his way until she convulsed to orgasm.

"I thought I'd just spread your legs and go down on you without asking, since you have this habit of keeping things from me."

She shook her head, breathless. "No more."

"No? Did you forget your nipple secret?" He reached over and surrounded one tip with his fingers. It hardened instantly under his firm manipulation, and she squirmed with languid pleasure. He kept working her nipple, just to watch her body undulate and arch.

"More secrets," he murmured. "It only takes playing with one hard nipple to drive you to an orgasmic frenzy."

She grasped his wrist. "It's too much."

"It's not enough. None of it is enough." His voice was hoarse with arousal, his body tight, taut, poised to penetrate.

There wasn't much room on the sofa, but he managed to spread her legs and position himself while still manipulating her one nipple. When his penis reamed into her, her body blasted into spasms.

"More secrets," he whispered. "I'm just going to fuck you for hours." But he could barely last five minutes before he exploded, unable to contain his volcano of lust.

He felt as if he had blasted out of his body altogether. A man could only fuck so much. But with her . . .

God, he never should have started. Never.

He looked at his watch. It'd been half an hour since he'd drained every bit of semen into her, and already he wanted more. He felt like he was perpetually erect, his penis in control, and his brain had nothing to do with it.

He was creaming to fondle her other nipple. But she slept now. Still, he couldn't resist touching her, sliding his hands all over her naked body, feeling her silky skin.

He never should have started, because now he couldn't get enough. It was complicated further by his having to confine her somehow—danger still lurked. He couldn't forget that, even though one minute of breathing the same air spiked his desire for her, and his thoughts went primal.

God, she was a gorgeous piece.

Just like her sister. *Don't forget.*

She woke finally and stretched, finding him lounging in a nearby chair, his penis erect, and watching her.

"I really like a man whose penis is always on point," she said through a yawn.

"I really like a woman with orgasmic tits."

"Yeah. Secrets." The word was like a bonfire as they stared at each other. The air grew sultry and tight with that greedy lust to possess.

"We're almost there," he said roughly. "I want your nipple. The one I didn't fuck."

She could barely breathe, the tension was so heavy. "My nipple wants you to come get it."

"If I come, I won't stop fucking you until this plane lands."

She twisted her body so the nipple in question could tempt him. He wasn't an easy get. She was awash with desire to have him fondle that nipple.

When he came to her finally, she reached for him first and put his penis in her mouth just as he touched her nipple. They reacted simultaneously—he, with a hefty spurt of cream, and she, with her whole body shuddering.

"Not letting go," she managed to tell him, through the hardness of his penis in her mouth.

"Not letting go," he echoed, squeezing a little tighter as she sucked and pulled at his shaft deep in her mouth.

Only when the pilot announced their approach to JFK did he let himself go, drenching her mouth, her chest, her hands with a geyser of semen as he sent her body into orgasmic spasms with one last tweak of her nipple.

There was a long silence as the plane banked downward.

"You can get dressed," he said.

"You mean, I don't have to walk through the terminal naked?"

"Maybe you do."

"Maybe I want to."

"No, what you want is to answer this question—and don't

answer now. The question is, do you want to be naked with me? And I don't mean get naked, whenever the urge strikes. I mean *be* naked—all the time when we're together, wherever we are."

He paused and then emphasized the question again, "Do you want to *be* naked with me? Your naked body open whenever I want to fuck. It's not about love or happily ever after or a future. It's about sex. Think about it."

She stopped dead as he said this, her breath catching hard and painfully at the thought.

Naked. Alone. All the time. With him. Whenever she wanted. Whenever *he* wanted.

She could barely ask the question, let alone any question. "*Are* we going to be somewhere together where that's possible?"

"I'm thinking about that."

"And if I don't want to be naked with you?"

He gave her a skeptical look. "Really? Fine. *If* that's your decision."

What was there to think about? It sounded like a no-brainer, except for the fact that they were almost in New York, and there were other factors coming into play. The mystery of Jillian's whereabouts; what Zach Leshan knew, figured out, assumed, and steps he might have taken on Jill's behalf; what she didn't uncover on Jilly's computer; her last message; the mysterious Ellicott; the overly cautious and irrevocably dead Mr. Baynard.

And her naive pursuit of the truth about Jillian.

Well, she'd found out *some* truths—chiefly, she had the temperament to become every bit as much a sexual courtesan as her twin—and the naked truth was she'd subsume all of the mysteries and puzzles into spending whatever time she had left with Doug Rawls.

"The safest place is probably your apartment," Rawls said after they got through customs and emerged from the terminal. "I'm assuming none of them know who you are or even that Jillian has a sister."

"No one knows—but I can't guarantee Zach Leshan hasn't figured it out by now. The night of the Crystal Ball, Jilly—*I*—got an offer Jillian wouldn't have refused, a trip to Monte Carlo with that Zoltan Brisco. Zach went to Jill's apartment to pack a suitcase and get her passport and things, which he wouldn't have found, of course. Along with not finding her suitcases or the clothes she would have needed for the trip. But he and I—"

She stopped as Rawls flagged a cab and helped her into it. "Zach and I had some strange conversations that week. He'll surely recall all the anomalies, including my claim to be Jill's twin, which apparently she herself used to get out of dates. He thought I was lying. He'll start counting all the ways I was different. Like I made coffee, when everything with Jill was takeout. It's a small thing, but telling. He must know now."

"Did you leave any trace of the real you in the apartment?"

She marveled at how he reverted to business on a dime, his attention on how hers and Jill's stories intersected.

She went on. "I barely brought anything with me when I decided to stay there—my driver's license, a credit card, my keys. But I brought some decorative items from my apartment—nothing identifiable, they're just definitively not *Jill*."

"Then your apartment is the safest place to be right now. What's the address?" The cab eased out of the taxi lane and whipped into the streaming traffic with expert speed.

The safest place to *be*. *Be* naked with him.

She felt Rawls's hand on her thigh. It was all about the sex. She'd do really well to remember that.

It was a long ride. She wanted sex, and somehow, he knew. His hand inched up to her waistband and unzipped her jeans. A moment later, he slipped his fingers deep into her cunt. He knew everything, even how to perform a stealth finger fuck in the back of a cab.

Her orgasm hit hard and fast.

She squeezed his hand to stop, but he kept his fingers embedded in her. "There's still a lot you have to tell me," he murmured.

"I know," she whispered. "You, too."

It took nearly an hour, with traffic, for the cab to inch its way to her apartment in the West 70s.

Only when the cabbie pulled up in front of the building did Rawls remove his fingers, and only because he had to pay the fare.

She lived on one of the top floors. It took forever for the elevator to get there, the lust factor multiplying exponentially with each moment they were in that small space.

God. Finally. She dug in her bag for her keys, opened the door, and flicked on the hallway light, revealing a large walk-in closet, a galley kitchen, and a wall overflowing with bookshelves. To the front of the apartment there was a wall of windows. The living room and a work area were just visible from where they stood.

He stopped her in the hallway.

"Now—answer the question—do you want to be naked with me?"

She didn't hesitate. "Yes." She started unbuttoning her jacket and tossed it on the floor emphatically. "Do you want to be naked with me?"

He started stripping, too. "Do you really have to ask?"

Already shaking with excitement, she backed into the living room. "The bed's back here." It was screened off for privacy from the living room. There also was a bathroom and another walk-in closet on this side, along with built-in storage.

But little of that registered as he tumbled onto the bed with her and without words, caresses, or foreplay, fused his naked body into hers—finally alone with her, the world at bay.

I am Justine.

Sometimes she had to remind herself. She stared at the ceiling, wide awake after yet another hour of pure concentrated fucking. Let her not forget that was what it was: sex for the sake of sex.

Of everything that had happened, how did she make any kind of sense of that? How did she explain the rest of it to him—hell, to herself?

Her breath caught in her chest at the thought. He had only to touch her and she was consumed with this volcanic urgency to couple with him. His penis was constantly monumentally erect. She could touch, fondle, pump, lick, suck to her heart's content.

And this was just the first twenty-four hours.

No talking, no backtracking. Just him, in the throes of that volcanic desire, turning her on her belly and fondling her bottom, arousing her again. Just him, sliding like a bandit between her legs, taking her.

Did she like it best when he just wedged himself into her body and held her, both superaware of the coming pleasure? Or was it when he opened her closet door, held her in front of the mirror, and inventoried her body as she watched him touch her? Or maybe it was the long, lingering kisses as he fondled her between her legs and pushed his powerful penis inside her.

Being alone in this relatively small space together added a layer of steaming urgency to the heat they generated. He could not contain his lust. She couldn't subdue hers.

It would have been easier if they stayed in London. Here, the question of Jillian's whereabouts hovered like a sword, became more pressing by the second. It was enough to quell their desire for oh, all of five minutes.

He'd mounted her again, taking her from the rear. She grasped the brass spindles of the headboard and held on tight as he rode her with the animal need to mark, to possess, to climax.

He collapsed on top of her, still hard inside her. She liked the all-encompassing feeling of his body covering hers. In the aftermath, it was the little things—his heaving chest against her back, the way her bottom fit just perfectly in the cradle of his hips, how deep he had been, his face buried in her neck, her hair sticky against her skin.

Don't read anything more into it.

Just take it while you can.

She snuck into the shower later that evening, needing to clean herself and check on her stash of protection.

She stared at herself in the mirror. What was her reality anymore? Naked with him, on her back or on her knees in full-bore penetration, apparently.

She exited the bathroom to the scent of fresh brewed coffee and found him lounging on the couch, looking through a folder, with the pot and two cups on the coffee table.

"What are you doing?"

"Research?" He held up the folder, in which, she remembered, were notes for her current project. It was the one she abandoned the day she phoned in to take her leave of absence.

"You're a researcher?"

"Maybe," she said briskly. "If they didn't fire me when I took an unauthorized leave of absence to pursue this folly, but it doesn't seem likely."

"Okay. I'm having a really hard time wrapping my mind around the research part. Labs and experiments and all that?"

"All that." Now she felt uncomfortable. He was the intruder, swiping her notes, digging for clues. What had he expected to find? Her little black book?

"Sit down." He motioned to the sofa opposite him. The living room was furnished with two small face-to-face sofas, a coffee table, and a multipurpose dresser by the window. She sat obediently while he poured her coffee.

For the first time in days his body was relaxed, but everything else about him was alert. If he hadn't been stark naked, it would have been just another day-after-the-night-before-breakfast scene, with a guy looking for a way to end a one-night stand.

"It's time to talk."

"Fine. You go first."

"No, you first. Jillian."

"No—I need to know what you know because I don't know anything."

He shook his head. "I don't believe you."

She shrugged. "Believe what you want."

He gave her a long, considering look. "You're good. Almost good enough . . ."

She shrugged and sipped the coffee. It was odd how the atmosphere had changed so completely just by him focusing his attention. The sex stopped for the first time in days. He was all business and still didn't believe her. Square one loomed again.

She was an anomaly, she realized. She was the thing that didn't belong, that wasn't what it seemed. She wasn't a sidebar, a distraction, or a red herring to him. She was a part of his puzzle—but he wasn't necessarily part of hers.

She waited. He waited. They were two people sitting opposite each other naked, eyeing each other, sipping coffee, a folder of research notes on the coffee table between them.

Something didn't fit.

He contemplated her with skepticism.

The hell with him.

She slanted a covert look at his penis, quiescent but interested. He had to know how irresistible it was to her.

The place where their interests crossed, she thought, was where Jilly had been with both Ellicott and Baynard two nights before he died. But Justine knew nothing about that place. All she knew was that sometime after that, Jilly had sent her the incontrovertible SOS. It sounded so fantastical. How could she tell him?

His penis stirred—he was reading her mind again. "Tell me," he said.

She had nothing to tell him. Honestly, *Justine time?* It was hardly the stuff of intrigue. But still . . .

She took a deep breath. "A little over a week ago, really late at night, I got a text message from Jill. I knew she wasn't in New York; she'd told me she had a modeling assignment in England and she'd be back the next weekend. So a text from her in the wee hours—it just never happens."

"And the text said what?"

Justine swallowed. "It was a childhood code, an SOS. So I went to her apartment because, a long time ago, we'd agreed that was what I would do. I found this hotel key in this little paper holder with a map of Manhattan folded into it."

It sounded worse and worse the simpler she tried to make it.

She'd have to tell him about Randy and her stupid decision to try on Jill's life for a day or two.

He waited patiently for her to continue.

"And then?"

She bit her lip. "The key holder mirrored her website. You know"—she knew he knew—"when I booted up, the site came up. She'd left it that way purposely; I didn't know anything about Jillian Dare."

She glanced at his disbelieving expression. "You don't believe me."

She forced herself to continue. "I went to the hotel, thinking she might have left something in the room—"

"I bet there *was* something in the room."

"There was something in the room."

"And did you make use of it?"

"He thought I was Jill." That was all she had to say. "I thought he wouldn't believe me if I said I wasn't. So it seemed like a plan to—"

"No one had a clue," he said, his voice neutral. "The sex blogs said Jill was back and doing her usual thing. How clever you were."

The sex blogs? Jesus. "I lucked out. She had no . . . appointments with regulars."

"And Leshan?"

"You tell me about Leshan," she snapped. "Obviously you know enough about him to make arrangements through him."

"And you got into Jill's life enough in the space of two days, taking everything you could get."

"Right," she said tightly. The night she'd met him flashed into her mind: the booth party, the two friends, her letting them feel and fondle her. Oh, God. "*Everything.* And you were into her life enough to *buy* her."

"I *thought* I was buying her."

"I hope they caught it on your expense account."

"It was worth every dollar, even if it wasn't Jillian I fucked."

"You fucked yourself those couple of days, so you can go to hell."

"Your story reeks of bullshit."

She bolted up from the sofa. "Thank God I just showered then."

"Sit *down*."

"I'm getting dressed. This being naked thing is over."

"This being naked thing hasn't even started. Sit *down*."

She sat resentfully.

"I have no patience for secrets."

She stared at him. "You've burrowed into and out of every part of my body. There are no secrets."

"Where's Jillian?"

"I don't know."

"That's what I don't believe. That it was you—in L.A., *and* at the Crystal Ball."

"Wait, wait." He knew about the trip with randy Randy? "How do you know about L.A.?"

"God, don't tell me you don't know about the Execs-Sex blogs."

She knew she looked appalled.

"They rate the raunch. They're exclusive members-only sites. If they're paying that kind of money, they want guarantees, reviews."

Oh, God.

He read the horror in her eyes. "Clever of you to play the masseuse card, by the way. Excellent crowd control strategy."

She felt like curling up into a fetal ball. "It worked," she said sharply.

"They rated it an over-the-top fantasy fuck. You definitely scored for Jillian. She'll have to add it to her repertoire. Or you'll have to keep it in yours."

"You don't believe anything, do you."

"Some things. Not much. Not you. But that won't interfere with the sex, if that's what you're worried about."

She shot him a scathing look.

"So you spread your legs for Jillian," he said. "After you went to the hotel? At the hotel?"

"I'm not answering that," she snapped.

"I'm trying to get a timeline. At this point, it's—what?—the next day? You've made the decision to stay at Jillian's?"

"I had no other option. She hadn't been missing long enough, I didn't know where she was, I didn't even know *if* she was missing. I didn't know what else to do."

"So you pack some things and move in and then what happened?"

"Zach happened," she said reluctantly. "He's obviously her confidant and pimp. He has a key to her apartment and he was expecting that Jillian had returned from London, so he had the vodka party and the ball lined up for her."

"And L.A.?"

"And L.A. I think Jillian had pretty much agreed to go to L.A., at least that's the impression I got. And the more I pushed to cancel, the more anxious Randy was to keep the date. He offered full freight, just for the weekend."

"I wonder how you managed that. Oh, it was the fantasy thing."

"It was a naked thing," she retorted.

"Yeah, guys like that *naked thing*."

She gritted her teeth and girded herself to tell the rest. "Zach didn't believe I wasn't Jillian. He didn't let up. I canceled one get-to-know-you date, but there was this other guy—"

"Not so hot? A hard lesson of the business—they can't all be gorgeous."

"Like you?" she interpolated, her voice dripping venom. "And then, as it happened, Zach had booked Jilly for the vodka party—and you."

"Me, tracking Ellicott. He monitors Execs-Sex regularly, and he took off for New York like a rocket right after Oliver Baynard's death. It won't so difficult to discover there were reviews about Jillian's L.A. trip and that she was scheduled to appear at the vodka party. And the Crystal Ball. You didn't imagine you saw him. But why the hell did you take off to London? How did you even know about Ellicott?"

"I knew Jillian had gone to London. Zach mentioned there'd been an accident the day Jillian was scheduled to return to the States. He wondered if she was held up because of it. But I didn't have time to play detective and connect the dots.

"I planned to get away at the ball. And then Brisco offered the Monte Carlo trip, and Zach insisted on packing for me, and, well, he was going to find her passport missing, her credit cards, and her suitcases. He'd instantly remember our conversations and the disparities there. I'm pretty sure he goes way back with Jillian, if you didn't know."

"I didn't." He thought for a moment. "I think Jillian knows something about how Baynard died."

"It was an odd accident."

"A deliberate accident. Too deliberate. But there's no way to prove it. I think Jillian might know what happened. But *we* know the unintended consequence. Her gorgeous, sonically orgasmic twin slipped into her skin and became a successful courtesan."

"You've always been a first-rate bastard."

"With no patience, don't forget that."

"You've tried my patience to the limit." She stood up determinedly. "I'm getting dressed, I'm going out, and I hope to hell you're out of here when I return."

"Well, no—no, you're not. You haven't gotten the larger picture. Because you turned up in her place, nobody knows Jillian's missing. They really think you're Jillian. You fill her Manolos admirably. And because of that, and because Jillian knows how Ellicott got his rival for a billion-dollar contract out of the way, he's still in Manhattan, and my guess is, he's hunting for her—that is, for you."

Chapter Ten

His assessment stopped her dead in her tracks. That, coupled with her little threatening phone call to him in London. But Rawls didn't have to know about that. The fact was, Jillian *was* the connection.

Jillian who in her note confessed she knew other kinds of secrets about the men she serviced, things that might conceivably put her in danger. Baynard *had* been a huge international public figure. He and Ellicott *had* been competing for that astronomical government contract. They'd been at the presentation point, and then Baynard died, Ellicott getting the contract.

And in the middle of it all was Jilly. Justine now knew Baynard had been with her two nights before. And Rawls knew why. Maybe it was a secret get-together, let's-join-forces kind of evening, with Jillian as the reward?

Justine cringed at the thought. But it wasn't much different from what she had done in L.A. Randy had hired her specifically to seduce and sex up his business associates so he could get what he wanted.

Only Ellicott hadn't gotten what he wanted; Baynard hadn't signed onto Ellicott's plan. So Baynard had been removed.

And Rawls was Baynard's surrogate. She noted that Rawls had not yet specified exactly what he did for Baynard. Private detective? Executive assistant? No. He was too powerful for that, and when she added to the mix his *no patience* edict, she could conclude that Doug Rawls waited for no one. Doug Rawls was ruthless, a man who got answers—no matter what he had to do.

Who was Doug Rawls?

He was Baynard's avenger. He wanted Jillian because she was with Baynard two nights before and might know something about Baynard's death.

Rawls didn't want to believe that someone just randomly ran Baynard off the road.

He didn't want *her*; he'd throw her to the wolves in a second if he thought she were lying or had betrayed him. He wanted answers.

It made him as dangerous as any of Jillian's enemies.

How had she wound up in her own apartment naked with him, ripe to have sex at the twitch of his penis?

This was not a good scientific method. Every choice she'd made had been impulsive, emotional, and ill-considered. It was best not to examine it all too closely. Better to concentrate on what he was telling her—that Ellicott was dangerous and he had dangerous friends.

If Jillian appeared anywhere, Ellicott would know. And he would find her.

But Ellicott didn't know about Justine—yet.

And that was the only reason she had her own in-house, vested-interest, bodyguard.

Justine slanted a look at him. He stared right back with that erotic intensity that had nothing to do with what he'd said or what she might be thinking. He was thinking something entirely different—something hot, raw, intimate.

The air felt charged suddenly, moist with potential, thick with the portent of pleasure.

Clothes didn't put a lid on it. Saying no wouldn't constrain it. Walking out the door just wasted time that could be put to better use.

"Did you save Jillian's message?" Rawls asked, sucking the steamy hot air out of the balloon.

"I saved it."

He waited. She didn't speak.

"And?" he said. *I'm waiting*, he didn't say.

There were good reasons to give it to him as well as bad ones.

She pulled up the saved messages in her cell and handed it to him.

"What does it mean?"

This was the bad part—revealing their past and the agony of their childhood. Less was more. Just give him the facts.

"It's a play on my name—it's supposed to read *justine time*, or *just in time*. It means she's in trouble. It started when we, and our newborn baby sister, were taken from our parents by social services, we were separated, and put into foster care." She turned her gaze away from his, away from the fleeting look of empathy she thought she saw there.

"Jilly wanted a way to covertly signal when things got really bad and she needed me. It just means the situation is critical and I have to come."

She heard the *beep* of Rawls punching numbers into her phone. "It's me. Backtrack on this number, every call, every text. Thanks."

He handed the phone back to her. "So this came in the early hours of the morning. And then what did you do?"

"I told you, I went to her apartment."

"Expecting to find what?"

She teetered—she hadn't told him about Jillian's letter. She didn't want to tell him anything more, but he would look at every angle, with her help or without it.

More secrets. More lies.

"She said whenever she left on a trip, she always left a note for me."

"What kind of note? Like funeral instructions?"

God, now how could she phrase this? He wouldn't believe for a moment that she hadn't known Jillian was a highly paid traveling companion.

"No, like a confession."

She let him figure it out. It took thirty seconds.

"That's rich. You really didn't know? No. I wouldn't believe you even if you had proof. God, that's good. And then you went off to the hotel to meet one of Jillian's johns? You should have run for your life *if* there was a *confession*."

She felt like running now. But let him believe what he wanted. At least she didn't have to go into Jilly's vault and reveal anything else. Jilly's letter was the least of it.

"Where is Jillian's computer?"

"At her apartment. Locked up. I didn't go back there after the Crystal Ball."

He rubbed his forehead. "Tell me again how you got onto Ellicott."

He didn't have to know about Jillian's meticulous client notes either.

"Zach. He let himself into the apartment that night expecting she'd returned. He wondered whether the accident had delayed her trip at all. He mentioned Ellicott's name. And I already knew she'd gone to London."

"Why did you think?" he asked curiously.

"Modeling assignment. Hands, feet. Body parts."

"You believed that?"

"We had a really shitty childhood, okay? Her life goal was to amass enough money so that she could feel safe."

"What about you?"

"Different foster parents, same shitty childhood. I channeled it into the certainty of the rational, provable, and explainable."

"I'd love to hear the conversation in your head about this last week."

"I just ignore it," she said cavalierly.

"But you don't."

Bam. "Neither do you," she retorted.

"You could say I'm up-front about it."

"And I'm barely dealing with it. Can we please get back to Jillian?"

"Yesss." He drew out the "s" in a hiss. "Jillian. What wouldn't Ellicott do if he found out Jillian knew anything about Baynard's death? She was in London with them both. She sends a distress signal to her twin. She's not heard from again. What did she expect you to do, not knowing any of this, because presumably she didn't expect you to *become* her."

Whatever you have to do—Jilly had given her permission to do whatever she needed to do, even take on her persona. But that was none of his business.

"She expected me to figure it out and then do whatever I could to get her out of the situation. Unfortunately, I screwed up."

"You *got* screwed, you mean. Don't pretend to be shocked that you loved every minute of it. You discovered you're more like Jillian than you knew, and you've been hiding behind a pristine white lab coat for years. Maybe you always wanted to *be* Jillian, because I don't believe for two minutes you didn't know how she earned her money."

"I didn't know," she said stonily. But of course it sounded impossible.

"What do you think Jillian knows anyway?" she asked.

"Maybe nothing. But I can't take that chance, now that I know about you. I need to get into Jillian's computer files."

"No, you don't."

His expression turned hard. "You're not going to deny me that. You haven't denied me anything."

"That's not sex. That's"—she didn't want to say the obvious—"forced entry."

His gaze sharpened at her tone, what she'd said. "You've been in her files."

Don't answer. Stay cool. Although not responding was already an answer.

She wished she'd thought to put Jilly's laptop in her safe deposit box. She was not cut out for this subterfuge. Or sex games. Or verbal duels with him.

She was a valuable commodity now. Jilly's computer. Jilly's men, money, notes.

She'd better not say another word. Because she was certain as sin he could easily crack Jilly's computer, and once he got hold of it, he wouldn't need her for anything more. She'd go from being indispensable to disposable.

Maybe the thing was over, anyway. They'd trace Jilly's phone, he'd know exactly where she'd been that evening, where to find her, and that would end her questions and his. Maybe he wouldn't even need the computer.

Her heart stopped at her next thought: Zach. Maybe he had confiscated the computer. What if Zach had the same kind of resources—the kind that could hack a computer or drill into a small safe, the kind that could act on the information in Jillian's files?

She knew nothing about Zach really. She had assumed he was the Zach from Jilly's past. She trusted him. He handled her dates. He got a cut of the money. He got off on her sexual adventures. He wouldn't betray her—or would he?

She let out a long breath. Every answer raised a new question.

Her eyes narrowed as Rawls leaned back casually against the arm of the couch. His eyes sparked with curiosity, his penis quivered with interest.

Why now, when she was least likely to feel in the mood?

She'd almost forgotten: this arrangement between them was about sex, whenever, wherever. Moods were not taken into account.

"Your choice," he murmured.

The problem was, she'd choose to make use of his fully loaded penis.

"I have no choices," she retorted.

"You have two choices," he contradicted, fully aware of the shift of her attention. "*Yes* or *no?*"

"You already have everything you want; the *be naked* part can just be over."

"I don't, and it isn't. But I won't argue with you." He levered himself up, took the coffeepot and cups to the kitchen, and then sauntered back behind her bedroom screen.

Damn. She could not let the thrill of sex with him dictate her choices. For one thing, it would mean reneging on her stance. And for another, he'd given in too quickly—she was no femme fatale.

He was up to something.

Think about Jilly. She looked at her flashing voice-mail light and decided not to do anything about that. She eyed her own computer. No, she didn't want to know what might be in her e-mail either.

The only other choice was to go back to bed. Right? And then he'd just use sex to coerce the password to Jill's files out of her.

It sounded like a plan he'd concoct.

She ought to have a plan, too, but she couldn't stay ahead of him. He was the poster boy for Eve's downfall. He was an amalgam of every man she'd ever met, wanted, rejected, or slept with—and especially of the men who had walked away from her.

But that had nothing to do with Jillian. Surely her only option didn't boil down to *being naked* with the mystery man with a magic penis.

Sex was a magnet, its irresistible pull drawing her into a web of desire and lies, furthering his quest to retrieve Jillian's computer. He wouldn't let go of that bone. Only he didn't know where Jilly lived, so maybe she was safe—for the moment.

Shit, scratch that. When that cell trace came back, he'd have Jillian's address, too.

She had to do something to protect Jilly.

Justine's bag was on her desk. Worst-case scenario, she could grab a coat and boots and get out of here faster than he could dress and follow her.

She looked around frantically. Her jeans, jacket, and sneakers were in a pile on the floor near the door. She didn't think twice as she grabbed her bag, swooped up her clothes, pulled out a coat, and—naked—slipped into the hallway, closing the door silently behind her.

She shimmied into her jeans and jacket in the cab. Rawls had surely discovered she'd gone by now. Maybe he could get himself together fast enough to follow her, but she saw no sign of him as she hailed a cab. She even kept her eyes on the rearview mirror as it barreled across town to Park Avenue.

She had all the keys—Jilly's apartment, the safe. She had her own passport, too, her wallet, and her cell. She could go to a hotel, she could get a flight somewhere. She could . . . couldn't do much without Rawls tracking her.

But she had to protect Jilly at all costs, against him, against Zach, against Ellicott. Did Jillian even know that everyone in her life was a potential enemy?

It was 3:00 A.M. She was dead tired, too, but she couldn't sleep until she and the computer were somewhere safe, out of everyone's reach.

Zach had to have searched the apartment by now. If he was Jillian's confidant, he might even know about the safe.

There was an unearthly stillness in the air as the cab drew up in front of Jillian's apartment building. She thrust a twenty-dollar bill at the driver and hopped out of the car.

Her hand shook as she waved at the doorman and made a beeline for the elevator, feeling as if the very shadows were following her.

Suddenly, her whole body froze as she was about to unlock the apartment door. What if Zach was there? What if Zach had moved in, much as she had done, to wait for Jillian, to search her things, to root out her secrets?

Oh, God. She girded herself to open the door slowly, the girl detective alert to every danger. The hallway was dark. The living room glowed with Jill's dim, ever-present night-light.

Zach could be asleep in one of the bedrooms.

Why didn't she have a flashlight on her? Rawls would have had a flashlight. He probably had a lock pick, too. He was prepared for everything.

There was nothing like a heavy darkness and a fraught imagination to make anyone feel utterly inept.

She should have changed the damned locks, Justine thought as she moved cautiously into the living room and down the hallway to the guest bedroom. She left the door ajar, slipped into the room, and flipped on the light, her heart pounding like a drum.

The room was empty.

Onto Jillian's room, swallowing hard, her hands ice cold. She held her breath and flipped the light. No one. Nothing.

The closet now, the panel and the safe. She pulled the handle, but it didn't move. Which didn't mean someone hadn't found it, tried to open it, hired a locksmith to blast it open, or that when *she* opened it that she wouldn't find it empty.

Stop it! She heard something.

She moved quickly away from the closet. A hand grabbed her arm. The shock nearly gave her a heart attack.

A voice growled, "Did you really think I wouldn't find you?"

She froze. Rawls. Her relief was instantly superseded by a wash of fear. He had a flashlight out and a bag slung over his shoulder.

"Guess not," she muttered.

"Where's the computer?"

"Find it yourself," she retorted.

"We don't have time to do another kabuki dance tonight. You don't know this place isn't being watched."

"No one knows where Jillian lives."

"What about Zach, the loose cannon? What wouldn't he tell and sell for the right price?"

Right—like his cut of the money Rawls had paid for her that booth party night.

It was always about the money. She didn't think she could take any more pressure, not even Rawls's hand on her arm. But the safe was Jillian's secret, and one she wouldn't give up easily. "You go in the kitchen."

He grunted.

"It's the only way."

"Don't climb out the window." He turned away and then stopped her, with a hard hand on her arm again as he flicked off the flashlight. "Damn it." He unceremoniously shoved her back into the closet and pressed his body against hers.

"Someone's at the door."

She made a move, writhing against his already blooming erection, to get to the door.

Instantly he immobilized her with his hands, his body, and with his mouth hard on hers. He pushed her back, off-balance, and into a domineering kiss that turned deep, rich, and arousing.

She couldn't, she wouldn't. She'd heard the sound, too, because he'd left the sliding door open just a crack, and she stopped struggling and she leaned into the kiss.

The noises were soft and unobtrusive. Like someone who knew his way around the apartment. It sounded like he was in the kitchen, going through the mostly empty cabinets. Then the noise moved to the living room, like furniture being shifted.

Footsteps came closer now, and Rawls eased his mouth off of hers, whispering, "Don't move" as the intruder slipped into the guest room directly opposite the closet.

"Shhh," he breathed in her ear as he relinquished her arms, eased the door open another inch, and edged out of the closet. He crossed the narrow hallway and flattened himself against the facing bedroom wall.

Then, as she watched through a crack in the door, he entered the guest room, and she heard the sound of a body hitting the floor with an awful thump. He appeared in the doorway.

"Get the effing computer. We have to get out of here *now*."

She couldn't keep secrets anymore, not with someone lying unconscious on the floor. She yanked the lever of the panel hard this time, and it slid open. She motioned for him to shine the flashlight into her bag, and she fished out the key, inserted it, and the safe swung open. She sighed with relief: the computer and the cell phones were still there.

"Good Christ," he muttered, scooping the phones into his bag while she grabbed the computer, locked the safe, and moved the panel back into place.

He flicked off the light and motioned her out of the apartment.

"Go, go, go. Down the stairs." He gestured to the end of the hallway. Ten flights down at nearly 4:00 A.M. God—a freaking nightmare.

She didn't have many more ways to evade him. But she had the computer. There was always a chance. It wasn't like that kiss changed anything.

She followed him down, hanging on to the banister, the thin beam of his flashlight showing there was nowhere to run.

Justine looked around covertly as they emerged from the building.

Rawls grasped her arm and directed her toward a black car parked down the block. "When are you going to realize you can't run?" He opened the door for her. "Get in."

James was in the driver's seat.

She felt too dazed not to just obey.

"I leave James to take care of things like bags and hotel bills, and then he follows later," Rawls drawled. "Luckily, he was available tonight."

"Lucky," Justine murmured. *Let this night be over.* She had a feeling it was only starting. "Now what?"

"We hide."

"Again?"

"It's fascinating that you haven't asked who the intruder was. That was Zach on the floor of the guest room."

"Oh." He meant Zach whom he'd *knocked out*, on the floor of the guest room. But Zach had had more than enough time to thoroughly search Jillian's apartment already, including all the times Jilly was away on extended trips.

Maybe someone had given him an incentive. A big monetary incentive.

And he hadn't yet found what he was looking for.

Nothing made sense. Including her going into hiding. Especially with Rawls.

He hadn't found what he was looking for either.

And he'd plainly said he wanted the computer. He'd known she'd jump at the bait and lead him to it.

"Where are we going?" she asked, feeling very weary all of a sudden.

"Not back to your apartment."

She didn't ask why. "What did you do to Zach?"

"That's not need-to-know information."

"You disabled him."

"That's a nice way to put it. I'd prefer to think of it as payback." He leaned forward and tapped James on the shoulder. James nodded, and turned west at the next light, and then uptown. *Way* uptown. They were near Columbia University in the West 100s before the car stopped at a nondescript, midblock brownstone.

"Home away from home," Rawls murmured. "Let's go."

James opened the door for her. It was the same scenario all over again. Rawls might be having mind-blowing sex with her, but he didn't trust her as much as she didn't trust him.

Rawls guided her up the stoop and into the hallway. There was a door to her left, a wall partitioning the lower duplex from the hallway and the door leading upstairs. He unlocked that door and motioned her up the stairs.

He waved her into what had been at one time one of two bedrooms, renovated into the kitchen and dining area for the upper duplex, replete with all the treasured details: walnut trim, a mirrored fireplace, original painted tile, gleaming parquet floors, wedding cake molding, and windows overlooking a garden.

She gave up then. She couldn't get a step ahead of him. Not an inch. She was almost tired of trying.

"This is the *be naked* part," he whispered as he led her into the living room.

She sank into the sofa, feeling unnerved and exhausted, and tried not to think about Zach, lying sprawled on the guest room floor.

"Are you Baynard's hit man?" she asked.

"That just killed my hard-on. Give me Jillian's computer."

She knew any fight would be futile, so she reluctantly pulled it from her bag. "I'm not giving you the password."

"I'll just hack it."

She believed him, but instead angled the screen so he couldn't see her fingers as she booted up Jillian's web page.

Even after all this time, and all she'd done in Jillian's name, she still couldn't believe this was Jillian's life. And worse, the naked, satin-wrapped Jillian looked so much like Justine, in her newborn sensual knowledge of herself, that it scared the hell out of her all over again.

She brought the computer over to a small table by the fireplace, where he sat. "You're not reading anything without my watching you."

"You should be taking off your clothes. We're having sex tonight."

"That game is over," she said stiffly.

"That game is just getting interesting. Where's her letter to you?"

"You don't get to read that."

"Don't fight me. Just bring up the letter."

"Why? You said you wouldn't believe it anyway."

"I changed my mind."

Resignedly, she opened the file.

He scanned the page and a half of text, his brow raising as he read and reread the note. "Something she knows. All that trust and discretion. It's positively heartwarming. It's always the whores that betray the trust. Why aren't you naked yet?"

"I'm not getting naked. Are you done?"

"No. I want to see what she has on Ellicott."

Justine prickled up. "I don't think so."

"Let me rephrase that—I *need* to see what she has on Ellicott."

"You mean you want to see what she has on *you*."

"You think? I think *you* want to see what's in that file about me."

So there *was* something to see. *Damn.*

"You know everything you need to know about me," he added brusquely. "As I do about you. Now bring up the goddamned Ellicott file."

"There's nothing in that file relevant to Ellicott's business. It's all personal."

"Even better," Rawls said. "Bring it up. You don't know what's important. And you know how impatient I get."

She wondered how far she could push that. But she hesitated because he'd also see other details—like the money that had been removed—and the descriptions of Ellicott's sexual idiosyncrasies.

It wasn't fair to Jilly, it just wasn't.

"She'll be compromised anyway by the time this is over," Rawls said. "She may not be able to go back."

"You can't know that." Why was she defending Jill's choices? She ought to be rejoicing. Jill would be out of that life, it would be over.

"I know."

"You know too freaking much," Justine muttered irritably. She turned the computer away from him, tapped in the password, and gave up Ellicott's file.

She read it with him for about a page and then wandered to the bow window to watch the dawn inching up over the city.

She felt so tired. Too tired. And not any closer to figuring out what had happened to Jillian or what to do about it.

Or if her lover was her enemy.

Just opening that file, she'd opened the Pandora's box of Jillian's sex life and the secret lives of her clients.

What did any of it really matter, though? As of this moment, she had no sister, she had no life. She probably didn't have a job. She had Rawls and an insatiable attraction that was quelled by his intense focus on Jillian's sex life and by Justine's own betrayal of her sister.

"Whatever you have to do."

Jilly, I had no choice, no choice at all.

After a while, Justine took the chair opposite Rawls and watched as he scrolled through the files on Jillian's clients. He wrote nothing down and made no comments.

She was edgy with curiosity. She bolted up from the chair and went into the kitchen to poke around. She had to do something.

Everything was antique, she noted, Mission-era and earlier. It was curiously low-tech and plain-Jane for someone so sophisticated on every other level.

"You can make some coffee," he called to her. "And get undressed."

"Coffee and no sex sounds fine to me."

His refrigerator was better stocked than Jillian's. Doug Rawls had a very healthy appetite in more ways than one, it seemed. The coffee was in a plastic container, readily visible. The coffeemaker was on the counter next to the filters.

It felt wrong to be in his space, acting domestic while he invaded her sister's privacy.

She sensed his presence behind her and turned to find him almost face-to-face with her. "So, did you finish pillaging Jilly's files?"

"Finished with the files. Not finished with you."

"And what did all that scouring prove?"

"Jillian is an excellent businesswoman. Her clients are creeps. I keep thinking about that kiss."

Justine turned away as the coffeemaker beeped.

"You didn't answer my question. Wait—which kiss?"

"The closet kiss."

"The one when we were hiding from the intruder you subsequently rendered unconscious?"

"Zach, the potentially dangerous intruder."

"Yeah. Coffee? And answer the question."

"I don't want coffee. I want you naked."

Justine poured her own coffee, determined to hold her ground, and walked back to the living room. "You know all about Jillian now. What did it prove?"

He moved closer to her. "It proved that she probably knows a lot of secrets. Only this time, something she knew got her in major trouble."

"None of that is news. And you surely noticed the son of a bitch took a nice refund on her services, probably thinking no one would ever know. He knew she wasn't coming back."

"Right, so you can't be wandering around like Alice in Wonderland in her stilettos because he won't rest until he finds you."

"While Jillian could be"—she swallowed—"a hostage, or injured, or dying, or dead."

"Or undercover somewhere because she knows Ellicott is hunting her. There was no way, there *is* no way, you alone can find her right now unless she contacts you."

"So we're both hiding from Ellicott? That doesn't make sense. You don't make sense. Who *are* you? Look at this place—this isn't the apartment of an A-level executive."

"I'm the guy who wants to be naked with you."

"I'm not feeling the love, frankly."

"Do the *naked* part. That's easy for you."

"I'm not doing naked. I'm going to keep searching for my sister."

"No, you are doing naked because there's nothing else you can do right now. It's too dangerous for you to be out there. You can be in my apartment and I can be in you. Which sounds like a better plan for the moment."

"You're telling me I can't walk out the door right now?"

"I'm telling you that you can take off your clothes and walk upstairs to the bedroom right now."

He meant it. But so did she—or at least she thought she did. But she saw his point. There was no getting around the fact that she'd been too successful being Jillian.

She held his sharp, steady gaze. That was always a big mistake. There was something about the way he looked at her—she read it in his eyes: Sex. Now. With. You.

She couldn't stop it, nor was she immune to her insidious desire to be naked with him.

Intellectually, she fought it. Physically, her body liquefied with lust. Her skin sensitized to every fiber of the irritating clothes she wore. She wanted to get naked for him. The was the crux of it. When they were together, she always wanted to be naked with him.

No words were needed. He started unbuttoning his shirt as she shrugged out of her jacket and jeans. He pushed her onto the sofa, canting her body toward him, and positioning her legs so that her knees were bent, her legs wide, her labia fully visible for penetration.

He stroked her there, kissed and sucked, and then, spreading her wide apart, he slowly nudged his penis head into her.

He held himself in control, holding her eyes, not letting her enter her own world but keeping her with him, in his world with just the rigid tip of his penis inside her.

Her body demanded more from him, but he kept his arms braced against the sofa, his penis just enfolded in her labia, connecting them, joining them without full penetration.

She went breathless with anticipation. And still he held back, saying not a word, letting what he did with his penis speak for him. He didn't move. He held himself with superhuman control just within her cunt lips, at an angle where they both could see their coupling. But she was so mesmerized by the feeling of her body enclosing his lush tip, by his eyes locked on hers, that she saw and felt nothing else.

He didn't move. He didn't thrust. He didn't speak. He just held himself there.

She nearly screamed with frustration. He felt it, too, she knew it, and it was deliberate. It was hot, raw, and something more—something that ought not to have been there but was.

She grasped his arms, urging him to complete her.

Everything fell away; her whole world centered on the feeling of him between her legs.

His arms bulged as he maintained control, his body straining not to thrust them both to orgasm. He never tore his eyes from hers. A different kind of tension started to build between them, as if his control of his body could not match his determination.

One move, she thought. Just one seductive undulation, and he could be hers, deep inside her, driving her toward that indescribable climax shimmering just beyond her reach.

She lifted her hips, mutely begging. *Come to me, come.* She swiveled her hips and tilted her body downward to force his penetration.

But he held on for dear life. Minute by minute, he was closer to breaking; she could see it in his face.

So close—push him, *make* him, *now*.

She braced her feet against his shoulders and lifted her body just as he caved and drove into her with a torturous fury. Her orgasm broke like thunder, crackling between her legs. The piercing hot pleasure was unquantifiable, and her body imploded on the hard ridge of his penis.

Her body shook and her tears flowed as he pushed her still harder, over and above, and into a final and simultaneous orgasm.

She needed nothing else—ever. Nothing.

Chapter Eleven

Being naked did not give her clarity; it fogged her mind and focused all her attention on her libido. Everything else felt vaguely irrelevant after the pleasure sapped her energy for anything but more sex.

Or maybe it was him. Or the combination of them.

She woke up suddenly to find that she was in his bed and in his arms without any awareness of how she got there.

She had a complete, overwhelming urge for more sex. His hands were on her body, gently stroking, imprinting himself on her, and his penis was fully erect, pressing against her bottom. He was wide awake, too.

She stretched her body, shimmying against him. His hands moved on her skin, all over her, between her legs.

She kept torturously still. She wanted him, but she wanted not to want him. The anticipation was as much an aphrodisiac as a kiss. As a climax. But she didn't think she could bear another one that powerful—she could still feel the tears on her cheeks.

And she didn't know what she was doing, but she wanted him with an all-consuming ferocity.

She slowly moved against his erection and the heat of his naked body, like the nights at the hotel after the booth party. In the end, it had been all about Jillian and the money.

In bed with him now was something different.

There was no question he wanted to fuck her, too, whatever his reasons, his feelings, and his motives. He felt her edgy need in the suppressed movement of her body and he followed with his hand, stroking her thigh, sliding his hand across her belly, up to her breast, taking her nipple, and rubbing it between his fingers.

The jolt of her body told him everything he needed to know. He played with her nipple and felt her squirm, heard her moan as he compressed the one nipple between his fingers again and again until her whole body spasmed with hot, streaming pleasure.

His hands were all over her now as she lolled against his hard body and let him feel her everywhere.

Let me—she whispered it, she thought it. She wanted his penis, to grasp it, hold it, bite it, own it the way he owned her nipples. But he wouldn't give her leeway to turn. He held her in thrall to the pleasure of her nipples and wouldn't let her go. She rubbed her bottom against the heft of his penis. *Make him come, make him give me all his luscious cream.*

And then, suddenly, he rolled her on her back. He covered her, mounted her, and drove his penis deep, holding her deliciously immobile.

They lay still, like before, without words, without movement, just bone-deep quiet in the dark. It heightened her every awareness—his naked body, his strength, his power, his dominance, and the primitive mystery of their connection.

Shhhh. She didn't know if he made the sound or if it was in her mind, but she heard it clearly. Words were not necessary. He wanted her to feel the length and breadth of him, to feel the part of him that was wholly hers.

He moved, she convulsed, and she was gone, racked again by the pounding orgasm that he banged into her.

Unspeakable. They fell asleep, with her still holding him at a place where words were superfluous and everything had already been said.

Waking up with him there was vastly different than it had been at the hotel. This was a different kind of bubble. Sex was on the menu first thing in the morning: coffee and her cream-coated nipples, her semen-soaked body, her swollen lips. After she gave him a heartfelt blow job, she retreated to the shower, and then joined him in the living room to sprawl on the couch.

But there was no rest in an atmosphere of nudity. Every movement had the potential for arousal. And in daylight, not a nuance could be hidden.

The way he looked at her was hot enough to fuel a fire. He was insatiable. He was powerful and an expert at what he did, how he did it, and how he made her feel—by a look, a touch, a word.

They finally drank the coffee Rawls had made two hours before, and he moved his chair away from the kitchen table to reveal his stiff penis.

"Sit," he ordered. "Because I'll fuck you on the table if you don't mount my penis right now."

His command was her desire. Mounting him was tricky—she had to climb onto his thighs and shift herself upward as she spread her legs because he was so long and thick. He watched avidly as she maneuvered her cleft directly over his shaft, parted her labia to guide him into her body, and then sat, hard, absorbing his whole shaft in her cunt.

"Just like that," he murmured, running his hands over her thighs. "Just like that."

She sat just a little higher than his head so that his mouth was level with her quivering breasts. He licked a nipple and she shuddered, bracing her hands against his shoulders.

"Look at me."

She met his gaze.

"Don't move." It was barely a breath of a sentence. "Just feel me in you."

"I feel you."

"Shhhh—just look at me."

His face was mesmerizing. The texture, the lines, the incredible blue of his eyes—he was arresting.

Don't look away.

Her body reacted apart from her will, undulating in little increments—she couldn't help it. His penis was made for her.

She flexed her body around his heft.

"Don't move."

He reached up and pulled her into a kiss. Long, passionate, devouring kisses. His hands moved then, down her back to cup her bottom. Feeling her crease, he penetrated anally as he ground himself more tightly between her legs.

She rode him hard, with bruising kisses as his expert fingers found the exact place for a moment of culmination that felt like gold melting through her core and pooling over his penis as he exploded inside her.

He kept her planted firmly on his lap afterward. He was still hard, still aroused, and holding her gaze. How could there be words for that? Feelings—there were feelings, and the reverberation of her orgasm, hot and glowing, inside her body. Words couldn't begin to explain what she was feeling, even as he eased her off of his shaft and easily carried her into the living room.

He felt something, too. He might be her adversary, but he was her lover, and that touched him somewhere deep within as well.

Or was she weaving a fairy tale from motes and moonbeams? Women did that—women hoped, women waited.

Already that hot look glowed in his eyes again as he looked at her lying on the couch.

If she sat up, she'd be right at mouth level with his penis. She could just reach out, handle it, pump it, and swallow his lust.

She arched her body and cupped her breasts to give him access to her nipples. No words. His kiss was hot with arousal as his fingers surrounded each nipple, pulling gently, meaningfully, as she maneuvered herself closer to him.

His penis invited her to enfold it in her grasp, to feel it and stroke it, to arouse it beyond orgasm.

She wanted to be the only one for his penis. His fingers, so expertly manipulating her nipples, drove her to a fever pitch of mindless urgency as she held on tightly to his penis.

He touched her nowhere else, he made no move to penetrate her. It was all in his kisses and his squeezing her nipples, and her body softened, moistened, ready for that ineffable moment of coupling.

But he prolonged it, exerting a small amount of pressure on her nipples, never breaking the kiss. She wanted to pull him in, but she didn't want to relinquish his penis. He was feeling the tension, too. She rolled that little involuntary gush of semen on the tip of his penis, around the head, onto her fingers. She wanted to rub it into her nipples, to wring every drop of it out of him.

Just when she thought she could take no more, he lifted his mouth a breath away from hers and murmured, "I want to hire you."

She dropped in a dizzying slide to pure confusion. "What?"

"Hire you. As my sex companion. Don't even pretend to protest. You want it all the time just like I do. Take the perks. Be naked all the time. I'll give you what you want. Same terms as Jillian."

She couldn't believe what he'd just said. She pulled away from him abruptly. She needed to be a hundred miles away from the magnetic pull of his sex.

"Are you crazy?" she asked indignantly.

"Am I?"

"I'm not—"

"You most definitely are."

She stalked away from him, her hands outstretched as if she were pushing him away. "I'm *not* Jill."

"But you are."

Stop him from saying those things. Stop him.

"For someone like me," he said, keeping his voice low, "time doesn't stop. I have things to do, places to go. When I want to fuck, I want someone who's ready for prime time. I don't want cheap pickups. I don't want bar bitches. I want a cunt I can't get enough of, because I get damned bored damned easily. And I'm willing to pay for what I want. Just like you were willing to *be* paid for what you wanted."

"That was—"

"That was you, uninhibited, in animal lust and loving every minute of it."

"Not me. I was pretending to be—" *Sex and lies.*

"Bullshit. And what about the past two days? What about five minutes ago? What about those hot, stiff nipples that couldn't get enough? What about that wet spot between your legs?"

"That's not me."

"What about—"

"Stop!" It was crazy. She was reacting to his words, to the image of them coupling. Why not? she wondered.

All I have to do is look at you and you go into heat."

"I don't want to hear a litany of—"

"Sure you do. Even now, you're all creamy for me."

"I am not. I'm dry as a bone."

"Want to test that?"

He started walking toward her, his penis jutting out so temptingly she could barely stand it. She knew how he intended to make his point, by thrusting his fingers between her legs into the ripe, moist heat already flowing with a forbidden excitement.

No—I'm not her.

But that didn't seem to matter to him, to his penis, or even to her body shuddering with lust. She had no plan B for this. She never expected his proposition.

He came closer, backing her up against the door. "What about how you didn't have one reservation about getting naked with me? Not one maidenly protest." His penis nudged her belly, and he grasped his penis and aimed it lower.

"What about"—he pushed her legs apart and positioned himself to thrust, hard and high—"I just fuck you right here and then you say yes." He shifted his hips and drove into her heat. "Because you never deny my penis, you never deny me any part of your body." He pushed deeper still, reaching for something only he could feel. "You never deny me anything."

He pinned her against the door, and she didn't care. He'd jammed himself so deep inside her, she could barely breathe.

He pushed her even tighter against the door, lifting her legs to wrap around his hips, so he supported her solely by the hardness of his penis.

Endless days and nights like this, she thought as he pounded into her core. *With him, like this. Why not?*

The thought sent her right to the breaking point—just one more thrust. She rode it hard and high, and her orgasm broke over his last barreling, ejaculating thrust.

"Yes or no?" he demanded, not a second after his wrenching release.

She felt barely coherent, but it struck her that if she said no, he would find someone to say yes, and the thought of him with someone else suddenly felt crippling. Every other thought, need, hope melted like snow.

"Yes," she whispered.

"Yes, what?" he demanded.

She girded herself as she lowered her legs slowly. She was still connected to him, the rock-hard reminder of just what she was saying yes to.

"Yes, I'll be yours. Yes, I want it all the"—she gasped as he eased himself from her, still erect and coated with her nectar—"time. Yes, I'll be your companion."

She wanted to eat him right then, right there. She looked up to meet the knowing look in his eyes. "Yes, you were right. I want it again."

He gave her a dark, sexy look. "Take it."

She grasped his penis. "Is there any cream left?"

"I'll let you find out."

She licked her lips and then surrounded his penis head with her mouth. She sucked on it, slowly, feeling his hands on her shoulders pushing her to pull him in deeper, feeling his urgency. She inched him into her mouth and began working the underside of his shaft with her tongue.

And then, she went wild, kissing, sucking, nipping, biting, swirling. With one long, hard pull, her teeth were poised around his tip to squeeze and nip, and he poured himself into her mouth. She took it, letting it seep from her tongue to the corners of her mouth and down to her chest, her breasts, her teeth still ready to squeeze every last drop of cream from him as he bucked and spewed. His knees buckled as she pulled and sucked the tip.

She had him on his knees, bracing on her shoulders, watching as she rubbed his semen into her breasts and her nipples. His eyes were hooded, his expression inscrutable, his inexhaustible penis still stiff.

It was amazing that she had so much power over him, because his sex had too much power over her. And even now she could see the light kindling again in his eyes and feel that little knot of desire unfurling again between her legs.

She was hardly a *companion*, with this ongoing ache always coiling deep in her core. More like a sex slave.

For however long it lasted, for however much he valued it, for whatever time it took for her to let it go, she'd do it.

"You want more." It was barely a whisper.

She knew the hot look she sent him said it all, but she said it aloud. "I always want you right between my legs." His mouth settled on hers in a rough, possessive kiss.

This . . . I want this . . . I want him.

He's looking for Jilly, too.

This is how I'll find her.

He kissed her all the way up to the bedroom, and for hours as they lay entwined, his penis rooted inside her. He didn't need to move; she didn't need the drive and the thrust when his tongue kept her aroused and occupied. And when he didn't kiss her, he gave her little sex-bites all over her neck and arms.

"A thousand a day, plus the usual perks, gifts, and bonuses," he murmured against her ear as he nibbled at the lobe.

She nodded, and he licked her lips and delved back into her mouth.

"Nor can you be naked with any other man," he added against her lips. "*Ever* while you're with me."

She felt a rare give of relief. Somewhere inside her she'd been a little afraid he'd use her the way she'd been used in L.A.

"Why would I *ever* even look at another man?" she whispered.

"Because you, like the others, want everything you can get."

"No, *you're* the one who taught me what I really want," she murmured.

"And just what is that?"

"That I just want to be naked with you." Her voice was husky with the confession. "And all the sex that goes with it."

"Even after all the fucking?"

"The first time—at the hotel—I remember everything we did. And after, I didn't know how I was going to be with another man ever again." *Oh, that sounded good.* "I was secretly thrilled when you said you wanted to hire me to be naked with you from now on." *Even better.*

"Were you?" His voice was skeptical.

Don't pile it on. It's a game. "You knew what I really wanted. I didn't. You showed me. I can't go back to how I was before. I need as much penis as I can get. So fuck me—you're ready, I want it, and you want to give it to me."

She reached for his mouth again and shimmied her hips. "Give it to me," she breathed. "I feel you—you're throbbing with it. Come on, come—"

He crushed his mouth over hers and drove into her hard. Once, twice, three times—gone, blasting hard and high between her legs, bucking and groaning as he pumped every last drop of himself into her cunt.

He went still as desire abated for a few minutes.

It was time for sleep. Except she was wide awake, both appalled and aroused by how far she'd gone and what she'd done.

A thousand dollars a day to be kept like this, have sex like this. *And* all the perks. And it was *him.*

And he had the resources to find Jillian.

She couldn't think of a single reason why she shouldn't.

When he was slack and sleeping, she could fit his entire penis in her mouth. When he awakened, aware of her lips around him, he went from half-staff to full-on hard, and two minutes later, he had eased his penis into her anal buttonhole, pushing and writhing his way in. He covered her body with his, top to bottom, and lay with her in a thick miasma of sensual possession.

"Oh, yes," she breathed, as he undulated his hips to heighten her pleasure. "Right there. I need that there—" She gasped as he pulled back and drove in. Unspeakable pleasure.

He came and then collapsed onto her and they rested again. He spooned her, one arm wrapped around her waist, the other on the curve of her hip.

This feeling of comfort was dangerous. She had to be hard-hearted and cold-blooded about it. Treat sex like business and her body like the commodity it was. And not enjoy it so much that she'd be lost without it when the arrangement came to an end.

And she must *never* be distracted from her main purpose: Jill.

But an hour—two—ten—later, something kept distracting her. Either his hard bar of an erection against her buttocks or his fingers rubbing her nipples, her body stiffened with lush arousal.

"Perfect," he breathed in her ear. "Put your leg over my thigh so I can get to your cunt."

"Hurry," she whispered, as she felt one of his hands slide away from her nipple, down her midriff and belly to spread her labia.

Her body convulsed as he penetrated her with his fingers, spreading her wider. He rooted his fingers in her, sliding them around inside her, circling her clit.

"What can I teach you now?" he growled as he pressed that hot nub, stroking and squeezing her nipple to send her instantly into orgasm. He prolonged it by pressing on her clit and whispering in her ear until she begged for mercy.

"No mercy for your cunt," he whispered. "Open it wider." He moved his hand downward and, at the same time, rolled onto his back so that she was lying back-to-front on top of him. With both hands, he pulled at her gently and began stroking her hot, quivering flesh.

Now his body convulsed, and he spurted cream all over her buttocks. But he didn't relinquish his erotic pull on her cunt lips.

"I can't bear any more." She barely got the words out, she was so shaken by the vulnerability she felt when he opened her up. It was too much. But he was adamant, aroused, paying her to open herself to him like this.

"You can bear it."

She needed to get away from his questing fingers. So she wiggled her hips and arched her body away from his incessant fondling.

Which only aroused him more.

"From now on, whenever I want you hot and raw, I will spread you like this. And you won't deny me what I want."

"No," she panted, her body slick and swollen.

A thousand a day. Her secret life.

"You'll see. You'll keep thinking about how it feels when your lover spreads you wide like this. The memory will arouse you, you'll want him to do it again each time before he penetrates you, you'll demand that he do it. You'll fall in love with that openness."

"I already have," she whispered.

"Have you?" He twisted his fingers just inside her labia. "Like that?"

"More," she moaned.

He gave her more, with his endlessly inventive hands, and finally let her close her thighs and her cunt around his pumping fingers to precipitate her rhythmic orgasm.

Without a word, he rolled her onto her belly and entered her from behind. He held her as he drove his bursting orgasm into her. She positioned her knees wide apart to give him the subtle message she'd willingly comply with his erotic lessons anytime he demanded.

I'm forgetting Jillian. Dear heaven, everything is getting lost in the morass of sex with him.

She barely knew how many days had passed. He had to have found something out by now, the trace on the cell, which meant he might well know where she had called from that awful night.

Being naked with him was too distracting—and unnerving. He'd been right. Lying quiescent next to him, all she could feel was the memory of his fingers pulling at her cleft.

Jilly's life is now mine.

Could she possibly get away with searching the apartment? Surely the elusive and mysterious James didn't lurk in the shadows of Rawls's private residence.

Nevertheless, she had to do something.

Keeping out of sight wasn't cutting it. Maybe it would make more sense if she lured Ellicott to her.

She didn't know what to do. Nearly two weeks had passed, and all she'd done was immerse herself in 24-7 sex.

She revealed all her secrets. What were his? How could he afford to spend so much money and take so much time away from whatever it was he did for the late Oliver Baynard? She knew nothing about him; he knew too much about her.

The balance had to shift. When her mind and her body weren't fuddled by sex, every time she cooled herself off in the shower, she felt absolutely sure of that. She'd allowed him too much latitude in bed and in Jillian's affairs, even though sex with him might lead to solving the riddle of Jillian's affairs.

Still, Jillian's computer files hadn't told him much more than he—and she—knew already. The question was what his undeniable corporate resources had uncovered that he hadn't told her.

He could have logged into his own e-mail while he was accessing Jillian's files. Oh, God, what if he had? She hadn't seen any kind of technology around the apartment.

On the other hand, she'd been busy. Occupied by him.

Sinking deeper and deeper into the quicksand of sex superseded everything else. And now she'd committed herself to servicing him anytime he commanded.

She caught her breath. Just the mere thought of it was erotic. The coil between her legs moved, little darts of desire pricked at her vitals. Her nipples hardened, her memory re-created the feeling of his fingers spreading her, and she immediately felt that telltale quickening, that ripening of her body.

She had to get out of the room, just to breathe, just to cool the roiling heat in her body. She swung her legs over the side of the bed, but the movement awoke him. His hand shot out and grasped her arm.

She had a quick response ready. "Bathroom."

He made a sleepy sound and relinquished her, and she eased out of the room, thankful that the bathroom was at the end of the hallway.

She made a quick stop there, and then before she could think the better of it, she ran downstairs. But where to look? He'd left Jillian's computer on his desk in the dining area. Justine's computer was still packed in his shoulder bag, if she remembered correctly, along with Jillian's cell phones, which they hadn't examined yet.

Nowhere did she remember seeing a computer, a cell phone, a BlackBerry belonging to him.

She groped her way to the kitchen. Why did she never have a flashlight when she needed one?

There was a ceiling light in here, she remembered, feeling her way toward the door and bumping into things. She felt like an idiot and nowhere near like an intrepid sleuth. A naked, clumsy sleuth.

She flicked on the light switch and froze. Jillian's computer was not on the desk where he'd left it. Her heart pounding wildly, she made a quick search of the desk, which was suspiciously empty of papers, files, and office equipment.

Where was his shoulder bag? Her pocketbook?

She paused before entering the living room, a feeling of dread in the pit of her stomach. There was just enough light from the kitchen that she could see the lamp by the sofa.

They'd tossed their bags onto a nearby chair. Or so she'd imagined.

Where were the computers and the cell phones? All her identification. All the answers.

She slumped on the sofa distraught. It wasn't enough that the choices she'd made over the past couple of weeks might have put Jilly's life more in danger, but now she was involved with a man who had mysteriously disposed of every conceivable clue.

Why had she not sought out help two weeks ago? Even though she couldn't claim Jillian was missing, she could have done *something* different, something *sane*. Now there was no way she could do anything without the proof of Jill's computer, files, and phones.

And she had committed herself to Rawls when now she couldn't even be certain he really *wanted* to find a connection between Ellicott and Baynard's death or if he had some other agenda.

Why else had all her stuff disappeared?

Yet he devoted so much time to sex. It was an odd strategy for a man seeking the truth of what he believed was a cold-blooded murder. How much of it was a lie?

Now that she was removed from the aura of his sex, and that insidious little coil of lust within her lay shriveled in uncertainty, she didn't know what to make of him.

"You already found what you're looking for." He stood in the doorway, his arms crossed, his penis elongating.

She knew one thing for sure about him: the sex games had to continue. It was all she could do right now.

"And what was that?" she asked without thinking.

"Permission to act on your secret sexual greed. But now, since I'm paying you an extraordinary amount of money, you need to understand what it means to be a companion."

He moved toward where she sat on the sofa.

"I know what it means," she said defiantly, quelling her suspicions. *Don't let him see you sweat.*

"No, you don't," he contradicted. "Because if you did, you wouldn't be down here in my living room, you'd be upstairs in my bed, servicing me."

He began pacing and she watched, fascinated, as his penis lengthened.

"You should be thanking me. You thought your dark secret was safe when it was perfectly obvious the moment Zach brought me to your booth party, you were itching to fuck. Remember, I was the one who sought you out afterward. I was the one who spent two days and nights in that hotel with you honing all your secret desires.

"I didn't have to coerce you to spread your legs; you were the one begging for it again and again. It was there for any man to see.

"So it's extremely bad business for you to be down here. Particularly after you accepted my offer, particularly after our last fuck. Because I know you were wide awake up there just now, remembering it. I know you could still feel my fingers inside you. You were squirming for more.

"And if you're going to spend this time with me going down your own path and not servicing *me*, then I'll find someone else who's more interested in my pleasure than snooping around."

She swallowed hard. It was time to play the game. "I'm sorry. How can I make it up to you?"

"Let me describe what a companion does. First and foremost, she keeps me happy in any way, shape, or form she can. She has a truck driver's appetite for sex. Her whole philosophy is to keep me well oiled and well fucked. That's it. She doesn't play games. She doesn't have any other concerns except her man and his penis. And for that he pays her for her level of sexual attentiveness and ability."

He paused for a moment and then went on, "You *said* you were thrilled when I offered you this opportunity. Now I wonder if you lied to me again. Of course, if you want sex without the exclusive commitment, I could offer you this: I'll fuck you when I can fit you in, but I'll hire another companion to relieve you of the full-time responsibility. It would mean you'd have to be available on *my* schedule. And since my new companion would be around all the time, you can understand I would spend most of my time fucking her.

"So think about it. I might be able to find time to fuck you on a casual basis."

He stopped behind her and leaned against the sofa. He watched her and waited. She hated his dark edge; he had too much power. And she was too hooked on sex with him.

"You do remember I'm not a patient man."

She remembered too well. And the thought of another woman wearing his penis, doing with that woman all the erotic things he did with *her*, was too much to bear.

"I want it all," she whispered.

"That tells me nothing. You want what?"

She took a shuddery breath. "I want to pleasure you however, whenever, wherever you command. You know I'm turned on every minute I'm naked with you."

"I know all that," he said impatiently. "That still tells me nothing."

"Give me another chance to be the companion you deserve. I don't want to be a sexual sidebar. I promise I'll spoil your penis, cater to your every desire, and leave you begging for more. I won't get distracted again. I just want to be naked with you for as long as you want me."

She didn't know what else to say. The silence lengthened as he digested her promises. Then he bent over her shoulder and whispered in her ear, "One more chance—since I've put so much time into your sexual education already."

She went weak with relief. She didn't have to give him up yet. She had time. There was time—

"But, I won't tolerate your sneaking around my apartment or my life. Ask me what you need to know."

"I need to know you still want to fuck me."

"Turn around."

She twisted her body, her mouth even with his thickly jutting shaft. She closed her mouth over it and started sucking the tip, maneuvering her body so she could get at the whole rock-hard length of him.

She felt her gratitude rising into a need. She needed to feel his scrotum, his thighs, that insanely sexy part of his belly just above the granite jut of his shaft.

She went wild with emotion, her hands touching him everywhere, sucking him hard. She wanted to devour him. He had no defense against her mouth, and when he seized up and blasted his cum into her, she took it and continued sucking until she wrung him dry.

He had to push her away, but even after she relinquished his shaft, she kept kissing, licking, and fondling it. "I missed you," she whispered. "It's only been a couple of hours since you fucked me and I still want you."

"Then you should have stayed in bed." He made a movement

to end her caresses. "That was a lost hour. I should keep track. I should deduct it."

"I won't cost you another hour," she whispered. "Take me back to bed with you."

He considered that for a moment. "No, I think, given the money I'm paying you, there needs to be a punishment for this behavior. Most companions never need any such discipline, but apparently you do. One night sleeping alone with no fucking privileges should be enough to keep you focused. You'll sleep in the guest room tonight, planning a dozen new ways to keep me happy."

Chapter Twelve

Her body ached for him the whole long, interminable night. Being naked without him made no sense. Every memory made her hot. She never thought this would turn into such a serious sex game, or that she'd have to beg for forgiveness and suffer a penance. What might he claim for the loss of a whole night's coupling with her?

The only thing that made it bearable was that he paid the penance, too. She pictured him sprawled on the bed, his penis towering with arousal, and nowhere to root except a pillow. *Good.* Let him pleasure himself then. It couldn't be nearly as pleasurable as fucking her.

Hurry, morning. A new day meant she had to relegate her twin to another place on the list—and trust that Rawls still needed to find her, too.

Ask if I need to know. She had a book's worth of questions, and tossing and turning alone in her bed only made her think of more.

She ought to have grabbed the *out* and run from his seduction, to let go of the hope that he had the resources to find Jillian.

But it was too late. She was in too deep, and too addicted to him.

And, of course, he wouldn't break. He'd spend himself ten times in the pillows before he'd give in to his "slave."

She despised him for making her crawl like that, even if it was a game. She'd make him pay somehow.

———

She awakened to find him sprawled in the club chair by the guest room window, waiting for her to sense his presence, his shattering tension, and his rampant erection.

She rolled to the edge of the bed, and braced her heels against the side rails of the antique bed so her legs were spread and her cleft visible.

"Did you sleep well?" she asked.

"Did you?"

She gave him a knowing smile. "You're here."

"You noticed."

"It's always the first thing I notice." It took virtually nothing now—a couple of sex-charged words, his gaze focused between her legs—for her body to melt for him.

"I like a companion who appreciates the penis she's with."

"But I'm not *with* a penis yet."

"Technically you are. It's in your room with you."

"Then it's my pleasure to admire it. What would your pleasure be?"

"My pleasure would be to hear that you couldn't sleep, that you were so aching hot for it, you couldn't stop yourself from . . . But that didn't happen, did it?"

"How would you know?"

"Not so humble now, are you. *My* room was unoccupied when I woke up."

"So this was a test of who wants to fuck more?"

"It was a test of a companion. Lesson two: she should never leave her penis unattended; she could lose more than she thinks she gains."

She stiffened. It sounded as if he were going to push this game to its ultimate conclusion, she thought suddenly with lightning clarity. He'd gotten what he wanted, and it wasn't her.

Jill's computer.

Maybe the no-holds-barred sex was a bonus, toying with her to get what he wanted and imposing impossible constrictions so the thing didn't go any further.

He'd come out of nowhere and softened her up with two days

of unbelievable body-bending sex, and then, when she was about to confront Ellicott, he was suddenly there to convince her that she was walking into danger. He'd combined that urgency with the lure of sex with the lurking threat stalking both her and her sister. And then he made all the evidence disappear, as if it had never existed.

That could be the scenario just as well as any other. Forget her addiction to sex with him, this went deeper. She had to keep playing to gain some advantage.

"You mandated the discipline," she said finally. "What if I'd given in and disobeyed?"

"Ah, the conundrum. I would have rejected you."

"And then raced to hire a properly deferential companion." Stop, she told herself. She couldn't let a jealous snit get in the way now.

He raised an eyebrow. "But then I would have wondered why I'm punishing myself when I hired you specifically for *my* convenience. Nothing else really enters into it unless you do something else to displease me."

So he didn't want her to go, either.

"But I don't displease you." She leaned back, bracing her upper torso against her elbows, to bring his attention back between her legs.

His eyebrow arched again. "I'm naked. You're naked. But it won't be that easy. The punishment still stands." He levered himself out of the chair and moved toward her.

"However, there's no reason for me to forgo certain pleasures just because you chose to." He bent over her, bracing himself on his arms, so he could lean in a breath away from her. "I meant it—no fucking tonight. And to make it even more difficult, because I am a *very* disciplined man, I will take your tongue for my pleasure tonight."

Her eyes widened and her breath caught.

"Just your tongue."

"We're going to make out for the rest of the night?"

He ignored the question. "Lie down."

She moved back toward the headboard. "Just kissing?"

"Just." He levered himself over her.

"You can't do——"

"I can. Can you?"

That was the question. Because once his mouth settled on hers, she wanted everything. He pushed her hands away when she reached for his penis, his chest, his buttocks, just to feel the texture of his skin.

"No touching," he rasped against her lips. "Just tongue."

It was licking and sucking and nibbling and kissing all night. He didn't cover her with his body, he didn't try to mount her, he refused to let her avid hands touch him.

Nothing but mouth-to-mouth contact, unbelievably carnal and arousing. Her body responded, whipped into a frenzy by his mouth on hers, using it to enflame and provoke and then deny her anything but his kisses.

Every now and again his penis inadvertently brushed her thigh, exuding semen as her body twisted to get closer to his skin, the hardness of his sex, the creamy wet of his ejaculate.

But no. Tongue only, his choice, his pleasure. He was adamant about it, with his hard-driving mouth, and ultimately his hands holding her wrists to keep her hands still, leaving her no recourse but to submit.

Her body felt like hot molasses between her legs, her nipples hard and neglected. She wanted it—him—so badly.

"My pleasure," he reminded her in a thick whisper. It was clear in his tone that he wanted her sex. He just wouldn't take it tonight.

He restrained his urges, in spite of the fact that his penis kept spilling his cream. He didn't touch her body, he ignored her nipples, he never looked at her cleft. It was all about her tongue, her kisses, his domination of her mouth, and his determination that she learn from her punishment.

She was the naked instrument of his pleasure until he decided she wasn't anymore.

"Show me your tongue."

She responded without thinking. "Why?"

He nipped her lip. "Because I want to see it. For my pleasure."

She slipped her tongue between her lips and he examined it intimately and then licked it.

Her heart beat wildly; she could barely breathe as her body arched frantically. He had to be made of iron to feel the spurt of his semen and not put his penis between her legs.

"Please," she finally begged him. "I need—"

"You need tongue," he breathed against her lips. "Only delicious hot tongue tonight. Don't beg. I won't relent."

She felt like a hormonal teenager, squirming and itching for the moment he spent his cream. She didn't need to be naked for an extended make-out session with no penis action. She needed to touch, to feel, to be the receptacle of all that lust and ejaculate as she felt his body jolt.

Leaving her without the gratification of that release, her body still ripe for penetration, he eased back on her mouth.

"It's a new day," he murmured, his voice husky. "Discipline is done." He relinquished her wrists, and he swung to a sitting position on the opposite side of the bed.

"That's it?" she asked in disbelief.

"You keep forgetting this is about *my* pleasure, *my* demands, keeping *me* happy."

"So you're just going to make out with me from now on?" She shouldn't challenge him, she shouldn't push the game.

"I haven't decided just how it's all going to go."

"Maybe I'm the one who should be seeking a new companion," she shot back, just to rile him.

"Do that if you feel you need to," he said coolly. "Let me know."

She took a deep, shuddery breath as he left the room, and then jumped out of bed.

She couldn't take another night like that, but she couldn't afford to walk away without the computers, the cell phones, and her bag. And she couldn't couldn't give up the sex. Yet.

It was not the conclusion she wanted to reach.

She washed quickly and went downstairs to the sunlit kitchen, now suffused with the homey scent of coffee brewing.

"Not gone yet?" he said mildly. "Don't make empty threats."

"I'm not so certain"—she stopped dead and then continued a little unsteadily—"they were all that empty."

Because on the desk in the dining area exactly where she'd put it yesterday, almost as if Rawls were taunting her, was Jillian's computer.

"Something wrong?" He was pouring the coffee, not looking at her, his tone deceptively casual.

She swallowed. If the computer was back, then her bag probably was as well.

She had to check.

"No. I just need some things in my bag—" She broke off as he handed her a cup of coffee.

"Coffee first."

It was the last thing she wanted, next to him following her into the living room like a cat. Sinuous. Silent.

She knew what she'd find: the bags would be exactly where they'd been the day before, everything inside intact.

But what were the odds that the information hadn't been copied? Or deleted?

In any event *need some things* gave her an excuse to check that her cell was there, even if she couldn't ascertain if Jillian's message was still in her in-box.

The only possible theory was that someone had taken everything from the apartment sometime after they'd arrived, and magically returned it all after Rawls had caught her sneaking around.

But why? Would he deny it if she really did ask him what she wanted to know?

Of course he would. She'd have to find out without asking him the time of day, let alone what else he—or some accomplice—had discovered in Jillian's computer.

She rummaged around in her handbag. Her maintenance kit was there, and she fished it out as an excuse for checking the contents. Her wallet, checkbook, passport. *Not her cell.*

And if not her cell, perhaps not her computer either.

But she didn't dare put a hand in his bag with him watching. She covertly glanced over. Her laptop was still there, but as far as she could tell, there was nothing else. Not Jillian's cell phones, not a folder, not even a pen, a business card, or a legal pad. Nothing.

"Everything where you expected to find it?"

She ignored his question and waved the plastic bag at him. "I need a shower."

"Good idea. Me, too." He put down his coffee cup. "Let's go."

There was no arguing with that tone. He gestured toward the stairs, and led her into the hallway bathroom.

She set her bag down on the counter between the two sinks. There were two oak-framed beveled mirrors above each in which she could see two of him.

Two jutting penises. Her heart started pounding. "No privacy?"

"Don't you think we're beyond that?" He turned on the shower. "Time for sex."

"I thought we were past that, too."

"That was just for last night, to make a point. Go on in. Face the wall. I can find my way."

The water shot out in a warm gush against her body. She sensed him moving in behind her and gasped as she felt his fingers at her crease, working his way between her legs.

There was something about the way he handled her body that was breathtaking. He spread her cheeks, eased his fingers down to her labia, inserted them, and readied her for penetration.

She tilted her lower torso toward his body as he positioned himself for the thrust. He drove into her hard, grasping her hips. It was just what she wanted, needed, after their long night of kissing.

He has your cell. What are you thinking?

And then she couldn't think. Her orgasm caught her, unprepared, in a bolt between her legs that she rocked and rode.

"Don't move."

"I can't." She closed her eyes and leaned her head against the wall, letting the water flow over them, still coupled.

"It's so tempting to do you again."

She had no control over the way her body reacted, that languid movement that invited him in.

"But anticipation is arousing in and of itself, don't you think?"

"You're a sadist," she muttered.

"I won't say what you are." He eased himself from her, and she felt the space within now utterly empty.

He climbed out of the shower. "I'll leave your clothes on the bench."

When she peered out through the steam, he was gone.

She towel-dried her hair and then slipped into her jeans, jacket, and sneakers, which after two days felt grubby. But it didn't seem to matter.

When she returned to the kitchen, he was similarly dressed in jeans, blue denim shirt, and running shoes, and was deep into the files on Jillian's computer.

"Coffee's still hot."

She poured some and leaned against the counter, watching him.

Who was he, really? Did it really matter to her? It wouldn't have mattered to Jillian as she pursued her hedonistic path to wealth.

He could afford private planes, a brownstone in Manhattan, a ten-thousand-dollar two-night hookup. He could also afford an accomplice, and he had the kind of stamina to keep a woman interested over and above all the intrigue. And for the first time, it really hit her. She finally understood how his money fit into everything that had happened. Baynard's corporation, like Ellicott's, dealt in high-risk security.

And if Oliver Baynard—as rich, powerful, and protected as he was—could meet with a random accident on a country road, what were the odds that an accident could be engineered to dispose of anyone who—

"Where are you? Bring me some coffee and pull up a chair."

She did as he said. He took the cup and gave her an unwavering look that roamed her face, devoid of makeup.

He shut the computer so she couldn't see the screen. "You are really beautiful, you know."

"I'm really damp and uncomfortable," she retorted. "And distractions don't work unless they involve a certain body part. What don't you want me to see on that screen?"

He gave her a considering look.

Eventually he said, "Jillian—"

She bolted out of the chair instantly. "What? What do you know? What aren't you telling me?"

"*Sit.* Jillian's alive, but we think she was involved in an accident."

Another accident . . .

She jumped up again and grabbed his arm. "Where is she?"

"I don't know. Yet. Now sit—and listen. You have James to thank for all this, by the way."

She closed her eyes in frustration. "I don't know what I'm thanking him for."

"Never forget for a minute that Ellicott has the same resources we do, but this is what we know so far. Ellicott hired a time-share corporate jet the day after Baynard died. It went down, outside London, where it wouldn't be fussed over by the press, at least not at first. The flight plan was filed for London from Paris. We think Jillian was on board and that she sent the text just before or as the plane went down. We think she survived.

"James stayed in London to find out what happened after that. The authorities were on the scene within the hour and reported that the pilot is in a coma. Forensics is sifting through the rest. They say there may have been a passenger on board, possibly a woman.

"That's all anyone knows right now except *we* know about Jillian's text to you. It's likely Ellicott tried to dispose of her. But since only the pilot was found in the wreckage, we have to assume she got out. Which means she could be anywhere. So where would she go, injured and needing help? Who would she contact?"

"She would contact me," Justine said instantly.

"She hasn't. No e-mail, no voice mail or text messages. What about Zach?"

"Conceivable. But I don't know."

"He might well have been paid by Ellicott to steal her computer, by the way, after you appeared on the scene."

She'd thought that herself, but hearing him say it sent chills through her. She knew firsthand that Zach was scum, a pimp with no morals and no loyalty. He'd have given Jillian up to Ellicott in a heartbeat for the right price.

"Who else?"

"I don't know. I don't know if she had any real friends, if she had any real romantic interest. I'm the only one I can even remotely see her contacting. I'm her safe house."

"Not anymore. Ellicott will have surveillance at the apartment and on Zach. Since Jillian—you—was up to the same old business days after the crash, and since Ellicott actually saw her perform at the Crystal Ball, he doesn't know for certain that she's dropped off the radar."

"But," Justine started, "he stopped payment on his fee. He knew she'd been in that accident. He thought she was dead."

"I know."

Of course he did. Mr. Security knew everything or how to find it out.

"I called his office that morning in London," she added. "I told the receptionist I'd speak with him *after* he replenished my bank account."

He went still for a long moment. "Shit. And you were planning to confront him again *after* that little stunt?"

She got up and paced into the kitchen. "I didn't know what else to do."

"Your impersonating her has complicated things almost beyond being salvageable."

"For *you*, you mean. You don't need me, and frankly, I'm still a little wary about why you need Jill."

"I need you."

The words hovered tenuously in the silence.

They stared at each other for a long moment, and then Justine spoke.

"You need a convenient body," she snapped, "and you're willing to pay for it."

"It's much cleaner that way. No emotional messes. And you

should be on your knees in gratitude that there's evidence Jill is still alive. My job is to find her before Ellicott does. So focus. Who else would she have contacted?"

She had no idea, and she had to admit it. Even if she'd known, she thought, she wouldn't have told him just then.

She shook her head. "I don't know."

"Anyone from her past, her childhood?"

Someone who'd been a part of their anguished ravaged foster home childhood? "I don't think it's likely."

"What about that baby sister you mentioned?"

She blanked out for a moment. She'd told him about that? "She disappeared into the system. All I ever discovered was that it was a closed adoption. I couldn't trace her beyond that—I tried. But I don't think Jilly ever gave her a second thought once we were taken away from our parents."

He sighed and went silent for a moment.

Then he said, "The other problem is that I have things to do while I'm here, and I can't trust you alone for thirty seconds. We also need a suitable wardrobe for you. And no, it doesn't make sense to return to your apartment or to Jillian's."

It surprised here that he was considering taking her out in public at all. Ellicott's people could be anywhere. But apparently, he had business here, in addition to his quest to find Jillian. No matter what else he had to do, though, Justine knew the end result was the same: Ellicott would pay for Baynard's death.

Chapter Thirteen

The sleek, black car was waiting for them when they left the house, with James behind the wheel.

She slid across the luxe leather backseat. "Thank you for finding out about Jillian."

"It wasn't much, miss, but we're not yet done."

"I understand."

Rawls gave him an address in the West 30s. "I'm taking you to the most exclusive fashion house in Manhattan."

Jilly was somewhere unknown, injured, bruised, possibly burned, and Justine was going to a fashion house. Her twin was incapacitated and probably feeling that Justine had failed her, resenting, perhaps, that Justine had stepped into her shoes and lived every inch of it to the fullest.

How could Justine ever explain, or make it up to her?

Traffic was horrendous as usual, but it didn't bother James. After a while he pulled up in front of a building on the West Side that could have housed offices, a TV studio, a warehouse—anything but a fashion showroom.

Rawls guided her through a steel door into a long, bare hallway, and up the elevator to the top floor.

There was a sign on a wooden double door before them as they got off the elevator: *Vous*. Rawls pressed the buzzer impatiently and they entered the showroom. There were several chairs along the wall, which was decorated with fashion sketches, and there was a brass door leading to the design studio.

A moment later, a petite woman bustled in, her hands outstretched. She had luxuriant gray hair and oversized rhinestone glasses.

"Helene," he said, "this is Justine."

"Come . . ."

Helene took them through an outer office and to a stunning workroom, as big and bustling as a hive, with cutters and fit models, and overflowing with bolts of material and sewing machines.

"Come," she repeated.

She led them through the chaos through yet another door. Here, everything was upholstered. The room had gray walls, dark blue carpet, and fitting rooms with gray satin curtains drawn for privacy. A couple of plush chairs sat against the opposite wall.

"In here." Helene motioned to one of the fitting rooms. "I will be right with you."

In the room there was a small dais in front of a trifold mirror, a chair, and a little table.

"Exactly what are we doing here?"

"We are getting you outfitted the way a proper companion should be," Rawls said. He held up his hand as she opened her mouth. "Don't protest. I'm debating just how much to use you."

"I think you've done a pretty good job of that already, she muttered, turning her back to the mirror. They were eye-to-eye and mouth-to-mouth. Bad idea.

He moved in for a kiss.

She wriggled away uncomfortably.

"Helene won't interrupt us."

"Really? And how do you know that?"

She shouldn't have looked in his eyes. He knew from other times, other women. She didn't want to know about *other*.

He started unbuttoning her jacket, and she stopped his hands.

"You have to strip," he murmured, his deep gaze on her face, reading her every expression. "It won't hurt."

She knew she was in trouble. She could turn away and have three of him in the mirror to contend with, or she could just take off her clothes and let him—do whatever he wanted.

A companion would not only *let him*, but she also would have suggested and encouraged him. She wasn't such a polished companion after all.

He continued unbuttoning her jacket, helped her slip out of it, unsnapped her jeans, and let her wriggle out of them. She kicked her sneakers off before he grasped her hips and pulled her close.

"You can kiss me," he suggested.

She touched his face—the planes, the texture of his skin, the rough stubble—and looked into his eyes. Her lips touched his, and they fell into the kiss.

"Keep going," he whispered. He moved his hands all over her body, thumbing her nipples, holding her hips, cupping her bottom. Her imagination followed, envisioning every movement as if she were watching it in the mirror.

If she kept going, she'd melt all over his hands.

"I know what you want."

"What do I want?" she breathed, her lips barely a lick away from his.

"You want to watch."

"No, I don't . . . I can't." She couldn't imagine looking at herself like that with him, doing—

"You can." Did she want to watch—everything he did, every tremor of her naked body in his expert hands? Her breath caught. Did she?

He did. He didn't wait for her consent; he turned her around slowly to face the mirror. Three of her. Three of him. She looked so sensual. Her body seemed to arch into him, seeking his touch, his heat, the heft of his penis.

It shocked her how totally comfortable she seemed, with his fingers circling her nipples, sending hot pleasure between her legs.

She watched her body undulate from three angles as he kept compressing her nipples, touching no other part of her until she felt she had to escape the ecstasy.

She leaned forward to force his fingers from her nipples and he persisted, holding them firmly, following her body movements until she arched against him again.

"You can," he murmured against her ear.

"I can't," she moaned, trying to pull his hands away.

"I'm not giving up these gorgeous nipples. And you can. You want it, don't fight it."

She couldn't fight a fly in the fog that enveloped her. He was right: she did want to, she wanted more.

He slid one hand down her body as he firmly compressed her nipple with the other. He enjoyed wreaking this kind of havoc with her, as he found her cleft, tilting her body slightly so she could see everything he did three times over. He spread her labia and inserted his fingers, bracing his thumb on her mound.

"Wet," he murmured, pushing deeper, feeling her convulse as he probed and felt for her clit. She watched as her body writhed with unspeakable pleasure as he played with her nipple and pumped his fingers between her legs.

Her orgasm, fierce and fast, caught her by surprise, shaking her to her very core. He rode it down with her, pressing her, pushing her, manipulating her clit until she could take no more and he let it spiral away.

She watched her naked body dance in orgasm, every intimate detail multiplied in the mirrors.

She'd wanted it. She wanted it again.

"Allo," came a call beyond the curtain. Helene discreetly announced her presence. It was time to begin.

"You wanted it," Rawls whispered as he eased his fingers from between her legs. "You always want it."

I want you, she thought, shaken. She wasn't experienced enough to know how to recover from such shattering pleasure in thirty seconds.

She wanted to bury her head, bury the memory, and make that little hornet of a woman go away so he could do it again.

"Come," Rawls called to her as Helene bustled in with a rack of clothes.

Helene nodded and said "*Bien*," then told Rawls to go away for an hour.

Rawls put his arm around Justine's shoulders and whispered, "Don't try to get away from me. You won't get far."

James, of course. The always lurking, ever-present, zealously loyal James. "I'll be here," she whispered back.

"Good. And I'll think seriously about a three-way mirror for the bedroom."

She couldn't have gone anywhere anyway; she was naked, for one thing, and the moment Rawls left the fitting room, half a dozen seamstresses began working on her.

"Monsieur was very particular about how he wished you to present yourself," Helene told her. "Say nothing. When a man wishes to dress you, it is never quite how you would dress yourself."

The seamstresses began choosing items from the rack and slipping them over her nude body.

"Everything is to fit you without undergarments," Helene said. "Monsieur was very particular about that."

Justine threw up her hands. She couldn't argue with Helene for following Rawls's instructions, especially when he'd be footing the bill.

"No, no," Helene said. "I know. It will not be as you think. I'm very talented."

But, Justine thought, *I don't know how to do it*. To be naked under her clothes, to feel the slide of silk caressing her bared nipples, to wear a power suit and be utterly naked beneath. She didn't know how to be comfortable like that.

But right now, it didn't matter. Helene chose everything. It was all expertly tailored to showcase her body. It was her basic companion wardrobe: the silk blouses, the tissue-thin gown, the fit-to-form skirt to match her suit jacket; the buttery knit top; the silk slip dress that barely covered her nipples. They were all beautiful, sensuous, and refined.

She was to wear the suit out. Rawls had arranged to have her hair and makeup attended to right in the fitting room, plus shoes and jewelry. He knew what he wanted. She felt like a blow-up doll, gilded in gold and peep-toe pumps. Her oversized handbag was filled with papers and a legal pad. No cell.

She hadn't forgotten her missing cell.

Damn. Damn him. Damn her for succumbing to him and becoming his compliant sex toy.

"Come, let's see," Helene said as the hairdresser finished.

Justine got up from the chair and stepped on the dais to see herself, clothed, in the three-way mirror.

The suit jacket molded to her curves and the skirt was tight around her hips, falling just above her knee. She wore black pumps, no hose, no bra, and she felt the weight of the light wool material against her skin, tightening her nipples.

Helene handed her the burgundy patent leather bag, and Justine hooked it over her shoulder.

"Perfect." But the accolade did not come from Helene.

She saw Rawls by the door, dressed for the corporate boardroom, and, just for the instant, was shocked to see all that male sexual power contained in a pin-striped suit.

"Pack the rest of her things, Helene."

Rawls held out his hand, and Justine took it and stepped off the dais. In heels, she was level with his mouth, close enough for a kiss. Had she ever worn heels with him? Had she ever been dressed with him? *Really* dressed?

It was a novel sensation, coupled with the fact that he knew she was naked under her empress's clothes.

He lifted the edge of her jacket. Her nipples thrust tightly against the blouse, and he drew in a deep breath as he cupped her right breast.

"We have a business meeting," he said. "We're presenting to the executive board of Century Sovereign Trust Company. You're my executive assistant. You'll pretend to take notes while I make some introductory remarks. After that, my staff will take over and walk the client through all the exhaustive details, and we'll be free to leave. James is waiting."

Apparently James already had her wardrobe tucked away in the trunk of the car. Rawls helped her in as she struggled with her new heels and tight skirt.

The feeling of being utterly exposed—and his being aware of it—turned her body to thick honey. The scent of sex was already fogging the air.

They pulled up to a building with a shallow plaza on Park Avenue, which, at the end of lunch hour, was filled with people eating, chatting, and idly observing the passersby.

The offices were on the top floor, elegant, and leather-upholstered.

Rawls was greeted by the receptionist. "Your associates arrived an hour ago and are setting up in the main conference room. You and—"

"My assistant, Ms. Durant."

"You and Ms. Durant will be joining the board members in the executive conference room. Follow me, please."

She led them through a quiet hallway to the far corner of the building and opened a large, mahogany door. Five board members were seated around a long table, bathed in a flood of sunlight from the floor-to-ceiling windows.

The board rose as one as Rawls entered the room, and Justine eyed an upholstered chair where she could sit while Rawls made his presentation.

They shook hands and Rawls introduced her before nodding and taking his place at the head the table.

"Gentlemen, let me introduce myself." He shot a look at Justine and went on, "I am Doug Rawls, the new CEO of Gilbraltar of London Risk Management."

Justine blinked. *Baynard. Ellicott. Jill.*

CEO?

"We are the most trusted name in risk management and, international and government security—the Praetorian Guard, as it were, of prevention and protection," he went on.

"We are discreet, and operate behind an invisible curtain so that our clients can carry on all normal activity while surrounded by rock-solid protection. Our risk assessors are trained in the best

covert operations departments in the world, are experts in pro-
filing, psychology, and forensics, and continually run and analyze
potential scenarios while working in tandem with government
and law enforcement agencies. We constantly monitor our clients
and are in constant communication."

Justine was still reeling. *CEO? He* was Baynard's successor? How
convenient, how stunningly, unbelievably convenient.

"Our field agents are put through rigorous training after they've
been screened, tested, and vetted for their ethics, integrity, loyalty, discretion, and discipline."

The ramifications were staggering. She could barely breathe. He'd
never thought to mention it, just turned up and announced it. What
wouldn't someone do if a billion-dollar corporation was at stake?
What if it were *he* whom Jillian could connect to Baynard's death?

No wonder he was searching so desperately for her.

"Nothing is left undone or unexamined in our duty to our clients. We consult, evaluate, and diagnose. We have offices in London and New York, but we dispatch worldwide. We can cover a
political convention or a politician's wife. We are unparalleled in
our global positioning and our ability to do the job and do it unobtrusively and effectively.

"We are, quite simply, the best."

He was the best at what he did; the man who hated secrets was
keeping secrets and telling lies. She felt as if the floor had dropped
out from under her and she'd just barely saved herself.

Except nothing had changed.

"Given that, you might ask why the British government awarded
their now notorious security contract to the Guardian Group.
The simple answer is that, due to the sudden death of Gibraltar
of London founder Oliver Baynard, we felt we should withdraw
our proposal—all proposals, for that matter—until the inevitable
transition of leadership took place."

Inevitable transition. He could have easily arranged to get Baynard out of the way.

She saw a tightrope walk stretching before her. What was true?
What was a lie? Was she sleeping with the enemy?

"That has now been accomplished, and I, as CEO, will go forward as Mr. Baynard would have, with his vision, his discretion, and his values. I thank you for giving us the opportunity to present to you, and I invite you to the main conference room, where my staff will demonstrate what Gibraltar can do for you."

God, he was impressive—and dangerous. Like a lion. And now he knew she knew it because surely everything she was thinking was reflected in her eyes.

She'd already plotted her course as she listened to him. Nothing could change; it was the only way she could protect Jill—to be with him, on the spot, whatever it took, whatever it cost her.

Nothing would change.

The departing board members shook his hand, and when the room finally emptied, he turned to her.

"The table is tempting, isn't it?"

She got to her feet, only to find that she was a little unsteady on the heels of this stunning revelation. She took a deep breath. It was always about sex. But now the undercurrents reeked of more than just animal lust. He could be a murderer.

"CEO?" she murmured, her voice unnervingly husky.

"Just named. Baynard's wishes."

Or his greedy ambition. But he must never have a clue she was thinking this way. She turned her head slightly so he couldn't read her eyes.

"And you, with all your resources, can't find Jillian?"

"Don't tell," he said mockingly. "Everything we do is primarily centered around preventive measures. Sometimes when people go underground, they go really low-tech. Anyone can disappear if they want to, if they're desperate. And no amount of situational diagnostics can pinpoint them, especially if they're on their own. You can't predict what kind of decisions they'll make or what their mental state is. I think Jillian is very much on her own, which makes it harder to deduce her movements and means we'll need to take other measures to find her. Let's go. My staff will be in there for hours. There's nothing more we need to do here."

He took her arm and guided her toward the door.

"What will your staff tell them?"

"They'll go into the specifics and use speculative scenarios to demonstrate how we analyze and predict potentially dangerous situations and then prevent an incident," he said as they walked down the hallway to the elevators. "In Jillian's case, we're backtracking to an incident no one knew was dangerous at the time. A situational analysis might have come up with a laundry list of possible problems, or none at all. That's why it's so difficult to make suppositions afterward. And why corporations—CEOs and political figures especially—need someone to manage potential risks behind the scenes. And then there's James."

"Who *is* James?" she asked as he whisked her through the revolving door.

"My other assistant." He opened the car door, and she slid into the rear seat. "So far today, you've played the role of companion to perfection."

"It's early," she murmured, trying to pull down her skirt. *Nothing* must change. She couldn't show an inkling of what she thought.

He put his hand on hers. "Don't. What's the point if I can't fondle you whenever I want?"

What *was* the point after all? *That* at least didn't change. It existed of its own volition.

"Do you want?" His companion's coy question to distract him. He was her enemy now. How much distance could she put between them? A naked body's length? Could she do any of this now that she believed there was a possibility that he—

His expression hardened. "I *want* to find Jillian. I deliberately approached Century Sovereign because Guardian Group pitched to them this week. I wanted to give Ellicott a good scare. He's the only one who knows what really happened to Jillian. I needed to ramp up the pressure. He's probably already wondering why Jillian hasn't contacted him again about her money, and he's waiting for the other shoe to drop."

Finally—he wanted to get Ellicott off the dime and do something to help Jillian.

Except clashing over clients wasn't going to cut it.

The locus had changed. *She* had intended to use *him*, and the new permutation to the story—the newly anointed CEO with every reason to grab all the money and power within his reach—made it even more imperative that she take control.

Making Jillian a moving target would do it. *Whatever I have to do.*

"So let me be Jillian again," she said suddenly. That at least would be lighting a match to gasoline. "Put me out there again. I'll do the companion thing as Jillian and draw Ellicott in."

He waved off her offer. "Too dangerous. You did hear the part about trying to kill you?"

"No, I heard the part about ramping up the pressure on him. I can do that. If I'm out in public with you, what can he do?"

"Something stupid, one would hope," he said acidly. "But he'd be much more subtle than that. However, I do have a business dinner tonight."

"Then take me, take Jill. See what happens. You said they're always on the lookout and posting on the blogs."

"Hmm . . . maybe."

"I'll wear that next-to-nothing dress," she offered.

"I'd rather you wear nothing at all," he muttered.

"You understand that *I* need to do *something*."

"I understand you are vastly underestimating how dangerous this man is."

This man. Which man was truly her enemy? What about Rawls's evasions and lies? Using her, using sex—it always came back to sex and how little it meant to him as opposed to what it could mean to her.

Sex was a diversion, to distract her and fill her.

He wanted Jilly. Period. And she was his only chance to get to her.

Three minutes after they entered his apartment, he pushed her down on the sofa and sank deep inside her, without a word.

How much deeper into hedonism could she slide? How did it help anything?

Damn it, she wanted the sex. In spite of her doubts, her suspicions, and her fears, she could not deny herself the sex.

And she had to stop wanting it; she had to *do* something.

She pushed at him, and he stilled his movements.

"No more." She was weighed down by all the guilt that she'd gotten nowhere but into Rawls's bed. "I can't," she whispered, levering herself up on one arm. "I can't."

"Can't?" He eased up a little. "Or won't? Having an attack of conscience? Companions don't have a conscience. Companions are compliant. Whatever it takes to please the client."

"Fine. Finish then."

"That's no fun. And not the point."

"I get the point."

"Good. Let's work on that."

And he did mean work. With torturously slow movements, his penis powered its way through her objections, her guilt, and the revelation of his CEO status. His mouth was on hers, wiping it all away with the swipe of his tongue. The naked soul of Jillian lived within her, and she could no more deny it than breathe.

She gave in to her nature, and she came, spiraling hard into her orgasm, and a moment later, his followed.

Her dress was a breath of silver material that hugged her body and revealed every curve. Her nipples pushed tight against the bodice, and Rawls didn't help by putting his arms around her as she gazed at herself in the mirror and fondled them.

She stretched toward his hands, winding her arms around his neck. *Nothing must change.* "This is the appetizer?"

"This is to make everyone who sees you tonight rabid with lust."

"As opposed to you?"

"Me? I'm in a constant state of lust."

"I see," she murmured, rubbing her bottom against his iron erection.

"We have to go to dinner."

"I know. I'm ready."

"Tonight, your name happens to be Jillian." He cupped her breasts and held them. "And later . . ."

She stared at Rawls in the mirror. It seemed to her that he always held her like this, made her feel like she was getting lost in him, and she had to fight to not let it happen. So much was at stake and so little information was concrete.

Don't forget how much you don't know. He's not Doug Rawls the henchman anymore. He's Doug Rawls, CEO. And he needs to find Jill. And he may be your lover, but he's also your adversary, and he needs YOU to find Jill as much as you need his resources.

Don't forget Jill.

Not tonight.

Rawls got her coat and her bag as she gathered her resolve.

She knew what she had to do: look beautiful, show off her body. Make the guests focus on her. Maybe he'd even scheduled a booth party.

James was waiting at the curb outside the brownstone.

"No poaching allowed," Rawls said to her as they drove to the restaurant. "Cards, however, may be exchanged."

"What about bodily fluids?" she retorted.

He gave her a look. "Only with me."

The restaurant was on the East Side, new and elegant enough that reservations had to be made a month in advance. Its particular attraction was that each table had a private booth.

It *is* a booth party, Justine thought mordantly, as she shrugged out of her coat and handed it to Rawls.

But there also was a second dining level overlooking the main floor, the most desired tables by the railing where celebrity-watchers could spy.

Rawls checked their coats and whispered to her, "I want those nipples hot, tight, and visible. Do something about it—or I will."

She shuddered at the thought and wheeled away from him and into the ladies' room. She went into a stall for a moment of privacy.

Am I crazy? What am I doing? Does he never get enough?

But she knew the answer to that. Her nipples thrusting against her dress were part of his strategy.

Her in the guise of Jill was exactly what he wanted, even if she'd suggested it. It was easy to forget that. She couldn't ever let herself forget that. It would make things easier later.

"Much better," he murmured, as she emerged from the restroom. He took her arm. "The client's name is Daventree."

The maître d' murmured his name, nodded, and led them into the dining room.

"Oh, God," Justine whispered, "is that—that's Ellicott—and the Principessa."

Why wasn't she surprised he already knew? Ellicott wasn't going to "hear" about their dinner; he would witness it.

"Exactly. Ellicott's been courting Daventree. But more importantly, he needs to see Jillian—your idea remember—out and about with his most despised competitor, exuding that Jillian sexuality."

They were just passing Ellicott's booth and he'd risen halfway up from his seat. Whether it was from shock or good manners it was hard to tell.

Rawls stopped and extended his hand. "Ellicott. What a coincidence. I know you're well acquainted with Jillian. And this is?"

"She knows who I am," the Principessa said, her voice sharp as steel. "And I know her. And how much she cost me."

"Jillian," Ellicott said stiffly.

"That," Justine said, infusing a snide edge in her tone, "is the Principessa."

"Nice to meet you," Rawls murmured, and as he pressed Justine's arm, she leaned into Ellicott and hissed so both he and the Principessa could hear, "I want my money, you bastard."

Ellicott reared his head and stared her straight in the eye. She stared back as his gaze moved to her breasts, the outline of her nipples against the fabric. Rawls possessively propelled her forward to follow the maître d'.

"Good job," he murmured as they were seated still within

Ellicott and the Principessa's view. "He's ready to shoot fire."

"I did it for Jillian. And if he explodes when he sees Daventree, well, so much the better."

"Nice to have you on my side," he said, handing her a menu.

"I'm not on your side. I'm on Jillian's side." She snapped open the menu to hide her anger. She could feel Ellicott's eyes on her and knew that the Principessa was studying her, too.

She leaned toward Rawls. "The Principessa will be able to tell I'm not Jill. She's taking in every little detail, probably still very angry with Jillian for blowing off the trip to Monte Carlo with Zoltan Brisco."

"Then be more Jillian than Jillian would be."

Exactly. *Exaggerate everything.* No one had seen Jill since the Crystal Ball—they wouldn't remember the little things.

The waiter hovered. Rawls told him they were expecting another guest. Justine pretended to study the menu. Ellicott's surveillance unnerved her.

"He keeps looking at me," she murmured to Rawls.

"He's thinking about what he's missing. He's jealous another man will be fondling those nipples tonight. He remembers how much you love that."

She felt her face flush. "Stop."

"I *know* how much you love that."

Don't let him seduce you with words.

"You're talking about Jillian, not me," she hissed.

"He's remembering how he sunk himself into your heat just weeks ago, and how thoroughly he'd be fucking you if you were with him tonight because your Principessa looks like a damned cold fish."

She knew she looked distressed, so she bent over the menu like it was a grail as Rawls added, "And he knows exactly how *I'm* going to fuck you tonight."

"*Jillian,*" she contradicted. "He knows *Jillian.*"

"And I know *you,*" Rawls countered.

"Mr. Daventree," the waiter said and they both looked up. Rawls stood, and Justine didn't know quite what to do.

She felt waves of hostility from across the room.

"Mr. Daventree," Rawls said as they shook hands. "This is Jillian."

She gave him her hand as he sat, appraising him as frankly as he was looking at her. Daventree was tall, thickly set, and expensively dressed. His hair was sprinkled with gray, and his face was as worn as an old shoe. His grip was firm and no-nonsense. And apparently he had a sense of humor.

"For me?" he asked, cocking his head at Jillian.

"For decoration," Rawls said. "What will you have to drink?"

Daventree was a wine expert as well. He ordered for the table, they chose appetizers, and Rawls got down to business.

The complexities of softening a client who knew there was a competitor in the room were as intricate and precise as the moves of a ballet.

At some point Justine tuned out, even though she was aware that Daventree, every once in a while, sneaked a glance at her breasts.

Maybe he was hungry for more than food. Maybe Rawls intended to give her to him. God, she hoped not, but this was the life Jillian lived—she had to be prepared for anything.

But if that were to be the case, she would refuse and leave. Maybe the disgruntled Principessa would take him on. She and Justine exchanged looks perhaps three times during the course of the evening, and the Principessa was curious. The Principessa, so young, so vigorous in her appetite for sex, would never understand rejecting an offer.

Why was she so fascinated with the Principessa and the Principessa with her?

Justine tried to pay attention to her food, but her mouth was dry as dust and she could barely swallow. The wine didn't help. It only made her light-headed, and that was the last thing she wanted.

She didn't know what Rawls wanted from this dinner though, except for Ellicott to see her with him, alive and sensual as ever.

And then there was the question of how the evening would end. How else could it end but him offering her to Daventree to seal the deal? She'd seen firsthand how that worked. But if that happened, she would just get up and leave—alone.

She felt Rawls's hot gaze sweep over her, as much as scolding her. She turned to Mr. Daventree, drummed up an innocuous question, and gave him her best smile.

Chapter Fourteen

Jillian never thought she'd survive. When the plane started to nosedive, she had scrabbled to pull on some clothes before crawling behind a seat, getting off a frantic text, and bracing herself for what would come.

She'd thought for one moment that this crash wasn't planned or calculated; Ellicott was hanging on for dear life, too.

She thought she'd imagined the scuffling somewhere above her, and then she thought she felt the cabin depressurize so abruptly she nearly stopped breathing.

And then nothing was clear except the wind howling and the engine whining and the plane spiraling downward.

She didn't remember any details after that, just the visceral drive to stay conscious, to get control and get out. How she managed it was a blur now, just a memory of searing pain after the staggering impact of slamming into the ground.

Her passing thought as the plane hit and there was a long moment of dead silence and then an ominous roar was that Ellicott wasn't there. And then it was an animal fight for survival. Crawling, choking, feeling the heat of the fire from the cockpit, she probably only had seconds before witnesses would arrive and try to save anyone on board.

Smoke went up her nose and in her eyes as she creeped along. There was a wailing siren in the distance. *Where was the goddamned door?*

Somehow she found it, and she tumbled out into the chill dawn air. Somewhere beyond where she lay, she heard voices, fire engines roaring up to the scene, and despite the injuries she'd sustained as she fell, despite her smoke-clogged throat and the burn on her leg. She had to get away.

She had nothing but the clothes on her back and the chain she always wore with one perfect little diamond—the first gift from her first grateful client. It was all she had to sustain her, to barter if she could get away, if she lived.

With fierce determination, she pushed her aching body to crawl what felt like a hundred yards to a cluster of bushes, where she watched as people gathered around.

Conceivably they'd gotten the pilot out already, but the plane was burning so furiously, she couldn't tell. She didn't care. She just needed a few minutes to gather her wits, an hour to sleep and recuperate, and a lifetime to relive how in the hell she'd survived.

No. Don't think about it. Just vanish.

In the end, it did seem as if she'd vanished. By luck or by accident, she held out until it got too dark for the searchers to forage the surrounding area. For the moment no one was looking for her, and she fell into sleep.

She woke with a jolt, in the midst of a nightmare, her aching bones stiff and fragile. Her body was ice cold, her mouth dry, her eyes still hazy, and her throat sore.

But she was still alive.

She didn't know where she was, though. Somewhere outside of London, where Ellicott would never find her, she imagined. And where was she going? She'd head to London and then vanish.

She had to think. She had to get warm without attracting attention.

Oh, God, she couldn't do this. If she went to the authorities, it would all be over. They'd know she was on the plane, they'd ask a thousand questions, and Ellicott would know she was alive.

Conversely, if she didn't go to the authorities, no one would find out that anyone else was aboard until the forensics were done, and by then—

She woke up with a jolt again. She could have been sleeping fifteen minutes or fifteen hours. She didn't know, except the daylight was creeping up beyond the branches where she lay. It was very cold, too, and if she fell asleep again, dressed as she was, she knew she wouldn't survive.

She had to get moving, before the authorities arrived, before anyone found her.

She could do this. It was paramount that Ellicott not know she was alive or she'd be dead for certain. It was just a matter of getting to London. She needed a plausible story, she needed clothes, food, warmth.

She felt for her necklace; she could sell the diamond. That was why she always wore it; it was her plan B. It wasn't big, and wouldn't bring much, but she could sell for just enough to get out of any bad situation she found herself in.

She could explain her appearance, too—an attack, a robbery, a beating, left for dead by a thief who'd stolen her car, her money, her credit cards, her passport. She'd hone the details as she went.

She got up slowly, painfully, and looked around. She was in a field well outside any town and could see the twisted wreckage of the plane. It must be a fragile thing if it could disintegrate so completely. She could have disintegrated so completely—*Exactly how Ellicott intended*.

She took a tentative step, shocked that she actually remained upright. This could work, as long as she was heading away from the crash. She might just be able to talk her way through to London if the news hadn't traveled that far.

One thing at a time was about all she could handle, though.

Her first tasks: take a deep breath and *move*.

And now weeks later, she was in London, at the embassy, staring at papers asking for all kinds of personal information for her to obtain a temporary passport so she could return home.

Name: Jillian Dare. Occupation: Being occupied; that is, courtesan. No, paid companion. God, that sounded awful.

Contacts. It was a trick question, surely. Who was her friend, really? She didn't know who was her enemy, now. *Nearest family?* She'd already dragged Justine deep enough into her dark world, even though there was so little Justine could do. This one she'd have to do by herself.

She'd already perfected her story of being attacked, driven out of town, robbed, beaten, and abandoned. In the small town where she'd finally made her way, she'd found sympathy and aid. Her diamond paved the way. Small as it was, it was perfect in color, cut, and clarity, and a jeweler in town was willing to buy it to help her out.

So she only needed to apply to the embassy, and the authorities didn't need to know anything else.

Name: she started to write Jillian and stopped.

Emergency passport applications were traceable. Ellicott had the connections. She couldn't take the chance.

And worse, she'd legally changed her name to Jillian *Dare* many years before so as not to connect her sins to Justine. Well, who needed redemption now? She could never have foreseen the consequences, and she couldn't afford to have the embassy vet her credentials as Jillian Dare with Ellicott on her heels.

Nor could she contact Justine, having no idea how deeply Justine had penetrated her secret life or how far she'd gotten in her investigation.

She *had* to get home.

She stared at the application. *Name.* If she put her name on a public document, how could she vanish? But they wouldn't just issue a passport in any old name she made up. She'd need an address, too, they'd want contact information, where she worked, closest relatives. They'd probably bill her for the airline ticket, too.

She was so close. According to the papers, the pilot was in a coma, and authorities had found evidence of at least one other passenger on board the plane. It might have been a woman, they said. And one of the parachutes was missing. The plane had been leased to a corporation that was still being investigated.

Ellicott sure knew how to hide his evidence. There would be no trace of his presence in the wreckage. They would assume the mystery woman had bailed out, and they'd look for her. The pilot might not survive. Ellicott might even try to kill him, since he was involved in the murder of Baynard.

She had to get back to the States.

Name. She stared at the word for a long time. She couldn't get Justine into more trouble now, not after the mess she'd already made. But it was such an elegant solution. Justine had an unsullied name, a job, and references. No one in Jillian's world knew about Justine. And, if she put Justine's name down, Ellicott couldn't track her movements postcrash.

Her enemies wouldn't be looking for Justine Durant. She'd be safe. It'd buy time so she could get home.

She closed her eyes, took a deep breath, and scribbled the name Justine Durant.

Oh, God. Justine, forgive me.

She stared at her sister's name for a long time, thinking how with the stroke of her pen, she'd made herself invisible.

Dinner seemed endless. Rawls was expert at keeping the conversation going, despite Justine's frustration and the fact that she had very little to say. It almost didn't matter. Her role was as the super-sexed eye candy they could fantasize about licking like a lollipop for dessert.

She noted that Ellicott kept drinking, watching them. The Principessa seemed bored, but not of looking at *her*. It occurred to Justine suddenly that Rawls was drawing this out specifically to irritate Ellicott.

Maybe Daventree was aware of it, too, but he had the good manners to continue until he could reasonably plead the late hour and excuse himself.

Rawls touched her elbow, signaling she should stand and allow Mr. Daventree to lean in and kiss both cheeks before they shook hands. At that angle Daventree got a good view of her chest, her protruding nipples, her body. He inhaled her scent, looked into her eyes, and regretfully said good-bye.

"Perfect," Rawls said, gesturing for the check. "And frankly, I don't care if we get the business. It's all about Ellicott now."

"You'll get his business," Justine said. "He was well aware of Ellicott's drinking."

"And Ellicott is well aware that I'm taking you home now to fuck you to oblivion."

"Should I be grateful you didn't offer me to Daventree?"

"Did you change your mind?" He looked up from signing the credit card receipt. "I could have. You did volunteer for duty tonight. And he wanted it."

"I didn't," she snapped.

"Good," he said simply. "Ready to face Ellicott again?"

"Whatever."

Rawls nodded at Ellicott as they wound their way to the entrance, with Jillian flagrantly on display. She felt the heat of the Principessa's scalding gaze as they walked by.

"I hate this," Justine hissed.

"Jillian wouldn't," he whispered back as he got their coats.

And then they were clear of the restaurant, out in the cold night air, and stepping into the waiting car.

She was in no mood for conversation. If what he surmised was true, Ellicott wanted Jillian dead, and had put her on an executive jet with the express intention of it crashing and burning. And it had crashed and burned. But somehow, after texting her, Jillian had survived. And disappeared.

But Jillian knew all about going under the radar. She'd done it for years, pretending to be someone else, living a secret life, telling facile lies to her gullible twin.

"He's been looking for you," Rawls said abruptly.

Justine stiffened. More secrets.

"So I brought you to a place where he could look."

"Was he looking?"

"My dear, naive companion, you can't demand money from a man who thinks you're dead without some ugly consequences."

Oh.

"And it was damned brassy of you to bring it up in the restaurant."

"Well, Jillian *earned* it."

"And Ellicott is definitely a man who weighs cost-benefit to nipple time."

"Stop it."

"I don't want to. I like talking about your nipples. I like the fact that I can make you squirm just by mentioning them. I'd rather be feeling them right now, but I understand Ellicott is a delicate subject. He still wants to kill Jillian."

"I'd rather talk about nipples than death," Justine muttered.

She knew Ellicott could be following them, that Rawls had deliberately dangled her in front of Ellicott. The man was a lunatic, really. Jillian's enemy.

"I wanted to give Ellicott an even stronger incentive to keep up his search for Jillian. Now, I can play with your nipples and he can dream about them."

"Are you serious?"

"Of course I'm serious."

"*No.* No more sex. This is it, it's over. I'll refund your money. I'll—"

"Just continue fucking me. That's all you can do now."

"No."

"It's all you can do until there's some trace of her or she contacts you—"

"And how would I know, since you took my computer and my cell?"

"I'll communicate with you."

"I know what *you* mean by communicate."

She felt him stiffening.

"All you need to know is, that as much as I want to find Jillian, my real interest is in fucking you as much possible. Maybe *your* focus should be on my pleasure. Maybe you should be aware that when I mention your nipples, I really want them naked, hard, and hot to play with. Or did you forget that you were *thrilled* I chose you to be my companion?"

She closed her eyes and took a deep breath. "I remember everything."

"Then show me."

"What do you prefer—cunt, tit, or tongue?"

"All three."

It was the last thing she wanted at the moment, but she shrugged out of her coat, out of her dress, and climbed onto his lap. She wound her arms around his neck. "Take what you want."

He didn't move; rather, he set her aside. "I can wait."

"You were just in a rush." It was a strange reversal to her. Almost as if he'd used sex as a diversion not to talk about Jillian and then changed his mind about it all over again.

But why? It took next to nothing to arouse her these days. She would have been into it in minutes if he hadn't pushed her away.

"You need to learn not to mouth off. Put on your coat."

It took another ten minutes or so before they arrived at the brownstone. They went up the steps and into the vestibule in silence. Something felt different; something felt strange.

She slipped off her coat and sank onto the sofa.

He slumped into the easy chair and gave her a long, measured look. "He would kill you too, you know."

That explained it. She started shaking. "So you flaunting me in a public place helped how?"

"It's like a grain of sand in your shoe—irritating. By letting him know there are two of you out there and one of you is conspiring with me, I cornered him, dared him to make a move, which he couldn't do in a public place. It should be enough to get him to do something soon."

"And while he's doing *something*, where is Jillian? Where am I?"

"You are protected by the premier risk management company in the world."

"You, you mean."

"No. The full range and scope of the operation is right under your feet."

"What?"

"Operations central is here, in the lower duplex."

More secrets. She couldn't quite grasp it. "Gibraltar's corporate headquarters is *here?*"

"Not the corporate headquarters. That is in London, with a branch here in midtown. But the brains of the operation is right here and focused on Ellicott's movements as closely as his operation thinks it is on mine. Except he's concentrating on the midtown office."

"And now he knows about me."

"But he doesn't know what you know and he can't take the chance you know anything—except that you're impersonating Jillian or might *be* Jillian—and you've demanded your money back. So, he'll be pretty certain you know *something.*"

She took a shuddering breath. "Right. And downstairs you have all the cells and the computers."

"Monitored minute-to-minute for incoming messages."

Justine shook her head. "She won't try to contact me. Too much time has gone by, and she'll make assumptions about certain things I might have done that could endanger us both."

"Like taking her place."

"Yes." Because she knew exactly what Jill would think.

"And you're so good at it."

"Aren't I?" she muttered. She'd goaded Ellicott twice now, in London and tonight. It was too dangerous to do it again. That adventure was over, and the real work of finding Jillian had to accelerate.

"Question," she went on. "What about the crash? Is the pilot still in a coma?" He nodded. "And the investigation concluded what?"

"There were two on board, a woman and the pilot. Engine failure was the cause of the crash, and it's thought that the passenger somehow bailed out. But they never found any evidence—not the parachute, or witnesses, or the woman. They know the jet was leased through a corporate time-share but they haven't traced it further than that."

"Did they identify the woman?"

"They got a partial on the name—i-a-n-d-a-r—not nearly enough to identify Jill on the surface. But some cryptographer is probably working on it now. Fingerprints, I don't know. They'll keep trying, but presumably Jillian counted on that and planned to be back in the States before she could be identified as the second passenger."

"But if she lost everything, how could she return?"

"She'd go to the embassy, apply for a temporary passport and whatever else she needed. But she'd have to explain, give some kind of identifying information—names of contacts, Social Security number, employer. And no passport has been issued in the name Jillian Dare, which, if you didn't know, has been her legal name for years."

Justine took another deep breath. "I didn't know." More secrets. More lies. Jillian had distanced herself from her past irrevocably by choosing to obliterate her birth name altogether, distancing herself from her twin, her only family. But she'd always been miles away even though she lived across town.

Given all that, Justine couldn't think of a single thing she could do for Jill. There had never been anything she could do, starting with the disastrous decision she'd made when they were children to call social services after the birth of their baby sister.

Jillian must have hated her. She'd wanted to stay because nothing could be worse than it already was, and at least they knew what they were dealing with. But foster care ended up worse on some levels. No wonder Jillian had chosen the name *Dare*. Everything she'd ever done was a dare, daring herself to run as fast and far from her past as she could.

All the while, Justine hid behind lab coats and microscopes in a world where answers were rooted in the laws of nature and science. No wonder she couldn't cope with practicalities, such as helping Jillian, such as knowing who Jilly even was.

Justine knew now though, and she couldn't think of one way this could end well for either of them.

She looked at Rawls to find he was eyeing her skeptically.

"You didn't know."

"I didn't know."

Rawls shook his head. "Hmm . . . well, there's nothing you can do now. Especially since she's probably still in England. My people are on it at both ends. I won't overlook anything."

"And what will you do when you find her?"

"Sequester her, get her testimony, bring Ellicott to trial, and—well, what is the proper punishment for the cold-blooded bastard who murdered the brilliant Oliver Baynard?"

Justine shivered. This was a side of Rawls she hadn't seen: cold-blooded and set on avenging Oliver Baynard. Rawls might kill Elli-cott himself if he had the chance.

She caught her breath as the realization really hit her. Doug Rawls was a man capable of mayhem, murder, plots, and deep secrets. He really could have killed Baynard himself. Which meant she had to decide what she believed.

She jacked herself up from the sofa and started pacing around the living room. "We have to stop this. I have to go home."

"You're safer here. And you're safer leaving Jillian to my peo-ple."

"No. I don't know your people. I know my people. And I'm not doing Jillian any good rolling around in bed with you. I'm leaving."

Rawls got to his feet, his expression tight. "Not tonight."

"In the morning."

"Not ever."

They stared at each other, her hostility emanating in such waves that she barely noticed the shift in tension.

"I don't think so," she spat, wheeling around to the door.

He didn't stop her, but she knew he wouldn't let her out of the building without a fight. Fine. She'd push him down the steps if she had to, but she would leave this place—leave him—tonight.

She raced unsteadily up the steps and into the bedroom.

Where were her jeans? He'd probably dumped them at Helene's showroom that afternoon, but she couldn't remember.

Where was that tailored suit?

She shrugged out of the dress and started pulling boxes out of his closet. The suit had to be in there somewhere. Her bag was somewhere, too. Everything was somewhere. Why hadn't she demanded to know where things would be and where he was?

No, forget that. Around him, she couldn't think. Around him, everything deteriorated to one denominator: sex. She couldn't afford the luxury of sex anymore. Or trust.

Her every pulse pounded with the urgency to get someplace where sex wasn't a distraction, where she wasn't constantly tempted and she could just be Justine, the clever twin sister with resources of her own. She could figure things out.

She found the pants to the suit and slipped them on. She found the white blouse. They were enough. She had no choice about the shoes. But she still needed her bag.

She pushed her hair back, out of her eyes. Damn it, where was it? Probably with him. Waiting downstairs, no doubt. Thinking she'd never get past him.

Her resolve flagged for a moment. It would be easier to distract him with sex, easier to spread her legs and work him out, and then sneak away.

She'd tried that before, though, hadn't she?

Listen to yourself.

No matter what, no matter how, she had to go. She just didn't know how.

She strode to the top of the staircase. He was waiting, with unusual patience, at the bottom of the steps.

She paused on the first step down and folded her arms across her chest. He raised an eyebrow. She took one step down. He waited. Not so patiently now.

She stepped down again. He made no move. She took another step as he watched, measuring, gauging, preparing.

She squared her hips, girding herself, if he made a move, to jab at his midsection with one well-placed stiletto. Maybe lower than his midsection.

Another step down. *Be resolute, firm.* "I *am* leaving."

He gave her a look from under his brows. She took another step down; she was about halfway now.

She took three more firm steps down. He was a wall she had to get around, climb over, or topple before she dealt with her own weaknesses, her own failures. There was a litany of them, starting from childhood, illuminated in a dimly lit stairwell between him and her own private hell.

"Don't," he said calmly.

"Don't stop me then."

He shrugged.

Damn him. Enough.

She took the final five steps with determination. She bumped right into his chest as he met her halfway and scooped her up over his shoulder, carrying her back up the stairs and into the bedroom, where he dumped her unceremoniously on the bed.

"There's only one way to keep you quiet," he murmured, as he pulled off her shoes, wrenched off her trousers, flung them on the floor, and climbed on top of her.

Her body fought but welcomed his familiar weight, the exquisite fit of hips against hers, his legs straddling hers, his erection nesting at the juncture of her thighs. His mouth settled on hers with a kind of repressed frustration.

She knew this position; it seemed inevitable that whenever he was near, she couldn't refuse him, no matter what he'd done, no matter what she felt.

Her rebellion felt like an aberration as she delved into the kiss and thrust everything else aside but her pure physical need.

"That's better," he murmured against her lips. "Be safe. Be with me."

Any woman would melt at the tone in his voice.

But she knew she wouldn't be safe, not with his secrets and hidden agenda. She could only be addicted to him, falling for him, and that was infinitely more dangerous for her.

She had to tell him her doubts, even if he could explain them away.

She pulled away from him. "You aren't safe. You had just as much to gain from Baynard's death as Ellicott."

He went utterly still.

"You really think that?"

"It's just as probable," she retorted. "One day you're second-in-command, the next day you're the CEO. *And* you've been looking for Jillian as rabidly as Ellicott. It's just as likely she knows something about you."

"Good God." He rolled over onto his back.

That was it; there was nothing more to say. She started to get out of bed, only to find herself pulled back by the unyielding cage of his arms.

"Not so fast," he whispered in her ear, as he rolled her over. "Don't talk, don't say a word, don't move."

His body was like a stone wall. She didn't dare wrench away from the fury she felt coursing through him.

He held her so tightly she couldn't move. It was a sexless hold, an angry embrace. The silence lengthened and he shifted, winding himself around her more closely.

She shuddered involuntarily and he pulled her in.

"You always cleaned up her messes, didn't you."

She didn't have to answer; he just knew. His body settled against hers again, softening now, enfolding her.

He held her through the night, his bare skin on hers. It was a different connection, a different kind of heat.

She wasn't alone. In that moment, she gave in to their undeniable connection, to the feeling in her heart.

She had to trust that he was everything he said he was, that he wasn't her enemy, that he needed just as urgently to find Jillian for the reasons he said, that Ellicott was responsible for Oliver Baynard's death.

At some point early in the morning, she heard the ring of his cell, his brusque answer, and then felt his mouth hovering over hers as he told her the pilot died.

Every warm thought went out the window, and her body constricted with a will to action.

"You're not leaving," he whispered against her lips. "Not now. Not ever. They'll kill you."

She believed him this time; she believed everything because with him enfolding her, it was impossible not to. Her body told him she was his now, in every possible way.

She dreamed that the pilot was dead; she had to be dreaming.

Reality was the feel of his shaft between her legs. Reality was Jilly getting to London after the crash, the premeditated crash.

In the lush state between satiation and sleep, she *felt* Jilly, she *was* Jilly, shivering in the embassy offices and refusing to answer any questions about where she'd been, how she'd gotten there, how she'd been left without money, a passport, or identification.

What would Jilly do? How would she fake it, fudge it? Justine imagined the application: Jillian Dare. Justine watched in her mind's eye as Jilly started to write her name, pausing, thinking of the ramifications.

She felt Jill's anguish, her weariness, the wheels spinning as she tried to determine what to do, how to get around the situation. . . .

She woke up with a gasp, pushing hard against Rawls's body.

She knew where Jillian could be.

She swallowed hard, willing her body to be still. It was nearly impossible when every impulse compelled her to act. She had to finish cleaning up the mess and get away from Rawls's seductive magnetism. And far, far away from the realization that she might never escape him, and she might not want to. But after this night, if she left him, there was no going back.

It didn't matter—Jilly took precedence.

Don't think about him. Just make certain all that exhausting sex sent him into a deep enough sleep, and then she'd make her move.

Till then she had to quell the urgency because he'd know something was up, that her tacit promises had been steeped in lies, and that she'd always choose her twin over him.

She moved, trying to shrug off his arm and reposition his leg, as if she were turning to get more comfortable.

Time crept. She had to get out before dawn. She moved again, this time successfully shifting his leg from her thigh.

She twisted, slipping out from under his arm.

Bad move. His grip on her arm was like a tourniquet. His voice, deadly cool, came at her like a ghost in the dark.

"You know something, don't you."

"I thought of something," she admitted.

He knew too well. He'd figure it out.

There was no hiding anything from him, especially the expression in her eyes when he snapped on the light.

"I think she impersonated me to get past the embassy requirements. I think she's at my apartment."

"And you didn't consider telling me for one minute." Not a question.

He reached for his cell and flipped it open. "Find out if Justine Durant came through customs anytime in the past three weeks. From London." He closed it with an emphatic snap. "It's time to end this. I want Jillian and I want Ellicott, and I need you: *you* are the plan."

The comment hung in the air as his hot gaze caught hers. A light sparked in his eyes, and she found it impossible to look away.

He snuffed out his desire. His eyes, now cold and assessing, swept over her. "You couldn't look less like Jillian right now."

She was naked, with bed hair and bad breath, feeling as wrinkled and touseled as the sheets.

"I want you in makeup, heels, and accessories. We're going shopping."

"I—"

"*We* are going shopping. I'm not letting you out of my sight. Ellicott's people are on you now, and they'll stop at nothing to find you."

"They don't scare me anymore," Justine shot back. "They could be ghosts, for all I know."

A faint smile rimmed his mouth. "Or you could be—sooner rather than later."

"But obviously not before I lead them—and you—to Jillian." But he knew where Jilly was already, he could easily take his revenge without her.

If only she'd just walked out the door and shut out every last memory of the past three weeks.

"If she's even there," Rawls interrupted her thought like a mind reader.

She hated when he did that.

"Which is why I need you," he said in that cool tone she despised. "Get dressed."

She crossed her arms. "I'm not—"

He shot her an exasperated look, swung out of bed, and began tossing her clothes at her. "You are. I'll dress you if I have to."

It was easier to concentrate on dressing than to think at this point. It was still early, too early to shop; the sun was just rising outside the window.

He took her arm forcefully. She ignored the electric shock of his touch and let him lead her down to the kitchen.

An hour later, she looked much more like Jillian. He'd taken her to Saks. A session at a makeup counter, a pair of platform heels, a big, shiny tote bag, a leather jacket, oversized sunglasses, and she was transformed.

"I hate this," she hissed as they left the store.

"Hate it all you want, but if you hadn't stepped into Jillian's shoes, things could have been very different."

She pressed her lips together. "I don't need you to castigate me for my choices, thank you."

"No, you're not seeing the bigger picture. If you hadn't, Jillian *would* be dead."

She shot him a startled look.

"He'd have hunted her down before she'd ever reached London. She'd never have gotten away. *You* were the complication he hadn't planned. You came on the scene before he'd determined for certain that she'd died in the crash."

"Oh." She'd actually saved Jilly's life?

"You're amply protected, if that makes you feel any better.

They headed east down West Thirty-fourth Street in a crowd of people. As they crossed Sixth Avenue, Rawls hailed a cab and gave the driver Jillian's address.

"She's not there."

"I know. But *they* are."

Justine digested the implications of what he said.

"So you're giving them something to sniff so they can corner their prey?"

"In a manner of speaking." The neutral tone of his voice hadn't changed. She felt a wash of dread. This was the endgame. And for the first time, it had nothing to do with sex, nothing to do with her. She was what he had always meant her to be: the fresh meat to lure Ellicott to a final confrontation.

She had to trust him, but she couldn't imagine how it would end. All she knew was that wherever she was, Jillian was safe.

And she, Justine, was the decoy in the duck pond.

Chapter Fifteen

Jilly is safe, that's all that matters, she reminded herself.

Justine's heart raced as the cab stopped in front of Jillian's apartment building.

Everything was normal from the outside. It was a perfectly beautiful day, cloudless and sun-drenched. Beautiful people walked down Park Avenue with its stream of honking cars. Nothing was out of the ordinary.

"Ready?" He motioned her to go.

Her hands turned to ice.

She hadn't been to Jilly's apartment since she and Rawls had found Zach snooping around.

Opening the door felt like she was opening Pandora's box. She swallowed hard, inserted the key, and pushed. It was dark as a tomb inside. Rawls pushed her aside and entered ahead of her, his flashlight at the ready.

Where was Jilly's night-light?

Justine followed behind him. A moment later, he turned on a table lamp in the living room.

Everything was just as she'd left it. There wasn't even any evidence of Zach's snooping. "So much for anything ending," she muttered.

"Trust me. They're watching us."

"That is *not* reassuring."

On the surface, the apartment seemed unused; Ellicott's people had not been there.

"Aren't we supposed to go find Armageddon?" she asked impatiently.

"Believe me, Armageddon will find us," Rawls said, flashing his light around as he moved toward the bedrooms.

He stopped.

"Shit."

Her heart beat wildly. "What?"

He pointed the light. She didn't have to move to see what he saw: Zach Leshan sprawled on the threshold of Jilly's bedroom. Rawls knelt and touched his neck. "He's dead."

"Her stomach turned.

"Not long. Maybe a day."

"Not today?" Like five minutes before they arrived, she thought. What if the police were on their way, ready to accuse them of murder? Was that Ellicott's plan?

It was just subtle enough. She felt faint.

"No. I'd say yesterday, no later."

"What if I say let's get out of here?"

A different voice answered. "I'd say you're just a minute too late."

Justine whirled at the strange yet familiar voice to see a distinct shadow behind her.

The Principessa?

"Hello, Jillian—or is it Justine? Weren't you clever?"

Justine froze as she caught sight of a pistol. Rawls sent her a cautioning look. "Weren't *you?*" he asked softly.

The Principessa swiped a gloved finger across a nearby table. "You know, Zach's fingerprints are all over this apartment. It wouldn't take much to convince a jury your precious sister had gotten fed up with Zach's demands and decided he knew too many secrets.

"And aren't twins' fingerprints identical? Maybe both sisters conspired to kill poor Zach. Of course, that will all come to light after we take care of you." She turned her impassive gaze on Rawls.

"Although we did think you'd take her to Justine's apartment. Jillian's there, isn't she? You knew this place would be under surveillance. And yet you brought *her* here." Her voice sharpened. "You knew he was waiting for Justine."

"We? He?" Justine didn't recognize her own voice. *This* was Armageddon, this jealous woman who spoke like an automaton and seemed determined to pin Zach's murder on her and Jilly.

"She means Ellicott," Rawls explained. He shifted his attention back to the Principessa "Why? You're not one of his."

The Principessa smirked. "You are both such powerful men. He came to me not long before you saw us dining together. He found some valuable information when he was looking for Jillian. Not only did he discover she was a twin, but he also found there had been another sister given up for adoption. Imagine his surprise when I already knew all about that."

Justine paled.

"And imagine how surprising that no one ever looked for her. They just gave up the baby and left her to whatever fate chose for her. She would be about, oh, my age now. Do you think her twin sisters ever cared? Or her stupid mother ever tried to get her back? Or her abusive drunk of a father even acknowledged she existed?"

Justine swallowed hard. "*I* looked for you," she said, her voice constricted.

The Principessa shot her a look of contempt. "So *you* say. But people will say anything when their lives are at stake. I *know* nothing like that ever happened. So this poor child was raised by a wealthy, alcoholic suburbanite who thought having a baby would solve all her problems. Left the child to a nanny, left her to her own devices, threw money at her to keep her happy, and didn't care when her husband took notice of her adopted daughter.

"So her daughter ran away with an older man when she was just seventeen. He taught her all about pleasuring men and being paid for it. It was kind of like Mother throwing money at me, except my men only demanded a pound of woman-flesh for their money.

"And so here we are, all these years later—and here is my so successful, scientist sister. It is rather ironic that you wound up on your back just like me, and what a trip being Jillian's adversary all this time, knowing that she was my sister and that she never knew, never cared. What a rush to finally have the chance at payback for all those years neither of you tried to find the baby your mother gave away.

"Now I'll make certain no one will ever find *you*. Imagine: Jillian's confidant, best friend, and business partner becomes the instrument by which I take *my* revenge. That dirty, nosy man wanted much too much, snuck around once too often. Death is too good for him. Except it *will* enable me to bury you both so deep in the prison system, you'll never get out. Not on appeal, not on extenuating circumstances, not on your sexual magnetism. Nothing, do you understand me?" Her voice rose. "Nothing!"

She looked at Justine, pale and in shock, and then at Rawls. "You know enough not to try anything. We're surrounded. Ellicott is waiting, Jillian is waiting, *I'm* waiting." She pulled out her cell, punched in a message, waited for a response, and then motioned them to the door. "Zach will be taken care of. Your escorts are waiting."

Four well-dressed but menacing-looking guards suddenly appeared. Two of them stayed behind, while the other two accompanied them to a limousine waiting at the curb. They opened the doors politely and waited. Justine climbed in unsteadily, her whole body bloodless and cold. *The Principessa was her sister?* It was beyond comprehension.

"Any questions?" the Principessa asked politely when they were under way.

Justine found her voice, as rusty as it sounded. "Did you ever try to find us?"

"Why should I have? I was the baby. It was *your* responsibility to find me. To *care* for me. Besides, by the time I was aware that I'd been adopted, I had lots of money to play with, I was spoiled, I had all the men I wanted, and I didn't need you," the Principessa answered carelessly.

"I see," Justine murmured. The baby. As if she'd forgotten the unnamed baby for whom she felt the guilt of having abandoned every day, the baby for whom she *had* vainly searched when she was old enough, only to find it had been a closed adoption and she couldn't access the records.

How could this, this bloodsucker ever think she had forgotten?

"So you see, when I discovered my history, all that enmity I felt for Jillian as a competitor made sense. I wanted revenge. You only cared about saving Jillian; you never tried to find me. That's the end of the story, and for that you, especially you, *and* Jillian, will be punished."

Ellicott had convinced her of that, Justine thought, shaken to the core by the Principessa's vicious desire for revenge. He must have taken her fractured fairy tale and used it as the instrument of his own revenge.

The Principessa was hell-bent though, and nothing would convince her otherwise. The truth meant nothing to her, except for the fact that she had known who her family was all along. The Principessa had nursed her own grudges for years, and Ellicott's desire to eliminate Jillian fit in perfectly.

Rawls hadn't said a word, hadn't looked at her. He never indicated for a moment that the Principessa's story had moved him one way or the other.

But why should he care? A woman had been a means to an end for him, too.

The limo glided through traffic over to the West Side and finally into the parking area of Justine's apartment complex.

The escorts opened the limo door, and Justine looked around as she emerged. Nothing out of place, nothing a novice and naif like her could identify, anyway. These people *were* ghosts. The Principessa seemed so certain of herself. And Rawls wasn't doing anything.

The escorts surrounded them as she teetered on those impossible heels into the lobby: one by her side and one behind Rawls and the Principessa.

Rawls, who easily have could taken the Principessa out in that short walk from the limo to the front door, was unusually quiet.

In the elevator, she sent him a searing look. He raised a brow.

She looked away, angered by the fact he really did know what he was doing. It wasn't just the Principessa.

Justine knew the drill: when the time came, he'd save himself and leave her to the mercy of Ellicott and the Principessa.

The Principessa took out her cell again and tapped a message. She read the reply and looked at Justine. "Uh-oh. The police have been notified that a body has been found in Jillian's apartment."

Her small smile made Justine's blood run cold.

"It's only a matter of time, no more than a day, I'd guess, before they come for you."

The elevator jolted to a stop and the guards moved toward the doors. Rawls's cell phone buzzed, the doors opened, and someone shouted "Drop it!" Rawls shoved Justine to the elevator floor as a shot rang out. Two bodies slumped down beside her.

When she looked up, three strangers had charged the elevator car, grabbed the escorts, and pulled them into the hallway. Rawls was on his knees, examining the Principessa and talking rapid-fire into his cell.

Justine leaped toward the Principessa. Blood was on the floor, on her clothes, on Rawls, on one of the strangers on his cell, barking orders. Rawls held his hand out to Justine.

"Nothing you can do. They'll take care of it."

"They who?" she asked shakily as she got to her feet.

"My people. They'll take care of everything."

The Principessa had said that, too, about Zach. They always had people to take care of everything. "Will she die?"

"Do you care?"

Did she? She was so stunned, she didn't know what she thought. It was her *sister*. She moved like a zombie into the hallway behind Rawls as his people nudged the two now-handcuffed escorts back into the elevator, and one of them took charge of the Principessa.

Rawls nodded, the doors closed, and he flipped his cell to check the missed call. "Shit. Ellicott's on his way back to London. Jillian's not here."

"No." Justine made for her apartment door. "She has to be."

She inserted her key in the lock, her hand shaking. At the same time she knocked and called out.

"Jilly? Are you there? It's me." Her voice wavered. "Jill?" No answer.

She entered the hallway and moved into the living room area. "Jill?" She made her way toward the screen that sectioned off her bed.

"Jillian?"

Please let her be behind the screen please.

No one was there. The apartment felt sapped of life.

She wheeled to find Rawls sitting at the kitchen counter, listening on his cell. "Who does she know in London?"

"Good God, how do I know?"

"We need that damned computer." He punched in a number and spoke briefly to James. "Let's go."

"But . . . the Principessa . . . those men . . ."

"Medevaced from the roof. The others will not be a problem. Ellicott's the problem." He levered himself off the stool. "Let's go."

"But she called the police. She . . . Zach—"

"It's all taken care of."

"Too many damned phantom people taking care of things," Justine muttered, resisting his hand. "And nobody taking care of Jillian."

"We'll take care of Jillian," Rawls said, touching her cold fingers. He met her fraught gaze. "We'll both clean up the mess. I promise."

"How?" Even she could hear how skeptical, how exhausted she sounded. It was all too much.

Zach had been killed because he'd gotten too greedy and he'd gotten in the way, she'd been threatened by her formerly unknown baby sister who had turned out to be a highly sought-after elite whore competing with Jillian for years. And Jillian apparently hadn't used the obvious identity switch to try to get back home.

Jillian was still out there. She could be kidnapped, attacked, murdered, or in jail. And Ellicott was on his way back to London.

She could barely wrap her mind around the idea that the Principessa was her sister, let alone the rest of it all.

"I'm going after Ellicott," Rawls said, his voice hard. He held out his hand again. "I hope you have your passport; you're going with me."

James was waiting with the car. He also had Jillian's computer, and he handed it over to Rawls as Rawls slid into the backseat after Justine. He carried a small duffel bag. They were going straight to the executive jet airport in Connecticut. Rawls logged in to the Internet, and his fingers flew over the keyboard.

"There was no temporary passport issued to a Justine Durant in the past three weeks," Rawls said. "So we have to assume two things: Jillian survived the crash and somehow got to London. How could she have done that if she lost everything when the plane went down? A woman alone, in dire circumstances, easy prey."

He rifled through another half dozen documents. "My sources found no reports of arrests, amnesia, or anyone at the crash site other than the pilot. So if she survived, how did she get to London?"

Justine had sunk into the leather seat, her head lolling against the cushion, too tired to think. "I have no idea."

He went back into the files. "Hold on—this is interesting—Ellicott doesn't have an apartment in London. He rents a suite at a hotel in Cadogan Square, where Jillian usually met him. I wonder . . ."

Justine closed her eyes. Maybe, if she slept, all of this would go away. Zach's death, the Principessa's shocking identity, Jillian's disappearance, all that sex.

Rawls's voice broke into her thoughts. "*If* she got to London, I bet she'd do something to goad Ellicott if she had no other recourse."

"Like I did at the restaurant?" Justine asked flatly. "She'd be crazy; he tried to kill her. He wanted to throttle me. Believe me, she has a strong sense of self-preservation."

"But she's also desperate, and in London, he's well known

enough that it would be much more dangerous for him to try anything there." He grabbed his cell. "I want a minute-to-minute report on Ellicott's movements after he lands. Just text me."

He went back to the computer. "The Principessa fully expected him to meet us at your apartment, which means his trip was spur of the moment."

"Maybe there was a crisis."

"Jillian turning up would constitute a crisis. Only it doesn't explain how she survived the crash or how she got there." He looked up as they turned onto the off-ramp to the airport. "Damn." He jostled Justine's arm. "She knows no one except the men she travels with? No female friends?"

"I don't know," Justine said wearily.

"She slept her way to London?" He kept racing through websites as he spoke.

He *would* think that, Justine thought. She mustered enough energy to say, "Screw you."

"But she was probably pretty beat up and bruised from the accident," Rawls continued. "She wouldn't want to be on scene when the first responders came; she'd be questioned, she'd have to give explanations."

He stopped abruptly as James pulled up to the hangar where the Gilbraltar airbus was prepped and waiting.

"All set, Mr. Rawls," James said before opening the limo doors.

Rawls would never give her an inch of space, Justine thought, when even a rat could see she was still shocked by everything that had happened. She got on the plane first and sank into one of the seats.

"Can I just sleep?"

"You can *just* help me figure out Jillian's movements." He motioned for her to buckle herself in as the plane started its taxi to the runway.

Justine braced herself for liftoff, her hands icy and her whole body stiff with apprehension.

Rawls got back on Jilly's computer the minute they attained altitude.

"Think. Jillian escapes this crash somehow. She's lost everything. She's bruised and maybe injured. She needs not to be seen, doesn't want to be rescued, especially doesn't want to answer questions or have her name dragged into an investigation. How does she do that?"

Justine leaned back and closed her eyes. "She would depend on the kindness of strangers."

"No. They'd bring the authorities into it. She'd have to get some distance from the scene of the accident to get any help where they wouldn't ask about the crash."

He went back into Jillian's files. "Her last trip to London, prior to this, also was with Ellicott. No help there. So Jillian's alone in a strange place after the crash. Everything's gone. Maybe she's injured, but she has to be mobile enough to move."

Justine tried to visualize it: a small plane, not unlike the one they were in, spiraling down, trees breaking the deadly descent? Impact, Jillian unconscious? Or just dazed, confused. Trying to get out, fighting to find the hatch, the smell of gas fogging her every instinct. Tumbling out, falling, tearing her clothes, bruising her arms and legs, hearing shouts, scrambling to find someplace she wouldn't be seen.

Suddenly a lightbulb appeared in Justine's mind.

"I have an idea," she said. "You're right that she'd have gotten as far away from the site as she could before she even asked for help. She'd have said"—*what I would have told them*—"that she'd been attacked, beaten, and robbed and that she'd lost everything. Which would explain it all—the bruises, no money, no ID—and create sympathy so somebody would help her. She wouldn't file a report because she'd have said she's a foreigner, her attackers were long gone, it happened at night, and she couldn't describe them. All she wants to do is get to London.

"But beyond that, Jilly always wears this necklace with a little half-carat diamond. She said it was a gift to herself after her first major modeling assignment."

"Right. A gift from her first paying customer more likely. Good. I like that." He got out his cell and punched in a message.

"She could have bartered that for money back to London."

"Okay, here we go. Jillian *is* in London. Someone treated themselves to a massive shopping spree on Ellicott's no-limit black card: designer clothes, expensive lingerie—sound familiar? A BlackBerry—oh, this is rich—delivered to the hotel. God, no wonder Ellicott bolted."

"How far ahead of us is he?" Justine asked sleepily.

"Three or four hours. He hasn't landed yet."

"So there's time?"

"You think? Oh, hell. James just sent a forward from your cell." He handed her the computer.

Her heart stopped.

On the screen was another Jillian SOS:

Justine time Drayton Hotel.

Chapter Sixteen

"Someone's got to be with her," Rawls said flatly. "Or interrupted her. There would have been more otherwise. Crap." He took back the computer. "And the battery's low. Shit." He logged off and set the laptop aside.

There was nothing more to say. A dozen scenarios raced through Justine's mind to account for the brevity of the message and what might have come next.

She had four more hours to think about it. It was too much time to root through the inexplicable events of the day. So much had changed in the past three weeks.

Even Justine.

She looked over at Rawls, who was deep in thought, staring out the window into the darkness, checking his cell now and again.

Keeping track of Ellicott from twenty thousand feet above, she gathered. *Don't wonder what he's thinking. Don't think about him at all. Don't think, just sleep.*

A driver met them after they cleared customs, and by the time they pulled away, Rawls was already on his cell, barking instructions.

"So what do we do now?" she asked in a muffled voice, not certain she wanted to know.

"We strike. When he least expects it."

"Which means?"

"We go to the hotel."

There was a stubbornness in his tone with which she didn't want to argue. But still, walking into the lion's den? It suddenly struck her what he had planned—*she* was to be the sacrificial lamb.

"I get it. I'm going to *be* Jill again, right?"

"It's the quickest and easiest solution to getting in."

"And, of course, I'm assured of seven layers of protection."

"Absolutely."

"Doing battle with Ellicott's seven layers of impenetrability."

"Not a problem."

"And then it's over."

"I promise."

Such finality struck a note of uncertainty with her. *Over.* She couldn't even contemplate what *over* would feel like. She had been living in another dimension for the past few weeks. And now she was different because of it, and she didn't know how to handle it.

Jillian was bound to be different, too.

The car slid silently through the city, turning onto Sloane Street and up to the arched entryway of the Crayton Hotel.

"Showtime," Rawls murmured. "Leave everything in the car, and just get the room key. I'll do the rest. Come on."

It was an impressive, elegant building, all brick with white stone tiered along the facade.

Rawls had melted into the shadows before she even opened the door. Everything rested in her shaky, ice-cold hands.

Maybe it was better that she went in quickly, before she had time to think, to rationalize, to be afraid.

She stared up at the windows overhead. Somewhere up there was Jillian, and the end of the adventure.

Be Jilly. She squared her shoulders, fluffed her hair, pulled some Jillian arrogance from deep in her gut, and stepped into the hushed atmosphere of the lobby.

The check-in desk was tucked discreetly to one side under a sweeping mahogany staircase. "Mr. Ellicott's room, please."

"I'm sorry," the clerk murmured. "Did we not issue a key several hours ago?"

Think fast. "Indeed you did. But I changed handbags and forgot to take my key."

He nodded and swiped a plastic card, made a note, and then handed her the key. Luckily, he turned his back to her, because she had no idea where the elevators were until she spotted a plaque pointing the way.

I'm never going to be a spy, she thought. *I don't even know Ellicott's room number. I'm going to mess this up big time. I just know someone's watching.*

The elevator doors slid open. Rawls was right there, startling her as he pulled her quickly inside.

"I hope you know the room number."

"I know everything," he muttered. "Calm down. We're not nearly done."

She let out a deep breath. *Oh, we're done.*

The elevator jolted to a stop, and Rawls waited a moment.

"You'll be taking Ellicott on by yourself for the first five minutes. Leave the key in the lock. I'll be right behind you, and my people are right behind me. Nothing will happen other than getting Jillian out of there. Understand?"

She nodded.

"Right there."

"Okay." But it wasn't okay. Ellicott was every bit as ruthless as Rawls, maybe more. If he was there, he wasn't sitting and waiting for *her*; he was probably trying to decide what to do with Jill, knowing there wasn't much time.

She hesitated at the door, then slipped the key into the slot. *What am I going to say? What am I going to do? This is too much. He's dangerous.*

But she didn't know which *he* she meant.

Jilly would do it. Jilly would just sail in and take over. That's what she's like. Justine is a coward and always has been.

Be Jill. She resolutely pushed down the handle and entered the room.

"Well, finally. Justine."

The sound of his voice stunned her for a moment; it was so deep, so British, so laissez-faire. He wasn't even looking at her—he was lounging in a chair, looking out the window.

Now what? She had a small advantage, with his attention diverted out the window. She needed a plan quickly.

There really was only one thing to do.

"Really?" she asked silkily, setting down her bag. "You really think *I'm* Justine."

That caught his attention. He swiveled around abruptly, and for the first time she saw him clearly—the sharp features in his narrow, aristocratic face, thinning gray hair, piercing dark eyes. He was older than she'd originally thought from his photo, but he was everything Jillian had written in her notes, though completely different somehow.

He moved like a panther, bolting from his chair and heading toward her. "My dear, Jillian just punished me by spending tens of thousands of pounds and charging it to me—information you would not have access to."

"My dear Clive"—she hoped Jillian called him by his first name—"you've been with me long enough to know I keep records of everything: likes, dislikes, sexual preferences. Or"—at the flashing fury in his eyes—"maybe you *didn't* know. I have every-thing, even credit card numbers. The no-limits ones especially."

She sashayed around him, looking for clues that Jillian was there.

"So where is Justine?" she asked casually and then called, "Jus-tine?" She spin around to face him. "I'm done with playing cat and mouse, Clive."

"Are you?" He was suddenly beside her, his anger radiating as he searched her every feature, because even though he was cer-tain, there was just that little bit of doubt.

She girded herself. "You owe me money. So just cut the check, tell Justine I'm here, and we'll call it even."

"God, you have balls."

"Haven't I always?" she purred.

There were two doors, one at each end of the large living room. She debated which was the bedroom.

"Justine!" She hoped her tone sounded firm rather than desperate. "You haven't done anything stupid like tying her up or handcuffing her to the bedpost." It was like swatting a lion with a rolled-up newspaper. "Justine?"

"Jilly?" Her voice was faint, coming from the opposite side of the room. Justine wheeled around, nearly knocking Ellicott aside. And there was Jill, at the threshold of the farther room, looking fragile, her arms across her midriff, her face pale, and her eyes huge.

Makeup only slightly concealed the bruises around her eyes and scratches on her cheeks. She'd never looked as good as she did that minute, though, as she came toward Justine. Justine took her hands and murmured, "Fooled them again."

Jillian's eyes slid from Justine's to the bedroom door. And then she blinked once and nodded.

Ellicott was circling around them. "You know, I've never diddled twins before."

"My money," Justine said loudly, taking Jillian's hand.

"No question," Ellicott said, touching her hair. "All your money," he murmured in her ear. "All you have to do is"—he stroked her arm—"what you always do so well." He turned to Jillian. "And all *you* have to do"—he touched her cheek—"is watch." He twisted his fingers in her hair.

He motioned toward the bedroom door. "If you want your money, that is." He looked at Justine. "You remember how good it was."

"Not recently," Justine hissed.

"Then you, my inventive bitch."

"It wasn't me," Jillian murmured.

"Then you're both doomed," Ellicott said dismissively.

Justine looked at Jillian. *We have to take him out.*

Jillian frowned. *There's someone in the bedroom.*

"You know how it works," Ellicott said, grasping Justine's arm and propelling her and Jillian forward, his other hand hard on Jillian's neck. "A threesome would be refreshing. And I'm curious whether twins—"

"Are you?" Justine interrupted forcefully, trying to wrench her arm from his tight hold. "And did you really think I was naive enough to walk in here without a plan?"

"My dear, where money is concerned, you *don't* think. You take. You devour." He kicked open the door. "You will not be missed."

He was speaking to both of them, still uncertain who was who. It was the moment to act, to *do* something.

"I haven't forgotten how you overcharged me for Baynard. You won't see that money again. You owe me for that." He thrust Jillian into the room, and Justine heard Jillian resisting whoever was in there. She immediately dove into action, kicking at Ellicott and twisting away from him.

It was useless.

"Don't worry about her," Ellicott murmured, "she'll be well taken care of."

She wrenched harder at his steel fingers.

"As will you," a new voice interjected. Rawls's voice was ice cold and unexpected, momentarily distracting Ellicott.

Justine didn't think: she took the opening, driving between Ellicott's legs with her foot, taking him by surprise, and toppling him to the floor.

An instant later, a trio of armed men emerged, one from the bedroom, two from the hallway behind Rawls, edging him into the room.

"I'd just as soon get rid of you, too," Ellicott muttered, getting up from the floor. He glanced down at Justine with a look of contempt. "You always were expendable."

He motioned to his men and they each grasped an arm and hoisted Justine to her feet. He gestured them to the couch. "Sit down."

Justine slanted a look at the bedroom door.

"She's among . . . friends, shall we say?" Ellicott said smoothly. "Sit the hell *down*."

Justine sat and glanced at Rawls, but he seemed as stoic and impassive as he had that fraught moment in the elevator days before. She sensed he was waiting; they were all waiting.

"So here we all are," Ellicott said. "Can you imagine? Two beautiful Jillians walking straight into my parlor, knowing what they know. It defies all logic. Can you even tell them apart, Rawls?"

"I can tell them apart," he answered flatly. Justine sent him a skeptical look.

"You know which one is which?"

"I know."

"He knows." Ellicott turned to his guards. "He knows." He looked at Rawls. "What else do you know?"

"I know you have layers of people, and I have layers of people, and it's only a matter of time before one of us runs out of people first. I'm willing to wait it out. Are you?"

Ellicott's face contorted. "You son of a bitch. Why am I wasting time when I've got the manpower, I've got the weapons, I've got the twins. And I've got you, too."

"And *I've* got you." Jillian's voice came from behind Ellicott as she dove out the bedroom door and slammed into him, knocking him off-balance. He went down, pulling Jillian with him. Simultaneously, Rawls wheeled around at the guards, kneeing one in the groin and thrusting the heel of his hand hard against the second guard's chin and then his throat.

They both went down, taking Rawls along as Justine grabbed Jillian's hand and pulled her to the door, Ellicott and the bedroom guard only steps behind them.

Justine opened the door just as Ellicott grabbed Jillian by the arm. Justine grabbed Jilly tight before Ellicott could wrench her away.

At that moment, Rawls tackled Ellicott, pushing Jillian out of the way. He didn't have to urge them to run. They tumbled over Ellicott's prone body and out the door.

They ran down the hallway, frantically punching the elevator button, looking for a stairwell—anything—as pounding footsteps followed behind them until they were virtually backed up against a wall.

Two more menacing men and nowhere to go.

Justine looked at Jillian, and Jillian shrugged. The men stopped short and one held up his hands. "We need to get you out of here."

"No, you don't," Justine retorted brashly. "Who the hell are you?"

"Gilbraltar."

"Sure. How do we know that? I don't believe you."

"Don't move."

They all froze.

"Okay, I believe you," Justine muttered as Ellicott appeared down the hall, a gun in his hand, inching his way toward them.

There was nowhere for anyone to go. Ellicott was dead serious. He didn't even care that it all could become public. Two competitors' sweepers on the scene meant he could make a plausible argument for self-defense, and he was ripe to kill.

Justine reached for Jillian's hand, reading the desperation in her eyes.

Do something.

Oh, yeah, that was a plan, with the barrel of a 9 mm pistol trained on them.

Ellicott motioned to Jillian and Justine. "I want them. *Now.*"

Justine moved in front of Jillian, taking her hand, and pulling her so she was slightly behind her.

"Come to me, my pretties." He held Justine's eyes as she edged around the Gilbraltar guard, looking for that opening, that nanosecond when she could attack Ellicott before he attacked them.

Where was Rawls? She couldn't wait for him; she had to *do* something—anything—to save them, to save Jillian. She couldn't think of anything, though, except to run. She dropped Jilly's hand abruptly and exploded toward Ellicott, hitting him full force.

The gun went off and they both fell, the guards right there, lifting off Justine and pinning Ellicott's arms before he could take another shot.

Justine gathered a sobbing Jillian into her arms as they backed away from the scene. The guard who seemed to be in charge directed them down the hallway to the elevator and the stairwell beyond.

"It's not over," he told them. "We need to go as quietly as we can out the back door."

They slinked down the dim staircase. Jillian hung on to the banister for dear life, Justine behind her, pushing her on.

A door above them opened and a shot rang out.

Rawls! There was no way to know where he was, if he was—

"Let's go, let's go." The sweeper pushed them as they scrambled down the steps and out into a service hall at the back of the hotel. He urged them down the hallway, down another flight of steps, and out the rear entrance.

A car waited. There was always a car waiting, Justine thought as she pushed Jillian into the backseat and collapsed beside her. A moment later, they were clear of the hotel and, it occurred to Justine, in the hands of a stranger whose name and allegiance they didn't know.

Oh, God, what have I done?

Justine swallowed hard and squeezed Jillian's hand. "That was amazingly low-tech," she commented drily to the guard. "Who are you? I want to see some ID."

She sounded as authoritative as a mouse. She wouldn't even know what kind of ID she was looking at.

She caught her breath and remembered Rawls. Up in that hotel suite, maybe unconscious, maybe . . .

Don't think that. Don't think.

"Here you go." Their protector handed over a card.

It told her nothing. A Guardian sweeper could have gotten hold of a Gilbraltar ID card easily enough.

"Where are we going?" she said, handing it back.

"To another hotel, miss, a safe place. Mr. Rawls took care of everything. You'll stay until we arrange a passport for Miss Jillian. And then you'll go home."

He took care of everything. Rawls was good at doing that.

But going home sounded so final.

What was home—for her or for Jill? Jillian didn't know a thing about Zach's death or the Principessa's secret, or all the things Justine had done in Jillian's name.

Rawls couldn't take care of *those* things.

It couldn't end well. She wished it wouldn't end at all.

Justine and Jillian were sequestered in a one-bedroom suite at a luxury hotel in Mayfair. Jillian's purchases on Ellicott's card were forwarded to the hotel, and they were provided with everything else they needed through an intermediary assistant who also was working with the embassy to procure Jillian a temporary passport.

They didn't talk much. It was as if Jillian didn't even want to know what happened. Maybe it was too soon. She was tired, bruised, waif thin, and still shaking.

Rawls visited the next day, brusque and aloof. He wasted no time getting to the point.

He turned to Jillian. "I need you to confirm what we think happened. That is, that Ellicott and Oliver Baynard had a dinner meeting two nights before his death. You were the dessert. Ellicott didn't close the deal, so he engineered Baynard's death and wrote it off as the cost of doing business."

Jillian sent a glance toward Justine. Justine nodded. It was better to just tell now than to drag things out any further. They were perhaps another day away from going home, and as far as Justine was concerned, the sooner Rawls left them the better.

She didn't need Rawls around when she knew she'd never see him again.

"I can link Ellicott to Baynard's death," Jillian said. "The so-called *witness* who CNN interviewed at the scene was actually Ellicott's private pilot and all-around go-to guy. I happened to see the news report. He made it back to Paris in time to fly us to England, and I made the mistake of reacting when I saw him. So Ellicott fucked me across the English Channel before he tried to kill me."

Her voice broke slightly as she said the words. "Stupid. I mean, you try to have some kind of personal relationship with these guys, some kind of trust. You don't think they're cold-blooded snakes."

"They are," Rawls said flatly.

"Are *you*?" Justine asked without thinking.

"Do you doubt it?"

"You'd resort to murder to eliminate a competitor," Jillian said.

He gave her a long, measured look. "Am I a murderer? No. Do I believe in justice and balancing the scales? Absolutely."

He looked at Justine. She looked just like Jillian. In that moment, he had the faintest doubt that they were who they claimed. But Justine had changed from her Jillian clothes, and Jillian was moving around restively, so very unlike Justine's deliberate movements. The puzzle snapped back into place.

He *could* tell them apart.

"And what constitutes justice for Mr. Ellicott?" Jillian asked.

"You tell me. What is justice for a man who's killed twice, attempted murder twice, and stalked with intent to kill—"

"Twice?" Jillian interrupted him.

Justine sank back on the sofa next to Jill and sent a despairing look at Rawls. She hadn't told Jill yet. He didn't move to help her, so Justine took her sister's hands.

"What?" Jillian sounded at the end of her rope.

"Zach. Zach is dead." *And God almighty*, she'd nearly forgotten that the Principessa had called the police. There could be a warrant out for their arrest in the States by now.

Jillian caught her breath. "Zach?" she whispered. "How? When?"

"Your apartment. Ellicott intended to frame us." Justine couldn't mention the Principessa, not when she hadn't told Jill about their relationship to her. Jillian wrenched her hands away from Justine.

"No . . . *no!*" Jillian shook her head violently. "Not Zach." She bolted from the living room, tears streaming.

Justine almost followed her and then sank back on the sofa, looking as if she wanted to say something.

She stared at Rawls for a moment, opened her mouth to speak, and then stopped.

"You didn't tell her about the Principessa either," he guessed.

"Not yet," she whispered reluctantly. "It seemed like too much. It's barely been a day." She stood up. "I have to——"

"You have to tell her."

"I have to *comfort* her. Stay or go——whatever."

She walked away and disappeared into the bedroom.

Rawls could hear her soft murmuring, and then the Principessa's name and Jillian's howl of denial. Then he heard the sound of the shower running, which conjured up other times, other places, things that weren't appropriate to think about as he eavesdropped on Jillian grieving over that piece of garbage Zach Leshan.

Everything, otherwise, was taken care of. He would take out Ellicott soon. There was no need for him to stay there any longer, but he didn't move. Maybe he wanted to know the end of the story, maybe he just didn't want to think about tomorrow and assuming the day-to-day duties at Gibraltar, maybe he was just so damned tired.

And then, as time stretched out, as Justine remained sequestered with Jillian, he had no choice: there was nothing he could do for her here.

It really was time to let go.

Rawls was gone. For a long moment, Justine just stood there, stunned that he hadn't stayed.

But then, she had run out on him many times.

"Justine?" Jillian was calling her, depending on her, still mourning that scum.

Justine sat down at the foot of the bed.

"We have to talk. We have decisions to make before we get home."

"About what? Zach is dead, that bitch Principessa is allegedly related to us——I will never, *ever* acknowledge her as my sister. But it's worse than that." Jillian lifted her sweater. "Look at me." She pulled down her jeans just to reveal a swath of cuts, bruises, and a very bad burn. "*Look at* me——I can't go back——it's over for me."

"It's over anyway the minute we get home if the police have linked us to Zach's death," Justine pointed out.

Jillian sank against the pillow. "Oh, God."

"I think Ellicott paid Zach to get hold of your computer."

"Did he?"

"Rawls has it."

Jillian groaned. "That's even worse."

"And he's gone."

"Good."

"Were you pretending not to know him?" Justine guessed.

"Kind of," Jillian said in a thin voice. "I think I dated him once, maybe." Meaning slept with him, Justine thought, filing that revelation instantly under *never needed to know*. "A year or two ago, maybe. I don't remember. It's probably in my files."

"I bet not anymore," Justine muttered.

"Oh, God. Do you know, do you have any idea what was in those files?"

"A vague idea," Justine murmured.

But Jillian didn't hear her. "How could you? How could you have let him—"

"How could I not?" Justine interrupted. "On the other hand, your late, lamented Zach could have gotten into them anytime you were on an extended trip, since you foolishly gave him a key to your place. How would you know if he were snooping?"

Jillian waved her question away. "That's not important now. He's gone. Anyway, this isn't a *total* catastrophe. I didn't keep everything on the laptop. You'll see when we get back home."

"Jilly, the police are probably swarming all over your apartment. There's no guarantee that Rawls's people took care of *every*thing."

"Except, those people *do* take care of those kinds of things. They're very good at what they do. But they can't change the fact that I can't be what I was anymore," Jillian said with a tremor in her voice. "Those bruises, that burn—they're not going to heal in any good way after a month of neglect. The men I deal with are buying perfection, among other things, but"—she looked at

Justine through hooded eyes—"I expect you know that already."

"That's why Ellicott didn't come after you, after the plane went down." There was a good example of less was more, but it didn't fool Jillian.

"I get that you walked in my shoes. You went to the Crystal Ball."

Time to bare her soul. "Among other dates."

Jillian bit her lip. "I hope you did me proud."

"I did you well enough so that Ellicott thought you were still alive. And it's Rawls's theory that my doing so kept *you* alive. Ellicott couldn't be certain I wasn't you."

Jillian digested it for a minute, thought it through, and then nodded.

"Fine. You can tell me the whole convoluted story some other time. My immediate problem is more urgent. Like how I'm going to go on from here."

"*We*," Justine amended. "How *we're* going to go on from here. First we have to get back home. And then we can deal with everything else."

Chapter Seventeen

They were able to leave two days later. During that time they dealt only with the assistant; Rawls did not return. The assistant took care of recording Jillian's testimony and then informed them that Mr. Rawls would be remaining in London for the foreseeable future. They would be traveling back to the States on a commercial airline, business class.

The whole adventure was over, and now that she was not operating on sexual tension and fear, Justine felt numb. No more private jets. No more hiding. No more sex. No more anything.

What now?

It was time for practicalities: Jillian's future, the possibility that Zach's death had not been resolved, and Justine finally severing ties with the employer she'd left in limbo.

They seemed such minor things in comparison to sex and death.

"I can't go back to my apartment—not yet," Jillian told her when they were passing through customs at JFK. "I have to think. I can't think there."

"So we'll go to my place to think."

"And sleep. Maybe I can sleep now."

They finished at customs and walked through the arrivals terminal. To Justine's shock, James was waiting to drive them back to Manhattan. "Mr. Rawls's directions, miss," he assured her when Justine questioned him.

Who was she to quibble with taking advantage of the last of her companion perks?

———

Her apartment felt strange, even though she'd been there less than a week before.

Everything was different. Justine felt different, and Jillian *looked* different.

"We'll talk in the morning," Jillian promised, taking the bed while Justine settled on the sofa, claiming she couldn't sleep yet.

Justine turned on the TV, tossed and turned, and couldn't get any of what had happened, what she'd done, out of her mind—or come to terms with the fact that it was over.

Jillian was safe. It was time to think about the future rather than gnaw on the past. That had been a dream, a fantasy. But now what?

The first thing was Zach's death. If they were in any way considered involved, it would end any future plans.

But they would have been arrested by now if there had been any suspicion of them.

Assume it had been taken care of.

The second was Justine's job. She had to smooth things over with her now former employer, try to negotiate some kind of severance and a recommendation.

Third, she had to find out what Jillian's concerns were, and hope that she'd give up *that* life. Jilly had money—from what Justine had seen in her account books—but she'd never have *enough* money to fill that empty void inside her, and that was a place Justine couldn't go.

One of many places she now couldn't go.

And her fourth task: forget everything and *everyone* else.

Jillian looked better in the morning, and apparently she'd made some decisions.

"I need to go back to my apartment. I need to get some things. Then I want to rent it out. I can't possibly live there right now, with Zach hanging over me there. It's bad karma."

"Then we'll do that," Justine said instantly. "Whatever makes you comfortable."

"Nothing makes me comfortable right now. I have no idea what is going to happen in the next five minutes."

"Okay, then let's grab a cab crosstown and see what we find."

Twenty minutes later, after inching along in rush-hour traffic, they were within walking distance of Jillian's apartment and paid the cabbie.

"Okay. Here we go," Justine murmured.

They warily entered the lobby to find it quiet and empty.

The doorman was taken aback by the sight of them. "Ms. Jillian?"

"Hello, Charles. This is my twin sister, Justine. I have a strange question for you. Did someone call the police to my apartment anytime in the past week?"

"Police? No. There's been no police here at all." He looked at her oddly.

"The police weren't here?"

"No."

"At all?"

"No."

Jillian couldn't push it any further. She looked at Justine, thanked Charles, and headed toward the elevator.

"This is strange," Justine said, feeling as if this were her own personal groundhog day. Jillian slowly opened the door and entered the apartment first.

Jillian took a deep breath, and Justine followed her. Jillian flicked on the living room lamp and turned on every other light in the apartment as they frantically went from living room to kitchen to the guest room to Jillian's room. They didn't find a scrap of evidence that someone had been killed.

"Omigod," Justine breathed. Rawls. Like it never happened.

No witnesses, no disruptions, no authorities, no questions.

"Where did you find him?" Jillian asked.

"Rawls found him sprawled across the threshold of your bedroom."

Jillian stared at the spot then started frantically going through her bedroom closet looking for something, and when she didn't find it, she whirled on her heel and strode into the kitchen.

"I can't live here anymore. I can't do business anymore. I have to radically change my life."

"Me, too," Justine murmured, following Jillian toward the kitchen. "What are you doing?"

"Plan B." Jilly wrenched open the freezer door and removed two ice trays. She turned to Justine. "The one where everything goes to hell. Like right now. My checkbooks are gone. Someone *stole* my checkbooks. I told you I kept them separate, right? So I can't access any of my accounts. If there's anything even in them anymore."

"What?"

Jillian went on. "But I digress. The point is, remember that little diamond I always wore? It saved me after the crash." She removed a dish from the cabinet. "And these"—she twisted one tray and turned it onto the dish—"will bankroll me now."

The cubes fell and in the reflection of the overhead light, Justine saw sparkles within that were *not* ice crystals.

"Dear God, are those diamonds? You froze diamonds?"

"Those are diamonds. And tell me, smart-ass, where would *you* hide them?"

"No one ever gave *me* diamonds," Justine muttered.

"I think I have some plastic bags and a tote." She started searching the cabinet and found some Ziploc bags in which to dump the cubes. "Everything else personal goes. I don't want any of it. Sell it, donate it, toss it, I don't care." She sounded frenetic now, rummaging in her closets, pulling out clothes, and dropping them on the floor. "And rent the damn place out."

"You're leaving *me* with all this?"

"We'll talk about it later."

They'd talk about it *never*, Justine realized as she rode back to her apartment and Jillian went to the bank.

Justine knew that Jillian *did* want her things, just not right now. And so her responsible twin would make certain everything she wanted or needed would somehow be preserved, and her apartment available whenever she *did* want to return.

Justine felt exhausted by Jillian's needs. She had enough of Jillian's needs. What about *her* needs?

No, better not delve into her needs. She had suppressed them, and she refused to acknowledge the little nub of erotic need that now throbbed incessantly.

Don't think about it.

Back in her apartment, she slumped on the couch. From where she lay she could see her phone, the blink of a voice mail beckoning her. *Best ignore that, too.*

She was so sapped, she didn't move a muscle until Jillian returned.

"Not completely wiped out," Jillian said, her tone neutral, as she entered the apartment. "A couple of accounts are still intact. Maybe he thought taking it all would raise suspicions. The withdrawals were dated after the crash, of course. Wasn't Zach the shitty little bastard? It was always money with him. He knew what kind of money I was putting away." She dropped onto the sofa beside Justine. "I'm going to get it back. I'm getting a lawyer, and I'm getting it back."

"That bad?" Justine interrupted her.

"It's bad enough. My only consolation is that he can't spend my money in hell." Jillian jumped up again and started pacing. "The son of a bitch bastard. And I *trusted* him."

Her futile rage threw a pall over everything; Justine had a vague idea how much money Jill was talking about. *A couple of accounts intact* was meaningless to her—they could have contained a thousand dollars or a hundred thousand. But Jillian had squirreled away millions. She could live off the interest on those accounts until she was eighty. Jillian couldn't recoup what she'd lost in a lifetime. All she had left were diamonds, dust, and an uncertain future.

"Hey," Jillian called to her the next morning as she was dressing, "I have a great idea."

"You couldn't possibly," Justine muttered as she replenished her coffee.

"We could start our own escort business."

Justine blinked. Someone knocked on the door, which saved her from responding to Jill. Justine went to the door.

The super stood in the hall, carrying a large box. "For you, Miss Durant."

She motioned him in, and he carried it to one of the bar stools. She rummaged in her purse for a tip, and he left.

Jillian came into the living room. "What's this?"

"We'll find out." Justine slashed the tape with a knife, opened the box, and peered in. Her heart fell as she removed the contents. "It's our computers, Jillian. Our cells. Everything."

She handed Jill her laptop.

"Any love letters?" Jillian asked lightly.

"No," she said, not examining the comment too closely. "It's better that way." Jill didn't even hear her because she was powering up her laptop.

"Hey, look at this," Jillian called, her tone bewildered.

Justine peered over her shoulder. "Zach's obituary?"

"First thing that came up when I booted up."

"Zach Leshan," Justine read, "died suddenly at his home on Central Park West of an aneurysm. Vice president, Account Affairs, Apple Agency. . . . Oh, my god. It's all so neat and clean; everything is perfectly accounted for."

"Except my money," Jillian muttered.

What wasn't accounted for, Justine thought, were all the nights Jilly had missed, the dates she'd never have, the men she'd never sleep with, the gifts she'd never receive, while her coveted "Plan B" diamonds sat in a dish on the counter, defrosting.

Who was Jillian, really? The sex goddess or the scarred beauty raging around the apartment?

And who was *Justine* if she was so upset over the differences between who she had been with Rawls and who she became in the aftermath?

Don't go there.

Nonetheless, curling in the back of her mind was the memory of the brownstone. It was the one place she was certain she could find him, and it took all her willpower not to wander by in the days after their return. It was enough to know it was there, that he might be there, even though she'd been told he would not be in New York anytime soon.

"We really have to think about what comes next," Jillian said after a couple more days.

"There is no *next*," Justine said wearily. "I don't even have a job."

She'd spent the whole morning with Human Resources at the university, trying to explain the extenuating circumstances that precipitated her month-long leave of absence. At least she'd negotiated a severance package that included unused vacation pay, two weeks' salary, pension rights, and a glowing letter of recommendation.

"I'm thinking I should pursue that escort service idea," Jillian said. It was the fastest way for Jilly to recoup her money, Justine thought.

"I mean," Jillian went on, "didn't you feel like a kid in a candy store? All those men?"

"No."

"Liar."

Justine didn't answer. She didn't want to answer. She just wanted answers to her own questions.

She took herself uptown the next day to get her answer. She walked down the long block from Broadway to the brownstone, prolonging the moment of truth.

And the truth was mind-numbing. The building was empty, everything closed up tight, and a FOR SALE sign on the front window.

The end.

Justine rented out Jillian's apartment on a short-term lease relatively quickly. She thought about selling hers, but she didn't have the patience to wade through the twists and turns of a co-op sale. Where to go and what to do next were the topics of discussion over the past week, when Jill wasn't railing about Zach.

"Why don't you want to set up a business with me?" Jillian asked as she typed on her laptop. "You enjoyed taking my place, I know you did."

"I did *not* enjoy it."

But Jillian knew better. She knew about the perks when you liked the client you were with. She knew about grateful clients. She knew the sex could become something deeper, something to guard your heart from if you were smart. And Jilly knew her twin hadn't been *smart* at all.

"You enjoyed Rawls for sure."

"He enjoyed me," Justine snapped under her breath.

"You have to admit the money's great," Jillian coaxed. "I need to get back my money, you do understand that. And I'll never feel secure unless—" She switched tactics. "We don't have to stay in Manhattan."

Justine shook her head. "I'm going back to the lab. I *understand* the lab. I don't understand the guy who'd pay that kind of money for a night of fabricated sexual adoration from a stranger."

"But what about Rawls? Nothing was fabricated between you two."

"I don't want to talk about him."

"I looked him up in my files."

"He was that forgettable, obviously."

Jillian ignored the brush-off and clicked into her files. "It was two years ago. Ellicott gave me to him. He really didn't want to but he couldn't refuse."

"Why would he?"

Jillian grunted. "Want to read what I wrote?"

"*No.*"

"*I'll* read what I wrote, then. *Fat cat, yummy sausage, luscious body, great stamina, cool, contained, focused—and not really interested.* Does that describe your sex with him?"

"It describes *your* sex with him," Justine retorted.

"You get addicted to it," Jillian said with a touch of longing in her tone.

Don't give in to it, not the memory of it, not even a passing thought of it. Because if she did, she'd have to acknowledge that she could easily be naked with über-powerful men for the perks and the money she'd commanded in Jilly's stead.

Jillian was right: she could become addicted to it. She *had* become addicted to it.

Stop it!

She needed to save Jillian again. She had to get Jillian out of town, get both of them away from the lure of her past life and start something fresh.

She'd call it rest and rehab, just for a couple of weeks. That'd be easier to sell to Jillian than the idea of relocating altogether.

She only had to notify her super that she'd be away for a while. She could pay bills online. The new tenants in Jillian's apartment had moved in already. Everything was taken care of.

Justine was always taking care of Jilly, cleaning up her messes, reassuring her while she rested and recuperated from *her* ordeal.

It was nice work for Jilly—on her back with no responsibility to please anyone but herself. And she now had the time and those blasted diamonds to fund any kind of life she wanted.

Why did she, *Justine,* always have to do the rescuing?

Maybe it was time for her to think about herself.

Would she relocate? *Where* would she relocate?

Wherever there was a decent job. A decent blow job?

Oh, God—she'd get *far* away from that. Go someplace new and different, she'd make this rest and rehab trip a way to scope out her next step. Maybe she'd go to Maine, as far north as she could go without hitting the Canadian border, a small town on a lake where she could put up her feet, regroup, and reinvent. Especially reinvent.

And *forget*—the most important thing of all.

Justine finally convinced Jillian that a trip up to Maine would revitalize them both and would give Jillian a chance to come to terms with her losses and figure out her next moves.

"I know what I'm doing next," Jillian had said. "Forget about

Zach, I'm going back to my apartment after that lease is up and I'm going to start catering to clients who want companions with imperfections. Sometimes," she added dreamily, "they pay more."

That was a goal and a goad if ever Justine heard one. She didn't respond, she just turned up the radio and tuned her out as they drove.

Jillian changed the station to a national all-news station just at the tail end of a story. ". . . Ellicott, dead at age fifty-six," the reporter announced.

Justine nearly swerved off the road. *"What?"* She pulled onto the shoulder while Jillian surfed wildly for a more detailed report.

"Clive Ellicott, CEO of the London risk management firm Guardian Group, was killed in a plane crash last night as he was returning to England from a business trip in France. First reports suggest the plane lost power over the Channel and dove into the water before more than a distress signal could be sent—"

"Oh, my God," Jillian whispered. "Ellicott is dead?"

It was the first thing that made sense to Justine in the past month. It was Rawls's kind of retribution—subtle, deserved, unquestionable, and *final*.

No witnesses, no disruptions, no authorities, no questions.

"The scales are balanced," she murmured. "Justice done." Rawls's justice: everything tied up in blue ribbons, leaving her in knots.

Justine had rented a cabin in the woods in a small lake town in Maine. It had some antiques shops, a church, a couple of convenience stores, and was within reasonable driving distance to Portland.

"Love those off-season rentals," Jillian murmured as they rounded a long curve and drove into town, but Justine could tell she was impatient already. Maine was far away from clubs, nightlife, crowds, excitement—men—and the potential for sex.

Being corralled in a small space really didn't appeal to Jillian, so the fact that the cabin was more spacious than they anticipated was a bonus. There was a large bedroom with two double beds, a good-size kitchen, and a stove-heated living room. There was a fantastic lake view from the deck, and it was within walking distance to town.

"Can we do take-out?" Jillian asked fretfully.

"Can we just relax for five minutes before you start getting antsy?" Justine asked irritably, a parking in a space near one of the convenience stores on Main Street. "Let's just walk around a bit and get some supplies."

"This is *not* my scene," Jillian groused under her breath.

"There's a news flash. Come on."

Main Street ran parallel to the town's ten-mile stretch of lake. There was a gas station and a nice assortment of stores and homes, along with the post office, the town hall, and two restaurants.

There were lots of stares as she and Jillian entered the convenience store and picked through the limited stock for coffee, milk, bread, butter, some cold cuts, and assorted other necessities.

"I guess they don't have a lot of twins up here," Jillian murmured, setting an armload of groceries down on the checkout counter.

"Shh," Justine whispered. She picked up a couple of local papers and added them to the pile as the clerk ran their items through the scanner.

"Okay, that was an enlightening country experience," Jillian announced when outside.

"It's enlightening how irritating you can be," Justine said sharply. "It's a goddamned vacation."

"Not when you think about where my clients have taken me. This is—"

"Rustic," Justine said. "Simple. Plain. And comfortable."

"Ellicott's dead. I can take back my life," Jillian said.

Justine took a deep breath. She didn't want her sister back in that life. Jillian had enough resources to make a *new* life.

Except she didn't want to.

As they sat on the porch after dinner, looking out at the water, Jillian made it clear just how much she didn't want to. "I want to go back home. I want sex. I want everything that goes with it—"

"You want the money," Justine interrupted. "That's all this is about. Even if that money hadn't been stolen, you'd still want the money."

Jillian looked away. "Okay. I want the money. There's never enough money. Our life with Mom and Dad? That's still a knife in my back. I never feel like I'm out from under it, and you know what? Zach knew about that, and he *still* stole from me. So this is the only way—the fastest, easiest, most enjoyable way—I know to get back that money."

"And when you can't anymore? What then?"

Jillian didn't answer for a long time. "I don't know," she said finally. "I never think that far ahead."

The words chilled Justine. She knew she couldn't reach her twin. Jillian would go back to Manhattan, go back to her apartment, rifle her phone book, and find the action she sought. And she wouldn't think further ahead than that.

Ever. Even if she were dying, which, on some level, she already was.

And Justine just couldn't save her from herself.

On their fourth day of vacation, after they had gone to an art show and a country fair, had kayaked on the lake, and heard a visiting band at a coffeehouse, Jillian was obviously still extremely restless. And she made certain Justine knew it.

Jilly hated the quiet; she didn't want to think, she didn't want to read the local papers, as Justine was doing, and she wanted money *now*.

She hated the fact that it was the same routine every morning: drink coffee, eat toast and eggs; sit on the porch; read the papers; stare at the lake.

Jilly sat on the porch with her coffee that morning and started making lists of things to do, people to contact, and more subtle ways to advertise her services.

"I hate it here. Let's go home."

"Another couple of days. Please, Jill."

"You miss it, too," Jillian jabbed.

Justine raised her eyebrows.

"We have to talk about it *sometime*," Jillian added. "That *being me* thing."

"Maybe *you* should try being *me*," Justine retorted.

"I'm *so* being you right now. Country girl steeped in flora, fauna, lakes, and locals."

"Nothing to talk about then."

Jillian bent her head over her list again. "What are we doing today?"

"Antiques show in Portland."

"Thank God. A city. Stores. Makeup counters. Shoes. Crowds. People. Yes!" She jumped up. "When do we leave? Say now!"

Justine resignedly set aside the paper. "Fine."

In an instant, Jillian was in the bedroom, changing and brushing her hair.

Justine moved more slowly, just grabbing her shoulder bag and her keys before she followed Jillian out the door.

"Uh-oh." Jill, muttering under her breath, had stopped short. Justine pivoted from locking up to see a black SUV nosing its way down the narrow, dirt driveway.

It stopped just feet away from them, the door opened, and Justine's breath caught as Doug Rawls stepped out. Doug Rawls, in a blue dress shirt, his sleeves rolled up, jeans, and a multipocketed suede vest.

Jillian looked at Justine, and Justine knew just what her sister was thinking.

Don't say a word. Let him sink himself.

"Did you really think I couldn't find you?" he asked.

"You said you could tell us apart," Jillian reminded him.

"I can."

Justine went cold. *Could he, really?*

"So who's who?" Justine challenged.

"You're Justine," he said firmly, without a pause or a comma.

"You sure?" Jill chimed in.

"I'd bet my life on it."

Jilly's brows went up. "You're wrong. *I'm* Justine."

"No," Rawls said firmly. "You're Jillian, and you can just take the car keys and go." He removed them from Justine's shaking hands and gave them to Jillian. "Go ahead."

"She won't be back," he said, as they watched Jillian maneuver the rental car around his SUV. "She's going straight back to Manhattan."

"Straight back to her own special hell, you mean," Justine muttered, mostly to herself.

"Maybe it's heaven, for her."

He was too perceptive. "And what's heaven for you?" she asked and then wished she hadn't.

She started for the path that led to the lake before he could answer.

"Not going to invite me in?"

"No. But sitting by the lake, talking to an acquaintance is something I can do."

"You're not going to get naked, you mean."

"Nope. Been there, done that. It's too emotionally draining. Plus, the weather is perfect. I love it here."

"Not too quiet?"

"Not quiet enough right now."

He ignored that. "What happens next?" he asked as she settled herself on top of a picnic table close to the shore.

"Nothing. Nothing has to happen."

"Oh, I think something has to happen. Something just changed."

She whipped around to look at his face, his startling blue gaze.

"Nothing can be the same," he added for good measure.

"I wish you hadn't come."

"That's a lie. Do you really want to go there?"

She stared straight ahead and didn't answer. He knew everything anyway. He knew how she felt, what she wanted, and what she needed. He knew what she was thinking, how she wanted to resist, and why she wouldn't.

Whatever was between them was just as strong in this small

lakeside town in Maine as it had been in elegant, A-list hotels in New York and London.

Oh, God. Forget London.

She bit her lip. She had nothing to say that wouldn't sound naive or ridiculous or give her away.

She ought to be channeling Jillian. Jilly would know what to say and how to say it. Jilly would've had him naked on the kitchen floor by now, nestled deep between her legs, reaching further still for that spiraling pleasure that—

She shook her head to clear it of all the sex-fogged memories.

"What do you want?" she finally asked.

He watched her—every reaction, every nuance of expression in her eyes, her face—picking his way carefully through the mine-field of her warring emotions.

"You," he said. "In London. Naked. With me."

She drew in a deep, shaking breath. "You see? That's the thing. Being naked, it gets in the way. It feeds everything and nothing. And then you're left with memories you can't satisfy and surely can't handle. Or at least I can't. So thank you, but no. I'm not doing that again."

He hoisted himself up next to her. "Sure you are."

She raised her eyebrow.

"This," he said, "is how I know you're Justine. Because in your eyes, and in your heart, you're hungry. But you're not voracious, you're not greedy. You don't have the eyes or the soul of a preda-tor. Not like Jillian. Jillian gnaws the meat right down to the bone and tosses it away. You want the banquet, the feast. You want me. Come to London with me."

She stared at him, surprised. It would be so easy to say yes. But she wouldn't be his companion in residence.

She'd done that already.

He leaned into her. The sheer physicality of him so close to her made her hot with lust. The body didn't forget. The heart always remembered. And the mind . . .

It could, almost at will, re-create the explosive pleasure until the memory petered into nothingness.

How could she stand to relive all that again and wind up with nothing in the end?

"I don't want a blow-up doll," he added very quietly, sliding off the table. "And I don't want a paid companion."

She looked away. Guys like him took what they were offered, wherever, whenever, and if he thought he'd convince her otherwise, he was crazy.

And it didn't erase the memories, nor cancel out everything she had done.

He moved closer. "I'm not going to touch you."

He didn't have to. She remembered his touch; it was imprinted on her memory.

He nudged closer still. "Or kiss you."

Instantly she thought of semisweet chocolate—when it melted in your mouth, the heart remembered its mind-altering sweetness, forgetting its bitterness.

He came close enough to touch, to kiss, to inhale.

"Come with me."

She shook her head. He could ask any woman in the world to be his sex toy. That was all he wanted; it was no different than being a companion. He wanted the comfort of someone he was familiar with, someone he knew to be sexual, someone with whom he would always be successful.

"Why?" she asked finally. "It doesn't have to be me. It can be any willing body. Why me?"

He held her gaze for a long moment and then suddenly stabbed his hand in her hair and twisted her head back slightly.

"Because, damn it," he fought not to kiss her, "because"—he bit her lower lip with a kind of suppressed violence—"this has to be about more"—his mouth crashed down on hers, and she tasted chocolate, rich, thick, seductive. He pulled away abruptly. "About more than just fucking. You."

They stared at each other.

"You're wrong," she murmured breathlessly. "It *is* only about the fucking." But she knew it was more than that. It was about *her*. And for the first time since she'd met him, she felt like herself. It was Justine he wanted, and Justine who offered herself to him.

"Now." She unbuttoned her jeans and wriggled them down around her knees as he whipped off his vest, pushed her back onto the table, ripped off one pant leg, and positioned her body at just the right angle to take him.

She tilted her body up, spread her legs wide, and braced her arms on the table so she could watch. Her breath caught as he exposed his penis, and she could barely breathe as he slowly nosed its bulbous head into her slit.

He looked up at her with burning eyes. "All about the fucking?"

"All," she whispered.

He grasped her thighs, pushing harder, undulating his hips to torque his penis inch by hot, hard inch into her. He was deep into the pulse of her sex, into the mystery, the need, and the mindless, primal drive to fuck *her*.

There was no rhyme or reason to it, nothing but his body's response to her, and hers to him. In no time, he pitched into a blasting ejaculation, meeting her bolt of an orgasm, leaving them, in the aftermath, still connected. Their eyes were locked as the pleasure eddied away.

Finally, he pulled himself away from her and pulled himself together. Not a word was said as she watched every movement until he was dressed.

He left her soaked in his semen and half naked on the table.

She watched him walk away in a moment of stark clarity. He would leave forever.

Instantly, she felt as if she were facing an abyss so deep she'd never find her way out.

That was what *forever* felt like, she thought. Endless. Dark. Empty.

Alone.

But he was here now. How often did anyone get a second chance?

The sound of the idling engine galvanized her.

She instinctively knew it was really all about something more, something tenuous and unacknowledged. It was as fragile as silk, as gossamer as morning mist, and burned by her searing memories of how it had begun.

His coming here was not a promise. It was an offer for a new beginning, one that wasn't wrought with conflict between her mind and her heart.

This was a *don't think* moment. *This was a moment to just grab your bag and go.*

She made her way down the path toward the drive, feeling as if she were in some alternate reality where she'd just had fantasy sex with the man who haunted her thoughts but who, in the end, was only an illusion.

The roar of the engine was *not* an illusion.

She picked her bag up from the bench by the door. She hesitated a moment, thinking of all hers and Jillian's stuff that was still strewn around the cabin.

Who cares? she thought. *James will take care of it.*

She hoisted her bag over her shoulder, walked to the SUV, and opened the door.

"Coming?"

"Did I not just?" she said as she climbed in next to him.

"Not enough," he growled.

"It's all about the fucking," she taunted him.

"It's all about the fact I'm now free to love you," he contradicted.

Her breath caught, holding the moment, loving the moment.

"So," he went on, "I want your hand—here." He unzipped his jeans and popped out his penis. "We have about an hour's drive to the airport. No blow job. Just hold it. Tight." He gunned the engine." I just want to feel your hand there."

"I don't have that kind of willpower."

"I do," he said flatly, shifting to turn the SUV around.

She tossed her bag in the back, buckled herself in, and reached for his hot, thick penis.

"Like that."

Just the size of him was breathtaking. It made her soaking wet with need and lust, made her nipples hard and her body squirm with fantasies of everything he could and would do to her when they were finally alone.

She could hardly stand it, holding his penis like that for an hour, having to control her desire for him.

It was an exercise in restraint. At which she was an abject failure because she *needed* to move her hand, to feel and caress and explore the heft of him.

When they finally boarded the Gilbraltar jet, she stripped her clothes from her superheated body, enticing him. He resisted fucking her even after the plane leveled off, and they *almost* made it to London without having intercourse. It wasn't *all* about the sex, after all.